"I fear you'll have to come to terms, Lafayette. Unless you put an end to your resistance, you shall never find the headquarters."

"What resistance?" Lafayette demanded. "All I want to do is get back home with Daphne and go on having a swell life."

"Precisely. Your conceptualizations of the swell life are no longer viable, Lafayette. You must accept the new order—willingly."

O'Leary rounded on him truculently. "If your 'new order' means I'm supposed to like being kidnapped, thrown in dungeons, kicked from pillar to post, and kept in the dark about what's going on, you can forget it . . ."

KEITH LAUMER

THE GALAXY BUILDER

ACE SCIENCE FICTION BOOKS
NEW YORK

THE GALAXY BUILDER

An Ace Science Fiction Book / published by arrangement with
the author

PRINTING HISTORY
Ace Original / February 1984

ISBN: 0-441-27280-0

Ace Science Fiction Books are published by
The Berkley Publishing Group,
200 Madison Avenue, New York, New York 10016.
PRINTED IN THE UNITED STATES OF AMERICA

Chapter One

It was a mild spring evening in the palace gardens at Artesia, and Sir Lafayette O'Leary, late of Colby Corners, U.S.A., now the trusted confidant of Queen Adoranne, sat on his favorite bench, at the end of the long mall with a view of the nymph fountain. Beyond stood the glittering bulk of the pink quartz palace itself, its towers atwinkle like the colored lights strung in the gardenia hedges.

Lafayette reached for Daphne's warm little hand. She responded with a squeeze and leaned her head on his shoulder with a sigh.

"Lafayette, honey," she said uncertainly. "Is something wrong?"

Lafayette shook his head and nuzzled the smooth cheek. "It's just that the big gala tonight reminds me of the night we broke up the big affair where that light-fingered no-good Zorro, masquerading as me, was just about to convince everybody that Adoranne and Alain were dead. That lousy Zorro! Tell me, Daph: When that stinker was occupying my body and pretending to be me, did he—that is, did you—did he try to get fresh with you or anything?"

"Why, Lafayette!" Daphne exclaimed. "After all, it *was* your body, so what difference would it make?"

1

"So you *did* let the skunk take liberties! Daphne, I'm surprised at you!"

"Don't be silly, Lafayette," she replied calmly. "I suppose things have just been quiet and peaceful for so long that you just have to try to stir something up; next you'll be going up to that dingy old magician's laboratory or whatever at the top of the east tower, and fiddling about with all the old necromancy equipment Nicodaeus left there. Please don't, Lafayette. I want you to promise me!"

"That's ridiculous, Daphne," Lafayette returned hotly. "You know perfectly well Nicodaeus was no sorcerer, he was a perfectly ordinary Inspector of Continua, operating out of Central, just like I was, once—"

"That's what's bothering you, isn't it, Lafayette?" Daphne said in a sympathetic tone. "You're remembering all those wild times you had, and wishing you weren't just a humdrum married man now, with a suppressor focused on you!"

"That's not true, Daphne," Lafayette protested. "Why, I'd be crazy not to appreciate the life I'm living here in Artesia, with you." He looked earnestly into her big brown eyes, thinking for the millionth time that hers was the prettiest face in all the worlds. "Anyway," he added, "they lifted the suppressor."

"Then promise," Daphne insisted, pausing to nibble at his lower lip. "Promise me you won't start focusing your psychic energies, or whatever it was you used to do."

"Sure, I promise," Lafayette said easily, after a prolonged smooch. "I have no intention of meddling; I've learned my lesson." He looked up into the ink-black sky and its familiar constellations which never changed, whether he was in Artesia, Melange, even Colby Corners—or any of the other infinity of alternate realities.

"Those old eyeball astronomers must have had oversize imaginations," he commented idly, "seeing all those animals and so on in the stars. Look at Orion: three stars for a belt and three for his sword, and they see a full-length portrait, complete with his dog, Spot. If it wasn't so boring, I could easily think up better ones that would come closer to looking like something. Take Ursa Major over there; 'Big Bear,' nuts. The most life-like part is the tail, and bears don't have tails. Now, if that little bright star on the left was just shifted over to the right a little . . .''

"Lafayette!" Daphne cried, clutching at his arm as if in panic. "What was that? Didn't you feel it?" she urged, giving the arm a shake. "It was—as if the film slipped, or —"

"Nonsense," O'Leary said laughingly. "This isn't a film, Daph—it's living, breathing reality. You're think-ing about the times when I succeeded in shifting things around a little—I guess you're hipped on that subject tonight. Forget it. I promised to stay out of Nicodaeus' lab, after all—and I won't respond to any more notes from the Red Bull."

"Do you remember our first meeting, Lafayette," Daphne cooed, "when you first came to Artesia? And nothing's been the same since."

"How could I forget?" O'Leary inquired rhetori-cally. "There you were, wearing nothing but a few soap-suds and a charming smile. I ordered up a hot bath . . . and got one with you in it."

"I thought I was dreaming," Daphne murmured. "One minute I was alone in my garret quarters, and the next I was in a strange apartment—with the cutest man looking at me—and you looked as surprised as I felt."

"That reminds me," O'Leary said. "We don't have to go back to the party; since Adoranne and Alain have already retired, we're free to do the same. Come on." He stood. A drop of cold water spattered on his fore-head. "We have to go in anyway," he said, turning to Daphne, and offering his hand, which she failed to notice.

"Lafayette!" she wailed. "It's going to rain!"

"Correction," he said as more drops impacted on his face. "It *is* raining." Heads down, they hurried along the gravel path, skirted the fountain, and made for the shelter of the great elm trees lining the walk. Rain on the foliage was a roar now, and cold rivulets were running down between Lafayette's shoulder blades. He unclipped the throat-latch of his short cloak of deep blue velvet with the argent device of the Axe and Dragon, and covered Daphne's shoulders and head.

"We can't stay here, Lafayette!" she cried over the drumming of the downpour. "Come on." Without awaiting assent, she was off, dashing out into the nearly opaque downpour. Through it, the palace lights were barely visible. In a moment O'Leary had lost sight of her, though he plunged after her at once. He nearly fell then, as the full force of the sudden storm struck. He stumbled ahead, calling, toward the blurry glow, but heard no reply, and could see nothing of Daphne. The soaked turf squished underfoot.

"Daphne! Wait! Please!" he shouted. *But that's silly, he added silently. Why should she stand out in the rain waiting for me when she can just as well wait inside?* He stumbled again, splashing through an ankle-deep puddle already formed in an unsuspected hollow at what he estimated had to be the foot of the wide, shallow steps leading up to the terrace. He felt loose stones underfoot. *Ye gods, it's already undermining the pavement,* he thought with dismay. *But it's hardly surprising, under a torrent like this; it's like massed fire hoses.* Totally soaked, shivering, half-blinded by the water in his eyes, he groped his way up the broken steps and across to the barely visible dark rectangle of an open doorway. Still no glimpse of Daphne. He staggered, reached the entry in a final lunge, and fell headlong.

For a long time, it seemed, the roar of the rain, from which he was now mercifully sheltered, went on. Lafayette wiped water from his eyes and blinked into total darkness all around.

"Daphne?" he called tentatively as he got to his feet.

"Not even an echo," he said aloud, and shivered hard. It was strangely cold. And why so dark? The palace was always kept warm, well-lit, and cosy in spite of its size. Maybe he had stumbled into a storeroom, he reflected, though he didn't recall any such facility interrupting the wide glass facade on the ballroom side—unless he had wandered off to the far left, where he seemed to recall there was a cluster of service spaces in the corner, across the corridor from the big party room. That must be it—and poor Daph had blundered into one of them like himself, and was alone somewhere now in the dark, wondering why he didn't come. He jumped as the door closed with a *slam!* There was no latch on the inside.

It took him five minutes to pace off the chamber in which he now was, it appeared, trapped: The room was an unadorned rectangle of rough-hewn stone, ten paces by six, with a crudely arched opening opposite the doorway through which he had entered. The opening was securely barred by a massive slab of iron-bound oak, abounding in splinters, one of which he removed from his thumb with his teeth. At his next approach, he proceeded more cautiously, paused before the door, set himself, and delivered a kick, partly in revenge, he acknowledged to himself. To his surprise, the heavy panel swung inward with a creak of rusty hinges. Lafayette took a tentative step inside and found himself at the foot of a steep flight of chipped stone steps which ascended into an even deeper blackness.

"Daphne?" he called, but his voice reverberated hollowly up the stairwell, eliciting no reply.

"She's got to be up there," he assured himself. "There's nowhere else she could have gone. So, here goes." The sound of his own voice talking to himself was unnerving. He started slowly up, then paused.

"Wait a minute, O'Leary," he commanded himself sternly. "This would be a good time to do something at least half-smart. You don't know where you are now; why get in deeper?

"Because if poor little Daphne is up there," he replied doggedly, "I want to find her and tell her everything's OK. But *is* everything OK?" He went on, unwillingly.

"OK or otherwise, she went up, and I've got to go,

too," he settled the dispute. He paused to listen. Other than the faint keening of the wind, there was no sound at all—unless that was cautious whispering down below. . . . On impulse, he turned and went back down, pausing just inside the half-open door.

". . . tell ya it's *him*," a hoarse voice hissed urgently. "All we gotta do to cop the reward is lay the scoundrel by the heels."

"That's easy to say, Marv," another raspy voice came back. "But if that's really the dread necromancer Allegorus, all the more reason to stand pat and send for the cavalry."

On impulse, Lafayette uttered a low, anquished moan, as of a spook in distress.

"Listen! You hear that, Marv? It sounded like maybe he's dying! Allegorus healthy is bad enough," he went on, "but wounded—and thirsting for revenge—lemme out of here!" The sounds of pounding feet and a brief scuffle followed.

Satisfied with the effect, O'Leary groaned again. More sounds of departing feet; and the chamber seemed deserted again. He stepped boldly forth, and at once found his head enveloped in a coarse and dusty cloth, held in place by more than one pair of hard hands. He managed to bite a thumb, eliciting a yell of pain, but the enveloping folds were only pulled tighter. He kicked, felt a satisfying impact against what felt like a knee, then swung both fists in haymakers which failed to connect. Then a rope clamped around him, both binding his arms and securing the dusty cloth tightly. He sneezed violently.

"Hey!" one of the coarse voices yelped. "No sneeze-spells now, or we'll hafta clobber ya good, which ya might never come to!"

Desperately, Lafayette suppressed a second sneeze, choking it down to a muffled snort. At once, a loose block of masonry fell from the ceiling, knocking him end-over-end. He had time only for a pang of dismay that he had somehow done it again, before all thought faded away.

It was going to be one of those tedious dreams, O'Leary realized, the kind where you know you're dreaming but having to go through with it, just as if you were awake. Only this one was surrealistic: nothing but a face, an angry—or frightened—face, yelling at him at close range, demanding, threatening. The face of a man. The man was dressed in a drab gray smock, Lafayette saw, and behind him in the dim gray-lit room he caught a glimpse of Daphne.

"Very well, then, fool!" the angry man said clearly. "If you refuse to cooperate, I shall consign you to the unresolved continua of your own meddlesome making. Begone!"

O'Leary tried to lunge past him toward Daphne, who was gone now, but he tripped and hit his head hard. He got to his feet shakily.

Chapter Two

He was standing—barely—supported by a man on either side who gripped his arms with hands like C-clamps. The ache in his head was approximately three feet in diameter, he estimated. He was back outside, he realized, smelling the fresh night air. Dimly, through a haze of pain, he saw a squat but mightily muscled man with bushy whiskers sitting on a broken gilt chair before him. The man was wrapped in badly cured furs. For some reason, O'Leary had the feeling the stubby Hercules had seated himself only a moment before. A small pink mouth opened amidst the whiskers, exposing chipped yellow teeth.

"Got any last words, traitor?" the pink mouth said. "Too bad if you do," the seated man continued after a momentary pause. "I'm Lord Trog. I got no time to listen to excuses." The beady red eyes which went with the whiskers seemed to O'Leary to be boring into him like hot pokers. Beyond the hacked-out clearing he stood in were some woods and, in the background, the pale silhouette of a ruined tower. He returned his attention to Lord Trog.

"You shoulda never of came out, hotshot," the gravelly voice went on. "Overconfidence, I guess."

"Where's Daphne?" O'Leary blurted. "I don't know

who you are, or what you think you're doing, invading the palace grounds and grabbing me. When the palace guard grabs *you*, you'll wish you'd been a little more subtle."

"Yeah, well, about the palace guard, they took the year off, see? And I don't know no Daphne." The squat man paused to poke a grimy finger into what O'Leary assumed was an ear, buried somewhere within the nearly spherical mass of untrimmed, greasy-looking hair which enveloped the fellow's head.

"Sounds like a dame," Trog added indifferently. "Boys," he turned his attention to one of the men holding O'Leary's arms, "boys, you seen any strange dames around the place lately?"

"Seen no dames at all, Chief," the fellow replied. "No dames, no booze, no smokes, no card games—we don't get to have no fun at all. Never figgered I was en-nerin a monastery when I joined up."

"That will do, Marv," the Chief grunted. His eyes flicked to the other man beside O'Leary.

"You, Omar? Any complaints? By the way, put Marv in irons at once, in the lower dungeon."

"Who, me, Chief?" Omar replied in tones of astonishment. "Why, no, sir, I'm perfectly content, just a loyal retainer glad to do his job. Do I really hafta stick old Marv down the hole? I mean, maybe he was just kidding, like."

The bearded man fumbled inside his furs, brought out a gray plastic object the size of a cigarette pack, and pressed a button on it as he brought it to his mouth.

"Top Dog to Pup One, over," he muttered. "Come in, Pup One. OK, skip the routine, but get the duty hit squad over here pronto. Over."

"Hey, boss, I was onney kidding around." Omar protested. "Me and Marv, we're nothing if not true-blue—" His protests were cut off abruptly as three louts in ragged blue knee-breeches and faded pink-and-yellow jackets with chapped elbows showing through the patches arrived on the scene, ominously clacking the actions of short-muzzled machine pistols.

"These here bums, Chief?" the foremost of the trio inquired, eyeing Marv and Omar dubiously. "Or this one?" He swiveled to cover Lafayette, who at once began mentally reviewing Professor Doktor Hans Josef Schimmerkopf's instructions for Focusing the Psychical Energies:

". . . whilst at all times aware of the distinction between the outer, or objective Reality and the inner, concentrate on those as-yet-not-realized aspects of the Scene the outcome of which remains problematical; and by an Effort of Will, bring into Focus that eventuation most conducive to satisfaction. . . ." In spite of the old boy's pompous style, Lafayette reminded himself, his methods had worked well enough to transport him to Artesia in the first place, and to several less desirable alternate realities thereafter. But at the moment, all that was necessary was to divert the whiskery fellow—

"I'm Lord Trog and I'm the Chief Honcho around these here parts, just in case you don't know it, Al," the whiskery chieftain growled, squinting at O'Leary. "And I don't put up with no guys on my trusty guard staff which they ain't trusty. So—throw 'em away, fellows," he commanded the duty squad. "These here two miscreants," he clarified, with a nod at Marv and Omar.

"Don't bother to shoot 'em up much, just yet, but a stretch in the lower dungeon will do 'em a lotta good, discipline-wise." He waved a calloused hand in a negligent gesture. "Take 'em away."

Gosh, O'Leary thought confusedly, *it worked, sort of! Maybe the old Psychic Energies are flowing again. That means . . . well, I'm not exactly sure what it means,* he conceded, *but now that I've got Trog's mind off having me shot, the first thing I've got to do is find Daphne. She must have gone up those steps. . . .*

"Where is the Countess?" O'Leary demanded sternly of Lord Trog, who, he thought, bore a considerable resemblance, under all that hair, to Yockabump, the court jester—and to Sprawnroyal of the Acme Novelty Company. The whiskers parted in a cavernous yawn.

"Back to that, huh?" His Lordship grunted. He looked about him as if suspicious of eavesdroppers.

"Level with me now, Bub, and maybe you can save yourself some trouble—and make a better-looking corpse, too: Are you *really* the fell necromancer Allegorus, like Marv and Omar said?"

"Where did they get that silly idea?" O'Leary demanded.

"Well, after all, ya *did* materialize outa thin air yonder in the Dread Tower, din't ya?"

"I came down the steps and they were waiting for me," Lafayette corrected. "Anyway, what's so dread about the Tower? It's just an old ruin." He smiled condescendingly. "I just ducked inside to get out of the weather, as it happens. So what?"

"You mean—you admit you were beyond the forbidden door, up inna top o' the Tower?" His Lordship drew a ragged circle in the air in front of him.

"A few steps up, was all," O'Leary explained. "You see, Daphne must have gone up there—unless Marv and Omar got *her,* too," he amended.

"If she did, pal, she's a goner. Too bad. We got a like critical shortage of dames here just now. What's she look like?"

Lafayette indicated Daphne's graceful contours with his hands. "Dark hair," he added. "Prettiest face in the known universe."

"Cheeze," Lord Trog mourned. "Wit' them statistics, she mighta qualified for my personal favor."

"I guess it's just as well she went up," O'Leary concluded. "What's up there that's so scary?"

"If you're really Allegorus, you already know," Trog reasoned. "And if you ain't, why should I give away any info?"

"It might weigh in your favor at your trial," O'Leary suggested. "What are you doing here in the palace gardens anyway?"

"Keepin' a eye on the Dread Tower, o' course, Al," Trog said as one stating the obvious. "And a good thing, it looks like, seein's you picked now to come out on one o' yer trouble-makin' raids."

"It appears," O'Leary said, feeling suddenly tired, "that you're in need of psychiatric attention, milord. Why don't you just go away quietly now, before your keepers find you; and I'll try to smooth things over with Her Majesty—as soon as you release Daphne unharmed, that is."

"Sounds like a square deal, Bub," Trog replied, showing his teeth in a wide grin. "Onney there's one little problem area: I ain't seen no Daphne, nor not even a Piggy-Lou."

"Stubborn, eh?" Lafayette said grimly. "You'll sing a different tune when you're clapped in irons with the royal PPS working you over with the latest in ball-bearing joint-presses and the fully automated hydraulic rack, not to mention the computer-controlled foot-roasters."

"Sure, I heard all that old jazz before," Trog said indifferently. "But you're in a funny spot to be threatening me wit' the attentions of a Physical Persuasion Specialist, which I got a pretty good boy on my staff my own self. Now, cut the comedy and give me the straight dope: Do you admit you're Allegorus the Awful, or don't ya?"

"Maybe you'd better tell me a little more about this fellow you're so scared of," O'Leary suggested. "Then I'll tell you if I'm him or not."

"Me, I'm a reasonable guy," Trog said, indicating himself with a grimy thumb. "Maybe you just like to hear people talk about ya, huh? Got a little ego problem, eh? Well, I'll play along: Everybody knows he comes out every three hundred years or like that, stirs up a bunch of trouble and then goes back inna tower for another three centuries—an' nobody never sends in no eats or drinks, so he always comes out wit a appetite on him like three harvest hands; and he likes beans—humern beans."

"Is that all?" O'Leary demanded sarcastically. "Sounds like a pretty dull fellow."

"Not when he gets wound up good, he ain't," Trog declared defensively.

"Anyway, I'm not him," O'Leary stated with finality. "And even if I were, what right do you and your gang of thugs have to interfere with the movements of a nobleman of the realm?"

"You was seen goin' into the Dread Tower, which nobody don't go in there except old Allegorus hisself!"

"I was merely taking shelter from the rain," Lafayette countered. "It was the only building in sight, so naturally—"

"Rain, huh? Well, Bub, you coulda picked a better alibi. All Aphasia's been in the like grip of a drought these last six years or more," Trog stated flatly, reaching down as he spoke to take a pinch of dust from the ground beside his chair. He rolled it between his gnarled fingers, letting it dribble away in a fine stream which spread and dissipated like smoke before it reached the ground. Lafayette looked down and saw dry mud caked on his elegant purple patent-leather court pumps, which were firmly planted in drifted dust. Not so much as a stunted green weed testified to the former existence of water here. Still, his shirt clung, sodden, to his back, though the air seemed noticeably warmer now.

"Oh, yeah?" he said in an attempt at a casual tone. "In that case, how'd I get soaked?"

"Marv and Omar figgered you'd fell in the well you must have inside the tower," Trog said. "Maybe that's why you come out—you was shook up from the misadventure which it coulda been fatal all alone in the dark and all."

"You referred to some place called Aphasia," O'Leary commented, "I thought Aphasia was a mental state." Then he added in a desperate attempt at rationality, "Well, maybe it is at that."

"Oh, I get it," Trog said, "ya poor slob, you're off your chump, huh? Well, Lord Trog ain't one to be too tough on a guy which he's afflicted of Allah. So relax, pal, and I'll leave my offficial leech have a look at your dome."

"I don't want any leech, official or otherwise, to look at my dome," Lafayette came back hotly. With an effort, he calmed himself. *Nothing to get excited about,*

O'Leary, he told himself sternly.

Somehow, he explained to himself patiently, *somehow, I've done it again—gotten myself involved in another of those ridiculous situations where everybody thinks I'm somebody else and nobody is who he seems to be. And it's not fair! This time I wasn't tinkering with gadgets swiped from the Probability Lab at Central, or practicing focusing the Psychic Energies, or meddling in Nicodeaus' lab, or anything else. . . .*

"No spells, now, Bub!" the hoarse voice of Lord Trog broke into Lafayette's self-instructive reverie. "Nor no prayers, neither," he added. "Don't worry, you'll get a fair trial and a relatively painless demise. Nobody ain't never said Lord Trog don't give a fella a even break, even if it's a compound fracture o' the femur." The barbaric lord snickered at his own wit, and shifted in his chair, which creaked ominously under his weight.

I know that chair, O'Leary realized abruptly. *It's one of the ones that used to be in the Great Hall, spaced between the mirrors! So these ruins really are the palace!*

For the first time, O'Leary took a good look around at the scrub woods that seemed to have sprung up where the south gardens ought to have been. His eyes went to the ruined tower of chipped pink stone looming above the treetops, the only structure in sight. Broken cut-stone blocks and drifted rubble were scattered all about, glowing pale pink in the moonlight. It was the east tower, where Nicodaeus' old laboratory occupied the top story—all that was left of the palace, Lafayette realized with a sinking feeling. He stooped and picked up an egg-sized fragment of pink stone, polished flat on one side, and felt a pang of regret as he realized that it had once been a part of the radiant facade of the palace; he dropped it into his pocket, silently vowing revenge on the vandals.

"I'm wasting time," he told himself sternly. "The poor kid is probably alone, scared—or worse yet, not alone and scared."

"Daphne!" he said aloud, and took a step past Trog and toward the ruin.

"No, you don't, Al," the seated man barked. "Hey, Marv, Omar! Where in Tophet are them bums which they're pulling the duty tonight?"

"In the lower dungeon, Your Lordship," O'Leary supplied.

"So you really *are* Allegorus, eh?" Trog grumbled. "Wit' duh second sight and all—"

"One sight was enough," O'Leary countered. "What happened to the palace?" He stooped and picked up another crumbling chip of pink quartz, seeing at once that it was severly weathered. Whatever had happened, it appeared, had happened a long time ago. That being the case, he must be suffering from amnesia, and Daphne couldn't have been caught in the collapse of the great building.

"Still," he said aloud, "that's where she was last seen —or almost seen: it was pretty hazy. So that's where I've got to start."

"Nix, Bub," Trog came to his feet, an unwashed gnome less than five feet tall, wrapped in foul-smelling half-cured hides; but he had the arms of a weight lifter and oversize, scarred-knuckle fists, which he thrust under O'Leary's nose. "One more step and I'll summon the boys, which dey'll trow yuz inna lion pit."

"Nope, lower dungeon, remember?" Lafayette said, and delivered a sharp kick to the boss's left kneecap. "Anyway, I don't have time to be bum-rapped right now," he added as he pushed past Lord Trog, now hopping on one leg and holding the other knee in both hands. O'Leary ran across the expanse of rubble-littered weeds past the last of the trees. He had reached the cracked and tilted slabs of the former terrace when a boulder struck him on the side of the head and sent him spinning down into a coal-black fog.

He was back in the gray room, back in the same dumb dream, he saw, except that the angry fellow had calmed down and was sitting across the table from him, speaking reasonably—or almost so:

". . . cut you in for a full share; I'm not greedy. Don't be a spoilsport." A serving-wench came up and put a full tankard before the fellow; as she turned away

O'Leary realized it was Daphne, a drab cloth tied around her once-lustrous dark hair in place of the diamond-studded coronet. He jumped up, knocking over the table on the man in gray, who yelled and leaped clear. His limbs strangely heavy, Lafayette tried to clamber over the fallen table, but it seemed to grow and elaborate under him. Daphne was gone.

It seemed to Lafayette that he had been climbing for a very long time, an exhausting ascent of a vertical wall, in total darkness. He paused to catch his breath, wincing at the ache in his head, and tried again to remember just where it was he was going—and whence he had come. But the problem was too complex; with a groan, he gave it up and reached up for a new handhold on the cold, wet wall against which he clung like an exhausted fly. He dug in his fingertips for a better purchase; they merely slipped painfully; then his other hand, groping upward, encountered something different from the unyielding texture of the stone wall. Cloth, it felt like, and under it, tough stringy flesh, which recoiled at his touch.

"Come on, pal, gimme a break, OK?" an aggrieved voice which O'Leary had heard before broke the stillness. "How's about you just relax now, and leave me do the same."

"Marv," O'Leary said aloud and, remembering his precarious position clinging to the wall, made a wild grab and secured a firm grip on a spongy mass of whiskers.

"Cripes!" Marv's voice yelled. "Come on, lay off the rough stuff, which me and Omar handled you wit' kid gloves all the way, right?"

"Pray accept my apologies, gentlemen," Lafayette said. "I have no intention of savaging you. Actually, I came along simply to assist you in escaping the unjust punishment visited on you by your ungrateful master."

"Yeah, after all we done for *him*," Omar agreed. "Right, Marv? The kid's got something there. We din't do nothing but follow orders, and—by the way, kid, how do you figure on springing us outa here?"

During the exchange, Lafayette had gradually become aware that, rather than crawling up a rough, damp stone wall, he had been creeping across a rough, damp stone floor. He relaxed gratefully and worked on getting his pulse and respiration back down into a range more characteristic of a patient with a positive prognosis.

"There's the way we come in," Marv suggested without enthusiasm, "only I for one can't jump no forty feet straight up and hover long enough to undo a tricky latch onna trap door before I start back down."

"Before we go," Lafayette said, "suppose you gentlemen fill me in on some details, such as what happened to the palace and all the people in it, especially Daphne? Are you sure you didn't grab her just before you waylaid me? And who is this Trog fellow, anyway?"

"Geeze, kid, we musta conked ya a little hard at that; sounds like you don't know nothing."

"Precisely," O'Leary agreed. "Start with Daphne. Did she escape up the stairs, or what?"

"If she done," Omar said gloomily, "it's curtains for sure for the poor broad, which you said she was a looker, right, Al?"

"Why do you fellows keep calling me 'Al'?" O'Leary demanded.

"Meaning no disrespect, Yer Honor," Omar said hastily.

"Just meant to be friendly-like," Marv added reassuringly. " 'Allegorus' is too long fer a name, anyways. No offense," he added.

"Suppose I assure you, once and for all," O'Leary said, "and for the last time: I'm not this Allegorus person."

"Ya must be, Al," Marv said persuasively. "Otherwise how could you of aced old Trog inta letting ya in here to help us out?"

"Oh, I know a few tricks, I'll admit," Lafayette acknowledged. "Who *is* Trog, and where'd he come from? Does he have anything to do with the palace being in ruins?"

"Slow down, Al," Omar suggested. "You're getting

ahead of us. Trog is just Trog, which Frodolkin hisself put him onna job guarding the Tower, they say.''

"Which brings us to the question of who is Frodolkin?'' Lafayette persisted.

"He's a shot which he's so big, nobody don't ever get to see him. He stays out at his fort, a few leagues west o' here, wit' a big army of, like, henchmen and cronies and guys like that,'' Marv contributed.

"What happened to the palace?'' O'Leary demanded. "Was it destroyed by this Frodolkin?''

"Naw, nothin' like that,'' Omar replied. "I mean, according to tribal legend and all, this here bunch o' busted rock useta be some kind o' palace, like, maybe three hunnert years ago; then it fell into roon, like they say, all but the Dread Tower, and you got that sealed off pretty good, Al. Now you tell me one: What's so hot about that crummy Tower, ya wanna stay in it alla time, huh?''

"Yeah,'' Marv echoed. "What ya got in there, anyways?''

"Nothing much,'' Lafayette conceded. "It's just that apparently Daphne's in there. Three hundred years, did you say? That's ridiculous! It was perfectly all right less than an hour ago.''

"Now,'' Marv said, "let's get back to how you're going to spring Omar and I. And we better get moving, which I got a idear His Lordship has got something on his mind, like that message he got from Frodolkin.''

"What message?'' Omar demanded. "I never heard nothing about no message.''

"You know,'' Marv replied glumly. "The usual: about the sacrifice to the vampire-god and all. Like every year. Only this time . . .''

"Yeah, *what,* this time?'' Omar persisted. "I guess we'll hafta round up some o' the local churls and villeins and ship 'em over, like always. So what?''

"So, Master Wise Guy, if you'd care to refresh yer membry, ya might recall we ain't seen none o' the local clods fer some time now, what wit' the tide of battle, like, surging back and forth acrost their farms. Ain't nobody left in these here parts except us loyal retainers;

including the hit squad, about forty souls in all. So who's gonna get to go and meet the vampire-god, except whatever guys happen to be on the gig-list at the moment? Here's three of us, onney four to go to make up the quota. We prolly got until daylight tomorrow."

"Have you went nuts, Marv?" Omar demanded without conviction. "You think a swell boss like Lord Trog would send his faithful boys off to a horrible end, just to save his own neck?" After a moment's thought he added, "Let's get outa here." He turned to O'Leary, "Now's yer chanst, bo," he said, "to get on our good side by working that nifty breakout you was telling about."

Lafayette heard sounds of fumbling in the dark. Then, with a sharp scratch of flint on steel, a spark glowed, and a moment later a candle-flame ignited, shedding a mellow glow on the stone walls. It showed a mildewed gray here in the tower base, rather than the soft pink of the outer structure; in its radiance, Marv and Omar squatted, heads together, a pair of hairy troglodytes eyeing O'Leary with inscrutable expressions on their rough-hewn features.

"Let's sum up," O'Leary proposed briskly. "I'm still in Artesia, although Lord Trog called it Aphasia—I'm not somehow shifted off into another continuum like Melange, or Colby Corners; but I've gotten myself shifted in time, three hundred years into the future, and this pile of rubble is all that's left of Adoranne's beautiful pink palace. I'll worry about 'how' later. And Daphne's here, too, probably hiding up in Nicodaeus' old lab at the top of the Tower, poor kid. But wait a minute: If it really *is* the palace, then the system of secret passages is still there, inside the walls. So—just where am I now, in relation to the palace? Marv, show me where this dungeon is in relation to the Tower." He smoothed the mud on the rough stone floor to create a sketching surface. "Draw me a map," he urged the barbaric ex-guard.

"Well, Al," Marv began reluctantly, "I ain't much of a one fer drawrin' pitchers, but if this here"—

he made an X with a blunt forefinger—"is the Tower, the upper dungeon is over here to the side, like this here. . . ." He added a rectangle adjacent to the X.

"On which side?" O'Leary demanded. "Which way is north?"

Marv hooked a thumb over his shoulder. "I got a keen sense o' direction, Al, but so what? Inside this hole, the onney direction innersts me is up."

"I mean on the map," O'Leary explained testily. "Now, if we're to the west, that's where the wine cellars used to be. And if the lower dungeon is under the cellars, say, that would put us just about in the unused storeroom where Goroble had his stolen equipment stashed; and if that's so—" O'Leary rose unsteadily on legs which felt as if they had been freshly molded of papier-mâché; he staggered, but righted himself and went across the room to study the crudely mortared blocks of rough-hewn masonry which comprised the partition. He identified the faint arrow he had scratched on the stone so long ago, reached, pressed, and felt the apparently solid masonry yield and swing inward, exposing a pitch-black passage beyond.

"Come on, boys," he said, and without waiting for a response, stepped through.

At once, he was at home, and memories came flooding back: creeping through dark passages behind Yockabump as the court jester led him for the first time through the system which gave covert access to practically every room in the great pile; later, exploring alone and finding the false king's hidden store of stolen high-technology gear; then, still later, leading Princess Adoranne and Count Alain to the ballroom just in time to cut short Quelius' bold attempt to usurp the throne of troubled Artesia. It was like the old days, Lafayette tried to tell himself—the bad old days when he was, at first, a displaced pauper in flight from the law and an outraged populace, and later, when he was a pampered favorite of the sovereign, in flight from the cops as well as from a gang of cutthroat wayfarers plus the Central Security Forces, all determined to cut him to small bits without trial. Compared with those days, he assured himself, this was a cinch: All he had chasing him now was Lord Trog's hit squad—and he was inside the ruins of the palace, with free access to the Tower, of all places, the one place he was likely to find some key to this mad situation; and surely Daphne was up there, waiting for him to rescue her.

But, he reminded himself sternly, he had promised Daphne to stay away from the lab, and now she was gone, poor trusting girl. . . . But she *had* to be in the Tower, unless Trog and his boys were better liars than seemed likely. . . . So all bets were off: His promise didn't count. And the pivot-stone opening on the narrow passage to the Tower stair had to be right along here. . . .

He found it and slipped through onto the landing outside which he had first been grabbed by Marv and Omar, which reminded him . . .

"This way, fellows," he called heartily. "Stick with me and we'll be out of here in maybe a trice and a half."

"Where are we at?" Marv demanded sullenly from the darkness hiding him.

" 'Where' means 'at what place,' " Lafayette told the uncouth fellow. "So you don't need to hang that 'at' on the end of your sentence; it's redundant."

"Skip all that jazz, bo," Marv returned. "But whereat are we?"

"Where we are at," O'Leary replied with dignity, "is right back where you two clowns clobbered me in the first place."

"You mean—?" Omar's voice choked up before he could utter the thought.

"I mean," Lafayette confirmed. "It's a lot better than the lower dungeon, right?"

"Excuse us, bo," Omar's voice floated back as the two exited hastily into the night.

"Daphne," O'Leary yelled up the stairwell, but only a sardonic echo returned. He started up into darkness, brushing aside cobwebs, tripping over small objects on the stone steps; doubtless, he thought, items dropped by thieves as they hastily looted the ruin. He paused to yell again: nothing, not even a good echo this time. But she *had* to be up there, didn't she? he thought desperately. There was one way to find out. He started up, one step at a time. Round and round the spiral stairway climbed. The steps continued to be littered with loose objects. It was strange that the Tower had survived, essentially intact, when all the rest had been reduced to rubble; but that was a good sign, he thought contentedly—that Central still maintained an interest in their only permanent point of contact with Locus Alpha Nine-Three, Plane V-87, Fox 221-b, known to its inhabitants as Artesia.

He was halfway up when he heard the first sounds of pursuit from below. Apparently Lord Trog had offered his loyal hit squad a fate even more dismal than the Dread Tower to any who failed to enter the latter in pursuit of the quarry. He sat on a step and listened. The pursuers seemed to be moving rather slowly. But even so, he'd be trapped at the top and would be able to do nothing but await their arrival.

O'Leary rose and went on. At last he reached the big iron-bound door. A ragged hole gaped where the big combination lock installed by Nicodaeus had formerly served to bar intruders. It was just as well: he wasn't sure he could remember the combination. He called once again for Daphne as he pushed the door open wide. For a moment he thought he had elicited a response, if only a faint sound of movement within, but as he stepped eagerly forward he saw that the room was empty. Of course, the old lab equipment of Nicodaeus was long gone: the tables covered with alembics and retorts, the shelves containing eye of newt and best mummy-dust, the crackle-finish panels crowded with dials, indicator lights, and flickering oscilloscope traces. Now it had the appearance of some ancient tomb, deep with dust, festooned with cobwebs, eerie in the moonlight streaming through the double doors which opened on the small balcony from which he had been forced more than once to flee to safety.

There was one more possibility, he reminded himself, sternly rejecting hoplessness: the most important item of all—the special telephone to Central, in the cabinet beside the door. He turned to it, ready to utter a cry of relief, but instead he groaned. The door of the compartment had been ripped from its hinges, and the interior was empty but for a scattering of dust and a number of bits of waste paper. A stub of wire, rudely hacked short, projected from the cabinet wall near one corner.

Aha! This was more like the old O'Leary luck. He could scrape the insulation away, cross the bare wires, and tap out an SOS. Surely some on-the-ball operator at Central would get the message, trace it, and—

"Move not, on your life!" A harsh voice called so close to O'Leary's ear that he uttered a yelp and started violently. Hard hands grabbed his arms, half-supporting, half-restraining him. He considered stamp-kicking the man behind him, but upon seeing the other man, in front of him, he chose discretion.

═══Chapter Three═══

Fists on hips, clad in a close-fitting outfit of
black trimmed with silver, a large businesslike handgun
in his fist, stood a man only half a head shorter than
Lafayette's six-one, his face thrust forward to bring its
expression of hostility within an inch of O'Leary's own
features. It was the face from the dream.

"Caught you red-handed, simpleton!" the familiar
voice barked. "Did you actually imagine you could
commit these outrages against the august peace and
security of Reality Prime with complete impunity?
Saucy rogue, eh, Chief, thus to bait Belarius in his very
den?" The stranger's gaze went past O'Leary's shoulder
to the man behind him.

"Did you say 'Belarius'?" Lafayette croaked.

"So, you recognize the name of the fabled Scourge of
Scoundrels, eh?" Suddenly Lafayette was spun from
behind.

"You're not Belarius," he blurted, nose-to-nose with
a stocky fellow, also in black-and-silver uniform and
gun, his outfit also trimmed with black-and-gold trac-
ings at the wrist and collar.

"You picked the wrong name, wise guy!" O'Leary
went on hotly. "I happen to know Belarius personally,

even if he *is* a big shot; in fact, I was instrumental in getting him out of a serious scrape once. He's a big fellow —six inches taller than you, at least, with these really piercing blue eyes, blue like a cave of ice, and a beak on him like an eagle; not that he's not a distinguished-looking old boy—and he's lots older than you. Go on, kid me some more. . ."

"The description you offer is that of my grandfather's grandfather, Belarius I," the self-styled Belarius said coldly. "Is your remarkable longevity another trivial detail to be dismissed with a wave of the hand?"

"I'm not really three hundred and thirty-one years old," Lafayette replied with dignity. "That is, maybe I was born three hundred and thirty-one years ago, but I've only lived thirty-one years."

"So, having been cut down in your boyhood, you rose from the grave after three centuries to resume your mischievous ways, is that it?" the imposter demanded sarcastically.

"That's not what I said!" O'Leary yelled. "Don't start trying to put me in one of those dumb false positions again! I'm Sir Lafayette O'Leary, and I *know* you're not Belarius!"

"Am I not?" the fellow replied coolly. "That would come as a great shock to my lady mother, who reared me as the fifth of that ilk."

"Oh, I forgot this is three hundred years later," O'Leary gobbled, his sarcasm lost on his impassive captor. "You can let go my arm now; I won't fall down. But that *was* quite a shock, having you creep up on me in this spooky place. How did you fellows get in here?"

"Rather tell *me* how you gained ingress to the Sealed Chamber," Belarius demanded, releasing O'Leary.

"And why, as well," his partner chimed in from behind. "What sought you here which was worth the forfeit of your existence out to eight parameters from your native locus?"

"Locus? You know about loci?" Lafayette babbled in relief. "So you must be from Central, right? You discovered something awful had happened to Artesia, and they sent you out to investigate, right? Boy oh boy, am I glad to see you!"

"A defense of insanity will avail you naught, wittold!" Belarius snorted. "As for Central, be assured that it is four levels of command inferior to Reality Prime, and that regardless of what chicaneries with which you may have deluded petty Central, your career of crimes against reality has now come to an end!"

"I didn't do anything, fellows," O'Leary protested wearily. "For once, I'm really innocent. I was just sitting in the garden admiring the stars with Mrs. O'Leary—I mean, Countess O'Leary, Daphne, my wife, you know, and all of a sudden—"

"Yes?" Belarius prompted, "go on."

"All of a sudden it was raining; and that's strange because I had just been reflecting that, from locus to locus, the weather never changes, even when everything else does."

"You may as well confess all, Mr. 'O'Leary,' as you have the effrontery to style yourself."

"I didn't style myself," Lafayette objected. "That's the name they gave me at the orphanage. In honor of Mrs. Beldame O'Leary, the founder, you know. And there's nothing to confess," he added. "What is it you think I've done, anyway?"

"The primary charge," Belarius said coldly, "is that you did willfully and with malice aforethought commit an act or acts of the third level of malfeasance, thereby creating an anomaly of Category Ultimate, the full repercussions of which act or acts having not yet been manifested. Shall I go on?"

"No. Go back," O'Leary suggested. "What's the third level of whateveritis, and what does Category Ultimate mean?"

"It means, quite simply," Belarius said harshly, "that you have forfeited whatever claim to continued existence you may have had. You're under arrest, and will be taken at once to a designated holding locus and there terminated."

"He means killed," the other man contributed, "all in compliance with the Code, of course. It's quite a coup for His Lordship: he deduced you'd be here—and we've caught you red-handed."

"I never heard of this code of yours," Lafayette stated flatly.

"Ignorance of the law is no excuse," Belarius quoted. "But you could hardly have failed to notice the class-AA security barrier around the Chamber, or the crack regiment of guards patroling the area, or the prominently posted notices reading 'NO ENTRY,' to say nothing of the type-Z combination lock on the door itself, all of which you somehow broached. Now, it will be of some interest to know how you did it, never mind 'why?' for the moment. Begin with the steel-and-concrete legtraps. The Chief of Security assured me personally that they were impassable. How did you pass them?"

"I didn't notice 'em," O'Leary said. "Where are they? Must be so well camouflaged they're invisible as well as ineffective."

"What of the Guards regiment, then? Do you claim to have slipped past the alert sentries of the most highly honored organization in the entire Service?"

"If you mean Trog and his boys, they're overrated," Lafayette said carelessly. "And I didn't *see* any keep-out signs."

"Clearly, Frumpkin," Belarius said to his partner, "the fellow has employed some highly sophisticated counter-security equipment thus to make mockery of my best efforts."

"Just used my head," O'Leary said bluntly.

"It's clear the rascal is even more dangerous than we had suspected," Frumpkin said. "Perhaps we'd best apply full Class One measures at once, after all. HQ would understand if we brought in a corpse under the circumstances."

"Seems rather drastic for such an insignificant-appearing young fellow as this," Belarius responded. "Just a few more points to clear up. What about it, fellow-me-lad?" he addressed Lafayette directly. "Will you cooperate in this inquiry or shall I be forced to invoke full Class One rigor? I leave it to you. Start with your motivation for your first disruption bombing at Nuclear City."

"Never heard of it," O'Leary said wearily. "Either Nuke City *or* a disruption bomb. Sorry."

"Glibness will avail you naught, fellow," Frumpkin said, wiping a hand across his face as one sore beset with frustration. He turned to Belarius V. "We've wasted enough time trying to reason with him," he said tiredly. "I suggest we simply stasis-file him and get on with the rest of it."

"I've got an idea," Lafayette offered. "Why not tell me, in simple nontechnical language, just what's going on? Maybe I could even shed some light on it if I knew what it was all about."

"So you think you're in a position to bargain, eh?" Frumpkin snorted. "You'll come clean in return for . . . what was your price?"

"Just tell me what happened to get you boys so upset," Lafayette said, feeling the futility of his request even as he spoke. "And save the jargon. Pretend I don't know anything about whatever it is you're so worried about."

"On October eight last," Belarius V said solemnly, "an attempt was made to destroy the Prime metering vault. An explosion of force seven on the TRAN scale. Inside the vault. You can see what that means. So could we all."

"I hate to sound like a dumdum," O'Leary said, "but I *can't* see what that means. Anyway, what does it have to do with me?"

"He's a resourceful devil, eh, Belarius?" Frumpkin commented. "No matter what one says, he has a disclaimer ready."

"But it seems it's always the same disclaimer," Belarius replied dryly. "See here, fellow," he said more briskly to Lafayette, "Just what excuse do you offer for your presence here in defiance of the Code?"

"None at all," Lafayette answered sharply. "I have a perfect right—or almost perfect—to be here. It's you two characters who have some explaining to do."

"I think that's quite enough," Belarius put in abruptly. He turned to a shabby steamer trunk or large suitcase beside him. Lifting the lid, he took out a complicated-looking apparatus and turned to O'Leary.

"Put out your hands, left palm up, right palm down," he ordered curtly, while Frumpkin fiddled with his gun. Lafayette complied warily, eyeing the gadget Belarius was holding. With a quick movement Belarius draped the thing across O'Leary's hands. He felt icy metal bands extrude, encircle his wrists, and tighten gently. There was a sensation of questing tendrils growing rapidly downward, searching over his body. He yelled once, tugged; there was no give in the complex shackle. When he tried to take a step toward Frumpkin, he found his legs were equally immobilized. "Hey!" he yelled again.

Belarius and Frumpkin were busy over the suitcase.

"Look at that, Frumpy," Belarius said grimly. Over Belarius' shoulder, Lafayette could barely glimpse a round glass screen like a cathode-ray tube, set in the trunk lid, on which glowed in pink a set of concentric arcs.

"This," Frumpkin said hoarsely, putting a well-groomed finger on a short segment of a curve looking squeezed between longer arcs. "Is this . . . our baseline here?"

Instead of answering, Belarius turned to O'Leary, stepping back to give him a clear view of the screen. He pointed.

"You can see for yourself what you've done," he grated. "You've trapped yourself in an abort. How you imagined you'd escape to make good your plot is, I confess, obscure to me."

"Me, too," Lafayette said. "What's an abort?"

"As the term suggests, an abort is a nonviable stem. As you see, this one ends in some seventy-two hours."

"How do you mean, 'ends'?" Lafayette asked. "All I

see is some kind of radar screen."

"Ends, terminates, discontinues, ceases to exist," Frumpkin spoke up. "That's a simple enough concept. And if we were still here then, we'd end with it. Accordingly, Belarius, I suggest we phase-shift at once, just in case your calibration is off a hair's breadth."

"What about this fellow, then?" Belarius inquired indifferently, indicating O'Leary. "Finish him off, and so report?"

"As you command, my lord," Frumpkin replied in an oily tone, disassociating himself from the murder.

"Why don't you just go home and leave me to my own devices?" Lafayette suggested. "Nobody would know the difference."

"No?" Belarius came back coolly. "You underestimate the subtlety of our Prime surveillance net. Nothing escapes the notice of YAC-19."

"Why bandy words with him, sir?" Frumpkin put in. "If we should simply shunt him into a holding locus, he'd keep until we could deal with him to best advantage. YAC-19 *will* want to interrogate him."

"True," Belarius conceded. "Set up coordinates for the nearest holding locus, then—"

"Wait," Lafayette cut in. "I *can't* leave this locus— Daphne's here, somewhere. And if I leave, I may never find it again!"

"The point is well taken," Belarius said. "Not that your petty concerns are of any merit, but there *is* YAC-19's policy to consider."

"Who is this yak you keep talking about?" Lafayette demanded. "Who's he to sit in judgment on a total stranger, and one close to the throne of Artesia, by the way!"

"YAC-19 is a computer," Belarius stated grandly, "and Postulate One at Nuclear City, of course."

"And *our* immediate supervisor," Frumpkin put in loftily.

"Its policy is to hold phase violations to a minimum," Belarius contributed. "To remove you from this your native locus would occasion a mild phase displacement; ergo, you'll stay here."

"It's not my native locus," Lafayette protested. "At least, I don't think it is—or maybe it's just the three hundred years. It doesn't look anything like Artesia—except for the Tower, that is." He glared sullenly at Belarius. "Artesia's my home," he stated, "not this dump . . . Aphasia, Trog called it."

"Locus designation?" Frumpkin inquired. "Of this Artesia, I mean."

"Alpha Nine-Three, Plane V-87, Fox 221-b," O'Leary replied promptly. Frumpkin looked grave and twiddled control knobs on the apparatus inside the suitcase.

"Doesn't check out, Belarius," he said tonelessly. "Something a trifle out of sync there." He shot O'Leary a hard look. "Why lie about it?" he demanded.

"I was born there," O'Leary said. "When I was a few months old, a renegade inspector from Central kidnapped me and took me to Colby Corners, U.S.A. I grew up there, and then I focused my psychical energies one evening, and was back in Artesia, where I belonged."

"Better change that story," Belarius put in after consulting a small handbook. "Artesia's listed, all right, but as a dead locus. What we call a traumatic abort. Ceased to exist nearly three hundred years ago."

"Nonsense!" O'Leary said, and after a thoughtful pause went on, "I was there half an hour ago—or three hundred years and a half hour ago. . . . I'm not quite sure about that. Anyway, Artesia is just as real as Melange, or Colby Corners, or Thallathlone, or any of those other crazy places I've been—and realer than *this* crazy locus, Aphasia."

"Not listed," Belarius said after a glance at his book. He turned to Frumpkin. "That's it, let's report back, and we'll just put this fellow on hold. Later, a brain-scrape will soon have the facts out of him."

"Wait!" Lafayette demanded. "You can't just go off and leave Aphasia to dissolve back into entropic energy—"

"Aha! So you *do* know something!"

"You told me," O'Leary said hastily. "Sure, I know about planes of reality and all that; I've been in enough of 'em. But this time I didn't meddle. I was just sitting in the garden with Daphne, and all of a sudden—"

"Get him over here, Belarius," Frumpkin cut him off. "The shift zone on this portable rig is pretty small, you know. We wouldn't want to leave even this poor boob stranded in half-phase." Belarius manhandled O'Leary into the indicated spot.

"Daphne's around here, somewhere!" O'Leary blurted. "If you leave her—"

"This Daphne is also a native of Colby Corners?" Belarius asked without interest.

"No—and neither am I—I just grew up there, in the orphanage, you know. Daphne's an Artesian, born and bred. . . . You can't go off and leave her stranded here!"

"What about it, Frumpkin?" Belarius queried his colleague. "Hadn't we best check this out?"

"Damn right!" O'Leary yelled. "You can't go creating a phase violation, remember, even if you *are* inhumane enough to strand a helpless girl in this dismal place. YAC-19 wouldn't like it," he added.

"I suppose we'll have to fetch her along," Frumpkin conceded. "Where is she, fellow, hiding in a dark corner?" He looked about the shadowy room in a show of confusion.

"How do I know, Flapkin, or whatever your dumb name is?" O'Leary demanded. "Release me, and I'll try to find her. I thought she must have come this way, but I was wrong—unless you two sharpies grabbed her and sent her off somewhere with that suitcase of yours."

"By no means, Mr. O'Leary. By the way, Frumpkin," Belarius shifted his attention to his associate. "Since he's had the effrontery to preempt the honored name of Lancelot O'Leary—"

"Not Lancelot!" Lafayette cut in. "Lafayette! And not Ladislaw, or Lohengrin, or Lafcadio, or any of those other nerds from other loci. That's L-A-F-A-Y-E-T-T-E!"

"To be sure," Frumpkin murmured, ruffling the

pages of his handbook. "*The* O'Leary. Of course. Why claim descent from any lesser O'Leary?"

"Descent my elbow!" O'Leary snorted. "I *am* Lafayette O'Leary! The same one who got your great-grandpap or whatever out of the soup the time Quelius made his play. Except for me, old B-I would still be fending off Jemimah in the royal swine-pen!"

Frumpkin was eyeing O'Leary intently. "I suppose a grand delusion is no more trouble than a petty one," he mused aloud, with a glance at Belarius.

"Just for the record," the latter suggested, "why not take a few Zeta readings on him? His mention of Quelius suggests he may know something. The Quelius file is top SBR classification, you'll recall: the hush order came from the top. So this chap can't be as insignificant as he appears."

"Very well," Frumpkin agreed, "but frankly, I think he's bluffing. A quick scan at about D-level?"

"A full class-A Zeta," Belarius corrected in a solemn tone. "If there's anything here at all, it's likely to be a major fault."

"A fault? Not in *our* records, I should hope," Frumpkin replied as he turned to Lafayette, extending what looked like an electrified acupuncture needle. "Just hold still, won't take a moment," he said soothingly, reaching for Lafayette's arm.

"How could I do otherwise, trussed up in this magic hair-net of yours?" O'Leary demanded. "You're not going to stick that thing in me, are you?" he inquired in a less-than-optimistic tone.

"Just a contact device," Frumpkin reassured him. The touch of the thin stiff wire was icy cold, and tingled. Frumpkin ran it along O'Leary's arm while consulting dials in his suitcase, his expression grave.

"I say!" Belarius exclaimed after a glance at the dials.

"Just so," Frumpkin concurred expressionlessly.

Both men turned quickly to eye Lafayette without visible approval.

"Where have you hidden it?" Belarius barked.

Before Lafayette could protest, Frumpkin said

sternly: "Young man, it is now quite clear that you have not only committed the gravest offence in the Civil Code, but have compounded the crime with a breach of the Primary Regulation itself—though how you managed such villainy remains obscure, I concede."

"A mystery which will be elucidated promptly, once the full attention of I-Branch is focused upon you, 'Mr. O'Leary,' as I assure you it will be in a very few minutes now," Belarius elaborated and gestured curtly to Frumpkin. "Power-up the shift-field," he commanded.

"Wait!" Lafayette yelled. "What if I really *am* Lafayette O'Leary; after all, your own gadgets are telling me I'm not just a routine case."

With a keen glance at Belarius, Frumpkin said quietly, "We *might* be justified in holding him for higher-level review. . . ."

"You *said* we've got seventy-two hours!" Lafayette cried. "Let me go, and I'll find Daphne, and you can at least shift her to a more civilized locus! Where's your chivalry?"

Belarius and Frumpkin muttered together; then Belarius touched a button on the panel in the trunk, and Lafayette felt the net fall away. He looked down, saw what looked like a wire coat hanger bent into a wad; he picked it up and, as Frumpkin jostled past him, dropped it in the latter's pocket, from which it at once extruded a questing tendril. Frumpkin halted abruptly, uttered a croak, and made an abortive grab at the filaments now busily trussing his biceps, before coming to rest red-faced, his arms half-raised.

"What is it, Frumpy?" Belarius inquired casually of his subordinate. "Just remember something?" Then he came over to drape a comradely arm over the other's shoulders, started back with a yelp, and froze, locked to Frumpkin.

"Seems your magic hair-net has a few bugs," Lafayette said. "It can't tell its boss from the other guy. So just hang loose, gentlemen, until I get back."

While the two Primary inspectors made inarticulate sounds behind him, Lafayette went to the telephone box, seized the stubs of the cut wires, and tapped the exposed conductors together. A tiny pink spark jumped. Encouraged, he went on, tapping out an SOS in Morse, then amplified his message: TRAPPED IN N'S TOWER BY BELARIUS V AND ONE FRUMPKIN FROM PRIMARY QUERY GET ME OUT OF HERE DASH DAPHNE TOO STOP.

That done, he listened at the door. Hearing nothing, he opened it half an inch and was instantly thrust backward as a small, whiskery man even shorter and uglier than Trog burst through. As Lafayette regained his balance, the newcomer turned on him, raising a stone ax, but froze at the boom of a resonant voice from across the room:

"Stop where you are, Murg."

"Geeze, Allegorus hisself!" Murg croaked, the ax dropping from his hand. Lafayette turned to see a tall, cloak-wrapped figure stepping in through the open French doors from the balcony.

The newcomer shot O'Leary a single sharp glance from piercing eyes which were the only part of his face visible in the deep shadows of the hood over his head; then he went directly across the room to confront Belarius and Frumpkin.

"Stand fast, O'Leary," he called over his shoulder before he began a low-voiced conversation with the two, who responded to the terse questions with excited protestations:

". . . line of inquiry!"

". . . desperate criminal!"

". . . got to be done!"

". . . my career!"

At last the hooded stranger turned away, and the two Nuclear agents fell strangely silent, still standing in rigid postures as if awaiting a command to resume activity. As the tall intruder approached, O'Leary began organizing his confused thoughts, readying his first question.

"Who are you?" he blurted instead.

"I am called Allegorus," the strangely authoritative man said impressively.

"I heard you only come out once every three hundred

years," O'Leary countered uncertainly.

"Nonsense," Allegorus replied coolly. "It's just that it's been three centuries since I was last here."

"Oh," Lafayette replied, as if enlightened.

Behind him, there was a scuttling sound as Murg made a dash through the door.

"No matter," Allegorus said with a careless wave of a long-fingered hand. "We can round up that lot when needed. But as for this precious pair you've cornered here," he went on in a lower tone, "I fear, my boy, you've gotten in over your head there. Top brass, you know. Still, we'll find a way out. As for yourself, Lafayette, you're in deep trouble, lad. I don't know how you managed to get involved in all this, but I'm glad I managed to intercept you before the next temporal segment assumed complete actualization; this way, there's at least a chance . . . if you'll lend me your complete cooperation, that is." Allegorus looked inquiringly, or perhaps hopefully, at O'Leary. "You *will* cooperate, won't you, lad?" He voiced the wish hesitantly, almost, O'Leary thought, as if he were worried he might be refused. Strange, what with Allegorus being the high cockalorum in these parts, and himself a mere intruder. . . .

"Perhaps," O'Leary said coolly. "Just what *is* the situation, as you see it?"

"Disaster, in the most literal sense," Allegorus replied promptly. "It appears an entropic disjunction has occurred," he went on grimly, his eyes fixed on Lafayette. "You're aware of what *that* could mean, I'm sure."

"Don't be so sure, Al," Lafayette countered breezily. "It sounds bad, but I never heard of it before." He paused, awaiting explanation. "But make it fast," he added. "I'm going to find Daphne. The poor kid's out *there*—" with a wave of his arm—"somewhere."

"All in good time, sir," Allegorus hastened to reassure him. "An E.D. is the most drastic sort of temporal anomaly—"

"I know about those," Lafayette cut in. "Central claimed I caused them whenever I focused my psychical

energies—like the time I shifted myself to Artesia, and
then when I turned that swill at the Ax and Dragon into
Chateau Lafitte-Rothschilde, '29. At first I thought I
was just sort of hallucinating, you know, my sub-
conscious trying to bring my inner conflicts to my attention; but Nicodaeus straightened me out. He told me I
was actually moving things around from one reality
level to another. Pretty simple, once you understand it.
But right now it seems I've gotten myself—and Daph,
too—into another locus, and I didn't even change a
daisy from white to pink! I don't get it. Maybe you
know something about it: Maybe *you* were twiddling
around with *your* psychical energies, and somehow
loused everything up. How about it: Have you ever
heard of Artesia? That's where this tower belongs, you
know—it was built by Nicodaeus, or not built—but he
fitted out this old garret as his lab." Lafayette looked
around at the dim, cobwebby stone walls, the littered
stone floor. "It used to be very impressive," he assured
Allegorus. "But now it's been stripped, since Nicodaeus
was recalled to Central."

The hooded man nodded. "But all this isn't helping
us with the main problem," he pointed out. "I'm very
familiar with dear old Artesia—spent some time there
myself once, long ago." Allegorus sighed, lost in
nostalgia.

"Then, let's *do* something!" Lafayette cried, ". . . if
you're as powerful as Belarius and Frumpkin said."

"Ah, yes." Allegorus turned to study the two under
discussion, still standing in their awkward poses.

"I see you took the precaution of stabilizing them
with your Mark V," he said easily.

"Not *my* Mark V," Lafayette corrected. "I took that
little gadget away from Frumpkin after he'd used it on
me."

"Indeed? And how, might I inquire?" Allegorus returned, sounding dubious.

"He got a little careless, and I got a little lucky,"
Lafayette replied modestly.

"You *did* activate the 'hold' capability of the contact
device, I trust," Allegorus said blandly. "Otherwise, of

course, its sphere of effectiveness is less than three minutes.''

"I didn't have time to read the owner's manual,'' Lafayette explained. "I just stuck it on them the same way Frumpkin stuck it to me—more or less.''

"In that case—'' Allegorus began with sudden urgency, turning toward the pair, too late. Already, Frumpkin was bending over the trunk—a portable command center, O'Leary now realized. Frumpkin raised his head, shot O'Leary a haughty look, and flipped switches even as Allegorus lunged with a yell: "Get them!''

Lafayette charged. There was a deep-toned *boom!* and the light suddenly dimmed. For an instant, O'Leary seemed to catch a ghostly glimpse of the misty gray room, where Frumpkin was fading from view even as Daphne came into sight. O'Leary yelled "Daphne!'' and lunged as the glimpse faded. O'Leary slammed against the wall, empty-handed, as his quarry—both men, plus their trunk—seemed to duck aside, slipping from his grasp. Allegorus was picking himself up, having fallen heavily as he missed his grab for Frumpkin. Lafayette gave him a hand, at the same time scanning the shadowy recesses of the big room for the two agile Primary agents, in vain.

He put a hand to his forehead, trying to orient himself. "I'm having visions,'' he muttered as Allegorus bent toward him solicitously. "Waking dreams, or something. *He* was there—'Frumpkin,' Belarius called him—and Daphne, too. I know it's silly, but I think he knows more than he's telling about her.'' He stepped back from the wall and looked around the room.

"Where are they?'' he muttered. "Let's get some light in here. I'll cover the door—unless they made it out the window; but they couldn't have moved that fast, even without their baggage.''

"No need, my boy,'' Allegorus said in his deep voice, "they've well and truly flown. Too bad. Might have cleared this whole thing up on the spot.'' He shook his head regretfully. "Harm's done,'' he concluded. "No point in mourning. We must get busy at once.''

"Sure," Lafayette said weakly. "Doing what?"

"Saving this entire manifold of loci from utter dissolution, for a start," Allegorus snapped. "Come, Lafayette, marshal your resources! This is your opportunity to display that dazzling ingenuity of which the Record speaks in such extravagant terms!"

"I'm wasting time," Lafayette cut him off. "I'm leaving here right now to look for Daphne. Sorry I don't have time for this E.D. of yours, but I've only got seventy-two hours. Ta." He headed for the door, ignoring Allegorus' urgent plea to wait. As he set foot on the landing, the stone slab cracked and shifted, affording him a glimpse, through a quickly widening gap, of open air yawning below. He noticed a dull rumbling sound; a stone block fell at his feet, slipped through the opening, and was gone. Dust and gravel were dribbling down around him; the entire Tower, he realized, was trembling, cracks appearing everywhere. More stones fell, went bounding down the steps, knocking off chips from the worn treads. Lafayette took a deep breath and followed, leaping down six steps at a bound as the walls fell about him. He arrived at the bottom in a cloud of dust and ricoshays, leaped clear of a heap of rubble, and was out the collapsing doorway and into sunshine.

Chapter Four

It was early morning, Lafayette realized as he stepped cautiously out onto the weed-choked vacant lot which had, back in Artesia, been the rose garden. All was silent. Lafayette went boldly across to the thicket where he had met Lord Trog and his minions. It was deserted now, only the gilt chair, now lying on its side, remaining as evidence of the hairy chieftain's visit. O'Leary set it upright and sat in it, remembering the long row of which it had once been a member, lining the mirrored grand hall.

There was a sound from the dense underbrush; then Marv, moving uncertainly, emerged into view. He had the appearance of a survivor of some disaster.

He eyed O'Leary warily, then looked aside, angling off as if to skirt his position rather than approaching.

"Where is everybody, Marv?" Lafayette called, his voice shocking even himself as it broke the eerie stillness. Marv shied and scuttled on. O'Leary called him back.

"Over here, Marv," he ordered. "We need to have a little talk." The former bodyguard paused and then obediently edged toward the chair, not looking at Lafayette. He reminded O'Leary of an oft-beaten dog with a guilty conscience.

"Glad to see you got clear, Yer Lordship," Marv muttered.

"Clear of what?" O'Leary demanded.

"Too bad me and Omar din't stay inside like you said —but climbing them stairs was too much. Like, not only is a guy sticking his neck out, but I and old Omar was getting pretty winded, too. So, when we heard the bugle go, natcherly we hadda report in on the double— just in time to watch Frodolkin's boys drag old Trog outa his fancy chair, which I think he'd pop a gusset if he could see you setting in it now, Sir Al."

"I'm Sir Lafayette, not 'Al,' " O'Leary snapped. "What's happened here? Where's Trog?"

"Like I was tryna say, sir—they got him. Prolly got him hung up by the heels right now, squeezing his secrets outa him. Onney it'll take a while, 'cause he ain't got none—secrets, I mean."

"Who's this Frodolkin you mentioned—and where?" O'Leary insisted. "I need to see the head man here, and if Trog's been replaced by Frodolkin, then he's the one I have to see—and in a hurry."

Marv scratched at his unkempt scalp with a fingernail like a black-rimmed banjo pick. "Lessee," he muttered, "he might be back at camp, celebrating the big victory and all—or maybe he's out scouting his new territory, kinda sizing up what he got here. Beats me."

"Listen, Marv," O'Leary said urgently, rising and going closer to the ragged fellow, who was intent now on capturing a flea. "Just before I showed up," O'Leary insisted, "didn't you see a girl—a lovely young woman with dark hair, wearing a silver-lamé gown and a blue velvet cloak that's too big for her? It's my cloak, you see; I just put it around her so she wouldn't get soaked in the rain. You must have seen her! She was only a few seconds ahead of me."

"Not a chanst, Al. A dame to fit that description ain't been seen in these parts since last Saint Filbert's Day anyways. And if she was, she'd of been grabbed by the first guy seen her. We ain't seen nobody. Forget it, pal. It's a nice delusion, but it just won't stand up. Why not go on down to town and find yerself one o' them nice friendly broads hangs around Ye Gut Bucket Bar and Grill?''

"Because Daphne's *here*, and I mean to find her," Lafayette replied staunchly. "How many of Trog's men can you round up in a hurry?"

"Depends what for," Marv replied lazily. "If it's easy and pays good, a lotta the boys'll volunteer, just outa sheer altruism. What you got in mind, Al?''

"For the last time," O'Leary snapped. "I'm not Al!"

"You come outa the Dread Tower, din't ya?" Marv countered.

"Of course, but—"

"You saying Allegorus don't hang around the Tower?" Marv challanged.

"Well, no," Lafayette conceded. "He dropped in while I was there, as a matter of fact."

"What *I* don't figger," Marv confided, rubbing his unshaven jaw with a horny palm, "is hows come you don't use some o' them snazzy tricks which you're justly famous for and all, to locate this Daffy broad you're hung up on."

"I wish I could," Lafayette mourned. "But ever since they focused the suppressor on me"—his thought continued after his voice faded—"still, I *did* handle old Trog pretty well when he was all set to give me the works. Maybe if I *really* concentrate—"

"Hey, Al, don't go working no spells while I'm around, OK?" Marv broke into his reverie. "I'm skeered o' witchcraft and like that. So just wait'll I take cover. Hark! What's that?"

"That's I and my boys putting the arm on you, dumdum," an unfamiliar voice replied to Marv's rhetorical question. A big fellow wearing a faded and patched but recognizable uniform resembling that of the Royal Artesian Pioneer Corps stepped from the underbrush, holding in his fist a naked short-sword with which he whacked idly at the obstructing brush.

"Uh-oh," Marv said in a stricken tone. "General Frodolkin hisself, if I ain't mistaken."

"None other, Marv," the great man acknowledged.

"Chee, sir," Marv said in tones of wonder. "Hows come Yer Worship to know my name and all?"

"Surely you recall, Marv: Last fall you turned your coat and for some days were one of my most trusted retainers. Unfortunately, after that you blotted your copybook badly by turning it again and redefecting to the upstart Trog with my second best dirk—with sheath—and wild tales of an imminent attack by me."

"I can explain, Yer Lordship," Marv came back uncertainly. "See, I got a idea to spy out old Trog, which he never did appreciate my loyal service, and come back to tip you off, which ya could beat him to the punch."

"Umm," Frodolkin murmured. "A matter into which my PPS will inquire later. Now, who's your companion here? Didn't I hear you call him Allegorus?"

"Ya could've," Marv conceded.

"Capital!" Frodolkin cried. "I have need of your services, sir," he went on, looking at Lafayette directly for the first time. Then he turned to yell over his shoulder: "George! Iron-Head Mike! Take me this pair at once! On the double!"

In response to this bellow, two surly louts came thrusting through the screen of trees, glowering. At sight of O'Leary, they moved in eargerly. At that moment, it occurred forcibly to O'Leary that he had definitely been hasty in leaving the shelter of the laboratory.

"No rough stuff yet, boys," Frodolkin said, easing into their path. "I got a use for this prisoner," he explained, deftly palming off the nearer of the two heavies. "Now, you just quiet down, George," he admonished. "You'll have your chance to hear bones breaking later, if he fails to cooperate."

"Aw, these pansies wit' clean fingernails always cooperates easy," George complained.

"Yeah," Iron-Head agreed, nodding his unkempt mop soberly. "We ain't had no fun since that little sapsucker in the fancy britches come pokin' around here, Monday a week."

Frodolkin turned to Lafayette. "Well, you see how

the wind blows, sir,'' he said silkily. "So, what is it to
be? Gracious cooperation, or grudging cooperation? I
assure you, in the end the result will be the same, so
you'd be wise to cultivate a bit of good will on my part
by willingly performing the trifling task I have in mind
for you.''

"Say, Al,'' Marv muttered conspiratorily from the
side of his mouth, "this here'd be a swell time for you
to pull one of them nifties outer yer sleeve, OK?''

"Sorry, General,'' Lafayette said, ignoring Marv.
"First I have to find Daphne—she's lost here somewhere. . . . Have you seen a beautiful brunette wearing a
blue velvet cloak? Probably scared to death, poor kid.''

"If I had,'' Frodolkin responded, "I'd not be here
now, nattering of trifles—not that your presence is to be
regarded lightly.''

Lafayette was thinking furiously: if he *could* manage
just one little trick now . . . After all, he didn't abso-
lutely *know* there wasn't a squad of the Royal Artesian
Household Guard concealed in the brush, awaiting the
moment to move in on these interlopers. . . . He concentrated on the details of their red-and-blue uniforms with
gold-braided white lapels, fancy-dress sabers hanging
beside polished boots. . . .

O'Leary blinked hard as a sudden vertigo seemed to
blur his vision. Then he was back in the dim gray room.
He looked around eagerly for another glimpse of
Daphne, but before he could complete his scan, Frumpkin hurried up, glass in hand.

"Sorry about the interruption, my boy,'' he said
hastily, "but as you see, my enemies are everywhere
—the blind fools! Now, as soon as you've decided to be
reasonable . . .''

Before Lafayette could reply scathingly, the dim light
faded and winked out. Frumpkin's voice continued for
a moment; then sunlight dazzled O'Leary.

There was a crackle of breaking twigs, and a paunchy
villein in a soiled red-and-blue coat staggered into view,
a decapitated wine bottle clamped in one gnarled fist. A
battered saber sheath dragged the ground, its gold-
braided decorations dangling in snarled loops.

"Oops, par' me, General," he said blurrily. "Have a li'l drinkie?" He proffered the bottle, which Frodolkin struck aside before George could reach it.

Almost, Lafayette told himself. *I came close, but my focus seems to be a bit off. Still, it's a start.*

"How's about it, Al?" Marv persisted. "How about a neat one, like the time you turned youself into a big bird? Or the time you had the flying carpet and all?"

"Not today, Marv," O'Leary said brusquely. Then to Frodolkin, who had turned the newcomer bodily and with a shove headed him back whence he had come, "Sorry, General. I'm just here for a few hours, and I have some very urgent business to attend to. But, just out of curiosity, what *is* this boon you're craving of me?"

"As to that," Frodolkin replied, "it happens that at present I find it necessary to chastise a rogue known as Duke Bother-Be-Damned, a chore for which I can ill afford to allocate my own valuable time just now. Ergo, I wish you to bring the scoundrel to heel on my behalf."

"Why should I do your dirty work?" Lafayette asked reasonably.

"Aside from George and Iron-Head Mike, there are a number of reasons," Frodolkin stated flatly.

"Sorry," Lafayette said. "I don't have time. Actually, I think I'll just nip back into the Tower for a moment; it seems I forgot something."

"Indeed you did, Sir Allegorus," Frodolkin agreed with a wave of his hand, which drew O'Leary's attention to a nearly solid ring of unshaven ruffians now surrounding the clearing.

"OK, *now!*" Marv hissed in the direction of O'Leary's ear. "Don't lemme down pal, after I sided witcha an all," he whined.

"Is that supposed to be some kind of threat?" Lafayette demanded of Frodolkin, ignoring Marv plucking at his sleeve.

"Supposition does not enter into the matter," Frodolkin replied coolly. "As for 'some kind of threat,' I think the nature of the threat is obvious enough." At his nod, Iron-Head Mike took a step closer to O'Leary.

"Perhaps," Frodolkin said, "after you've completed your mission, I'll consider permitting you to revisit yon fell ruin—though why you should desire to do so is, I confess, a riddle."

"Look, General," Lafayette said desperately. "You don't get it. I'm not just some picnicker you happened to roust. I've got to get back to the lab—it's my only link, maybe, with Central and Artesia. And meanwhile, my wife, Daphne . . . uh, Countess Daphne to you, is out here somewhere, lost in this crazy jungle full of maniacs!"

"The Countess, eh?" Frodolkin echoed. He turned to the nearest of his bodyguard. "Any of you boys seen the Countess around?" he inquired in a bored tone.

"Uh, Chief, old Mel-the-Smell's got him a sow he calls Dutchess," a whiskery fellow volunteered doubtfully.

"He don't mean no pig," Iron-Head dismissed the suggestion. "He means a dame, a real snazzy piece too, eh, kid?" He leered at Lafayette and belched comfortably. "Maybe we're missing a bet at that, Chief, not collecting duh broad."

Now's the time, Lafayette told himself grimly. He eyed the seven-foot bruiser, thinking of the heavy lunch of lobster-tails and pizza the big fellow might well have gulped down half an hour ago. *Focus the old psychic energies,* he urged himself. Was there a slight *flicker*, or did he imagine it? He looked at Iron-Head Mike.

A stricken expression crossed the blunted features of the bodyguard. He put one large hand tenderly against his abdomen. His color was no longer good.

"What's wrong, Iron-Head?" Lafayette inquired genially. "You look hungry. How about a pizza and a gallon of warm sweet port?"

Iron-Head shuddered, looking distinctly green now.

"What's all this about pizza?" Frodolkin demanded. "I've warned you fellows to stay out of my private mess tent. You wouldn't appreciate the subtleties of smoked oysters, caviar, escargots, artichoke hearts, pickled onions, and rare wines; that's why I sequester such comestibles as my portion of our forage."

"Ulp," Iron-Head said blurrily, using both hands now.

Oh, boy, Lafayette said to himself, feeling a surge of enthusiasm. *It's just like the old days, like the time Count Alain was trying to keep me from getting to know Adoranne. I'm back in business!*

"Hey, Mike," George said, emerging into view from the underbrush with his unshaved jaws working hard and holding in his unwashed paw a vast sandwich minus one sizable crescent.

"Wanna bite o' my sardine-peaner-butter-and-banana samidge?" he inquired, offering the construction, the edges of which oozed ketchup and mayonnaise—or possibly blood and brains, Lafayette reflected, averting his eyes. Iron-Head passed him at a trot, bound for the shelter of a raggedly overgrown hibiscus hedge whence there emanated almost at once sounds reminiscent of a brontosaurus in labor, combined with the eruption of a small volcano. As Frodolkin stared concernedly after his stricken minion, Lafayette unobtrusively edged off toward the vine-grown and mildew-stained tower still, surprisingly, looming above the trees against the clear morning sky. He was halfway there when Marv's voice overtook him.

"Hey, where ya goin', boss? Not back inside the Dread Tower, huh? I mean, I been inside wunst and got out in one piece—I ain't innerested in, like, tempting fate and all by venturin there again!"

"Certainly, Marv," O'Leary replied firmly. "That's where the action is. Come on." Even as he spoke, O'Leary heard his voice take on a hollow, echoic quality. Mist was settling in, blurring things, and again he saw the gray room around him. Frumpkin rose from an overstuffed chair, and at once Lafayette grabbed his arm, no longer clad in coarse gray, he noticed, but in the elegant silver-trimmed black he had worn in the Tower.

"Where's Daphne?" O'Leary demanded. Frumpkin jerked his arm free and spoke to someone out of sight behind O'Leary. He heard a movement, ducked too late, and fell endlessly; he struck hard, and the light of day glared around him.

"Grab them, lads!" Frodolkin's command cracked like a whip. Lafayette turned as Marv hurried back the way he had come, giving a wide berth to George who was advancing supporting Iron-Head Mike, who came protesting. As they approached, O'Leary stepped close to Mike.

"You may have an iron head," he said, "but I'll bet you've got a glass gut." He feinted a jab to the midriff; the big fellow staggered back, hands extended, fingers spread as if to fend off an advancing juggernaut.

"Have a heart, pal," he groaned. "I ain't in my best form right now, OK? So maybe I'll give ya a break this time, see? I'll just play like I din't hear him."

As Lafayette eased around the giant and continued quickly across the broken flagstones to the no-longer-collapsed doorway, Marv caught his arm. He turned to shake him loose, and from behind him an iron clamp closed on his shoulder, yanked him inside, and dropped him. The door slammed and he was in darkness.

The darkness lightened and he caught a glimpse of the wide, featureless gray room. Daphne stood a few feet away, dressed in a gown of pale yellow Lafayette had never before seen. He croaked her name. She turned, seemed to look through him, and walked away to be lost in dimness. Frumpkin hurried up. "This won't do, you know, my boy," he said in mild reprimand. "We must come to terms."

O'Leary knocked the Man in Black aside and hurried after Daphne, but there was only darkness around him now.

"Come back here, you vandal!" Frumpkin's frantic voice shouted after him. "You'll ruin everything!"

"It occurred to me, my boy," the resonant voice of Allegorus said from the gloom, "that you'd be in need of a trifle of assistance about now." There was a scratching sound, and light flared. The tall figure of the mysterious Primary agent loomed over O'Leary, holding a candlestick in one hand. With the other, still as hard as an iron clamp, he hauled Lafayette to his feet.

"Come along, lad," he ordered curtly. "We have work to do—and not much time to do it in."

Chapter Five

"I was sure you'd have second thoughts, my boy," Allegorus went on expansively, "when you realized what you'd blundered into out there."

"I thought the tower was collapsing," Lafayette said. "In fact, I *know* it was collapsing. How'd it get put back together so quick?"

"A mere temporal faultline, Lafayette," Allegorus replied soothingly. "For a moment there, in transit to Aphasia II, you were occupying a locus in which the tower happened to be falling as a result of all the probability stresses set up by current events centering on the lab."

"What about the lab?" Lafayette demanded, feeling a sudden stab of panic. "Is it still intact?"

"No fear, lad. As I told you earlier, the volume of space-time occupied by the installation has been thoroughly stabilized; in some loci, where the tower itself has fallen, it appears to float unsupported in thin air, a circumstance which is helpful both in rendering it inaccessible to curious locals and engendering the aura of supernatural dread which you've encountered here in embryonic form."

"I just came back to get a few things straight," Lafayette demurred, but he followed his rescuer up the rubble-littered stairway. "By the way, what *did* I blunder into? It seems there's been a change of administration out there in the last few minutes."

"That, my dear boy, is the least of the changes which have occurred," Allegorus replied patronizingly.

"Let's hold it right here," Lafayette said, and halted. "Until we clear up a few things. And I'm definitely not your dear boy. Anytime someone starts calling me 'dear boy,' I know I'm being set up for something. Why not come right out and tell me what it is? I might even volunteer. And what do you know about a big gray room where Frumpkin's keeping Daphne?"

Allegorus, three steps above, turned to face him. "Lafayette," he said almost kindly, "I have no wish to delude or confuse you, but the situation in which we find ourselves is one of the most extreme gravity, aggravated, I regret to say, by your own hasty actions since you arrived here."

"Sure, you mentioned the entropic disjunction. Now tell me what it means," Lafayette demanded grumpily. "Maybe we'd better hurry on up and just make sure the lab is still there," he suggested, edging past Allegorus. *Especially the phone*, he was assuring himself urgently. *The phone is still working.*

"You're well aware, Lafayette, of the manifold nature of what we choose to call 'reality,'" Allegorus pontificated. "What is not so generally realized is that the laminar paratemporal structure is more fragile than is at first evident. You found you were able, of course, quite voluntarily to shift your personal ego-focus from one plane to an adjacent one by a mere effort of will, which quite clearly is only a slight extension of the inherent faculty of all matter to coexist on multiple levels, shifting freely from one to another under pressure of circumstance. But it is just there, at the question of circumstantial pressures, that the crux of our problem lies. You see," Allegorus continued less glibly, seating himself on the step and warming to his subject, "when circumstantial forces are modified on a sufficiently wide scale, it is not the individual who slips across the interplanar gap, but the locus itself, this being the principle of the Focal Referent, a device with which you are familiar. Vast events on a cosmic scale can equally exert such pressures. And when such an event is triggered out-of-matrix by a freak occurrence, whole categories of foci can suffer dissubstantiation, while in accordance with Newton's well-known law, commensurate changes of equal and opposite scope bring unrealized foci into substantive status. It appears, Lafayette, that is what has happened. The ramifications are too complex to consider in any detail. The least of such repercussions is the realization of this bundle of defective foci known locally as Aphasia, replacing in the grand scheme the legitimate Artesian bundle, and relegating the latter to the void of that which might have been.''

O'Leary jumped up. ''You can't pin that one on me,'' he yelled. ''I told you, I was just sitting on a bench with . . . uh . . .'' Lafayette paused, frowning. ''Anyway, all of a sudden it was raining, and from then on everything went to pot. *I* didn't do anything!''

''You see, already those identities which have been relegated to nothingness fade from your memory,'' Allegorus pointed out. '' 'Daphne' was the name which escaped you just now, by the way. Now, I want you to think carefully, Lafayette. Precisely what did you say and do—and even think—as you sat on the bench? Try. This may be of monumental importance.''

''Nothing,'' Lafayette said defensively. ''We were just admiring the stars—''

''Any specific star?'' Allegorus cut in quickly.

''No! I mean, well, maybe. It was in Boötes, near the Great Bear, Ursa Major. I was just thinking bears don't have tails, and that it looked more like a duck—or it would if it had another star for the beak.''

''Lafayette,'' Allegorus said in a stricken tone, ''you didn't do—actually *do* anything? I mean to say, it was no more than an idle thought, eh?''

''I just played around with the idea of moving a near-by star over to make the beak, as I said.''

Allegorus leaped up and slapped his forehead with a

crack like a pistol shot. "That's it! The Great Unicorn! Greenwich was right! The E.D. does emanate from the vicinity of M-51!"

As O'Leary was about to voice his impatience with the renewed spate of nonsense he had once again received in response to his request for a simple explanation, he felt the stone tip and shake beneath him. A block of rough-cut masonry fell from the ceiling, just missing his left foot. Allegorus seized his arm, tugging him upward.

"Into the lab, man!" he cried, as more stone fragments rained down and the stair bucked under him like a flatbed at speed on a gravel road.

Frumpkin's frantic face seemed to be swimming, disembodied, in gelatinous mist.

"Stop now!" he yelled. "This will avail you nothing, O'Leary! And if you expect to see Daphne again—" His voice ceased in mid-word and Lafayette caught a fleeting glimpse of Daphne's face, her hair in disorder, her eyes wide with fear. He reached for her, but there was only mist and dust and a deep rumbling underfoot. The powerful grip on his arm urged him upward.

"This is no time for wool-gathering, Lafayette!" Allegorus' resonant voice shouted as from a distance. With an effort, O'Leary focused his vision on the breaking stair-slab underfoot, and managed to leap over it before it fell. Allegorus steadied him on his feet.

"It happened again!" O'Leary shouted over the rumble of falling stone. Allegorus hurried him on.

They paused on the landing to catch their breath, fending off a rain of gravel.

"I thought you said the tower didn't really collapse!" Lafayette remonstrated.

"Oh, it collapsed, Lafayette, it collapsed indeed—in a wide belt of loci into which we have no business straying just now. I fear we've not yet felt all the repercussions of your folly."

"*My* folly, nothing!" Lafayette yelled. "Let's get out of here!"

"The abnormal density gradient in Boötes was first noted some decades ago," Allegorus said a bit breathlessly as Lafayette urged him up the disintegrating stair. "A clear case of a collapsed Schrodinger function on a vast scale, but as it was extragalactic in orgin, nothing was done. Then, mere hours ago—but you know all about that."

"All about *what*?" O'Leary yelled.

"Consider for a moment, lad," Allegorus urged quietly, thrusting Lafayette toward the plank door to the lab. "Refresh your memory on the basics of quantum mechanics."

"I never got around to the higher physics," Lafayette protested. "I was too hung up with *Getting Into Radio Now,* and *How to Speak Spanish Without Actually Trying ,* and *Auto Repair Made Easy,* and continental-style techniques of fencing, and my synthetic rubber experiments, and making sardine sandwiches."

"A full schedule, without doubt," Allegorus commiserated.

"If you knew how bad I hated those sardine sandwiches!" Lafayette said bitterly. "I liked taffy OK, up until I got myself stranded in the desert with nothing else to eat."

"Yours has been an adventurous existence," Allegorus agreed. "But just now we'd best take steps to ensure the present Adventure is not permitted to deteriorate into a Terrible Experience." Then they were through the door and in the comparative calm of the old laboratory, though the floor still vibrated underfoot. The walls, Lafayette noted, were now decorated with zebra-hide shields, voodoo masks, stone-tipped spears, a moth-eaten lion's head, and gaudy posters advertising a weekend tour to tropical Antarctica. He pointed out the changed decor to Allegorus, who waved it away. "A shift in locus of a few parameters can often produce extensive superficial modification. Not to fear, my boy. Our link to Central remains secure."

"What happened to Marv?" O'Leary inquired

vaguely. "He was right behind us."

"Inasmuch as the fellow is indigenous to Aphasia II," Allegorus replied blandly, "it hardly matters."

"But he was the nearest thing to a friend I had in this nuthouse," Lafayette objected. He stepped out on the landing and looked down through dust into darkness. At that moment a despairing cry came from far below:

"Al—gimme a hand. It's me, Marv, your old side-kick—and it looks like they got me!"

"He calls you 'Al'?" Allegorus queried.

"He thinks I'm some spook," Lafayette explained briefly, then added, "I mean, they've got this super-stition about some weirdo with your name who pops out of the tower every three hundred years and shakes everybody up. When I came out, they assumed I was him—or you, if you're really the one they were expecting."

Allegorus pulled at his chin. "Hmmm," he mused. "That's rather curious, actually, Lafayette, considering that this is, as I mentioned, a spurious locus. It entered on its quasi-existence less than an hour ago. Yet it has traditional memories of a long history. This suggests a meddling hand. It is a matter I shall take up with the Council on my return."

"Sure, do that," Lafayette replied absently, ducking as a dislodged stone fell past him to make a resounding smash far below, followed by yells.

"OK, Al, that did it. Thanks a bunch," Marv's now cheerful voice rang from below. "Oh-oh, here they come again!" Marv's voice died away in a wail.

"I've got to help him," Lafayette said, ducking back as other, smaller stones fell rattling down the steps.

"Stay here!" Allegorus said sharply. "The lab is the only stable fix in this entire locus, which seems to be on the verge of derealization. We'd best get back inside at once!"

"Well," Lafayette stalled, "it won't hurt to just sneak a look. . . ." As he took a cautious step sideways, an egg-size rock impacted heavily against his skull just above the ear; he pitched forward and tumbled down into the rolling dustcloud obscuring the stairway.

Out of the swirling dust a dim room materialized; this time Frumpkin was nowhere to be seen. But another figure, slim and graceful, hurried past.

"Daphne!" O'Leary yelled, and lunged after her. She seemed not to notice, pausing only to switch on a standing lamp which illuminated a bulky easy chair in the depths of which, Lafayette saw with a start, Frumpkin was curled asleep; he seemed to wake with a start, then waved a negligent hand in dismissal, at which Daphne turned away. Except for an expression of disappointment on her sweet face, she seemed just as O'Leary had seen her last. He started after her and tripped. When he looked up, she was gone.

"Look here, Lafayette," Frumpkin said testily, "this interference will have to stop!"

Lafayette peered into the dimness but saw nothing of Daphne; he tried to rise, but collapsed; his hands were painfully restrained, he realized as he fainted.

The dungeon, Lafayette reflected, *is, as dungeons go, not too bad. No rats, and the straw is almost dry. The manacles, on the other hand—or on both hands—are large and rusty. Perhaps too large?* He tried to slip his right hand through the broad iron bracelet; he winced as the scaly corrosion rasped his skin, but maintained the pressure; his hand was free, if a bit bloody—but the film of blood had helped lubricate it, no doubt. The other hand came halfway and wedged tight.

Perhaps, Lafayette told himself, thinking frantically, *perhaps I left the flat-walker in this suit. I could have. I never got around to returning the gadget to Ajax, in all the excitement, and I haven't worn these britches since then, so it ought to be right here in my side pocket. . . .* Reaching awkwardly around himself to check his left pocket, he felt a lump under the cloth, managed to get a finger into the mouth of the pocket, groped, felt cloth tear—and grasped the miniature device which had once enabled him to walk through the three-foot-thick wall of the cell under the palace of Duke Rudolfo in time to rescue the Lady Androgorre, as dear little Daph—or her alternate self—was known at Melange, a dreary locus indeed. But he had succeeded in his mission, and now, with the flat-walker in his hand (he had his old stuff back for sure now), he could do it again. But first he had to find out just where he was: It would be a pity to pass through the wall only to find himself treading air fifty feet above a paved courtyard. Perhaps if he just took a peek, without committing himself . . . As to which wall to penetrate, there was no choice—not as long as he was still linked to one wall by his left wrist, which was far too tender from his earlier attempt to pull free even to contemplate submitting to that ordeal again. He turned to face the rough-hewn wall; as he fingered the tiny flexible flat-walker, his thoughts went back to the moment in Ajax's rough-hewn cavern lab when Pinchcraft, the research chief, had instructed him in the theory and practice of flat-walking. . . .

". . . It generates a field which has the effect of modifying the spatial relationships of whatever it's attuned to, vis-à-vis the exocosm. It converts any unilinear dimension into an equivalent displacement along the perpendicular entropic axis, at the same time setting up a harmonic which produces a reciprocal epicentric effect. Or in other words, it reduces the user's physical dimensions to near zero and compensates by a corresponding increase in density in its quasi-two-dimensional state."

It sounded just as silly now as it did then, Lafayette reflected. Still, it *had* worked. All he had to do, he remembered clearly, was to orient the device with its long axis parallel with his own, and the smooth face aligned with the widest plane of his body. He adjusted the device as required, felt over the roughened surface, then found and pressed the small bump at its center.

Nothing changed. Lafayette stifled his disappointment. The outfit had been dry-cleaned at least once since he had last used the flat-walker, years before, and it was probably ruined. Too bad: it would have been a big help. He raised a hand to brush away a cobweb that was touching his face; the sensation of a gossamer touch persisted. Then he noticed a faint glow in front of him —emanating from the stone wall? Suddenly excited, Lafayette took a cautious step, and felt the almost impalpable sensation he remembered from the last time he had walked through solid masonry.

For a fleeting instant he glimpsed the misty gray room, and Frumpkin's angular face shouting at him, "For the last time!" Then, without transition, he was out of doors, smelling fresh air. The sudden blaze of full sunlight dazzled him. He groped, feeling his way across uneven turf.

"Well, so you decided to come back and take my offer after all!" Frodolkin's hearty voice boomed at him. Hard hands clutched Lafayette's arms. He opened his eyes, saw that he was back in the ragged clearing from which he had fled only minutes before.

"You move good, kid," Iron-Head Mike declared. "I din't even see you until you was halfway past that stretch of wall. That's good. It's gonna be a big help to you when you get to the duke's camp. When I seen the phantom arm come outa the door and haul you in, I figgered you was done for. But I guess you know a few angles after all. Mike? Help our pal to sit down and give him some eats; he looks beat."

A hearty shove against his back sent O'Leary stumbling forward until a foot hooked his ankle and he fell heavily.

"Turn over, Bub," Mike's hoarse voice commanded. "The boss wants you sitting, not laying," Lafayette turned over and sat up. In the shade now, he was able, by squinting ferociously, to see through the glare an unfamiliar patch of neglected garden stretching across to a battered but intact granite wall, above which the tower reared up, intact, but stripped of its ivy. He was in yet another locus, he realized with a stab of panic. How would he ever find Aphasia II again, where poor little Daphne was probably crying her eyes out, expecting him to appear at any moment to take her home. He stood, ignoring Mike's yell: "I ain't told you to stand up, Bub!

You wait right where you was, and I'll rustle ya a peaner butter and sardine samidge and some good sweet port!''

This new locus, O'Leary realized, was a close relative of the one he had just left, differing largely in that it seemed just a few stages less deteriorated. General Frodolkin, he saw, now wore a virtually intact, though faded uniform. His beard had been trimmed and the rust was gone from the sword blade. He was approaching, idly whacking at dandelion heads with the weapon. As Mike drew back a booted leg to sweep Lafayette's feet from under him, the latter dropped to a sitting position and promptly kicked Mike's knee, causing the big fellow to collapse like a condemned tenement under the wrecker's ball. As Mike snarled curses, Frodolkin came up, tsked mildly, and ordered the fellow to abstain from further drinking on duty on pain of beheading, a fate he dramatized by lopping a blossom from a wild-growing rose bush with a quick sweep of his bared blade.

"As for you, young fellow," he said, turning his attention to O'Leary, "if by any chance you should fail in your sacred mission, your fate will be no less dire, though slower."

"Where's Marv?" O'Leary demanded, ignoring the threat.

"Oh, yes, poor Marv," the General echoed. "I seem to recall that I turned him over to my PPS for a friendly chat. Hark! That's him now, I don't doubt," he interrupted himself as hoarse screams echoed from the middle distance.

"Free him," Lafayette ordered. "He's my partner, and he goes with me. By the way, where am I supposed to find this Duke Bother-Be-Damned?"

"Not at all a bad idea, O'Leary," Frodolkin said expansively. "I shall take it under advisement. Meanwhile, I'll do as you suggest. Oh, Percy!" he concluded with a yell. There was a crashing in the underbrush and a short, roly-poly fellow wearing a soiled leather blacksmith's apron appeared, dashing sweat from his brow.

"Yeah, boss?" he said in an anxious tone, his small beady eyes flicking to O'Leary. "A new client, eh?

Swell. Just gimme a minute to fan old Marv and put Band-Aids on his hurties. He was a stubborn cuss, but he finely spilled the beans. You better keep a eye out for a ruffian name of Old Eerie or Something, which Marv says he's planning to pull one o' them cooze-like. You know, worm his way inta yer worship's confidence, then turn the tables. Seems like he's got a lotta magical gear stashed in the Tower yonder, which he can turn hisself inta a big bird and all."

"Thank you, Percy, a succinct report," the general replied blandly. "Now you may bring Marv into the presence. Conscious, mind you." He turned a stern eye on Lafayette. "So," he murmured, "you plot treachery, eh? You disappoint me, lad; I'd great plans for you."

"I haven't plotted anything." Lafayette demurred. "I don't even know which way is up yet. All I want is to find Daphne—but I don't suppose she's here anyway," he concluded hopelessly.

"I assure you, she is not," Frodolkin said firmly. "You may as well abandon that fantasy. After your triumphal return, you shall have second choice, after only myself, of the nubile wenches of the region, which I hear the Duke's got a nice little seraglio of his own."

"I don't want a seraglio, I just want Daphne," O'Leary replied doggedly. "And if I'm going to kidnap this duke for you, I'd better get started." He rose, brushing leaf mold from his seat. "Do I get any weapons or supplies?" he inquired, "or do I just walk into his armed camp and bring him out barehanded and eat when I get back?"

"That's the idea, lad," Frodolkin concurred smoothly. "I knew you'd know how to go about it. His camp is sort of in that direction," he added, pointing vaguely. "I wouldn't send a man out unbriefed," he explained. "Only about half a day's walk, if you avoid the bog, of course."

"Don't you think you ought to give me some sort of ID?" Lafayette inquired, "so I don't get scragged by your own troops along the way."

"No need, Al. Just tell them you're under my personal protection. But mind you stay clear of ambushes and the like."

"And when I get back, you'll let me go back into the Tower, right?" Lafayette specified, starting off uncertainly in the direction indicated.

"To be sure, dear boy," Frodolkin agreed absently. "Though I, for one, couldn't be dragged in there by wild Caucasian ponies. Still, I suppose you have your magical apparatus stored there, eh?"

"It's not that," Lafayette demurred, heading for a trail which seemed to lead more or less in the direction Frodolkin had indicated. "It's just that the lab's my sole link with Artesia—and my only hope of getting back to wherever I left poor Daphne stranded, with Central's help of course—unless Allegorus has other ideas. I don't really trust that slicker. Well, bye, I'm off."

"So you are, lad, but on such a mission as yours, perhaps a trifle of brain-fever will be more help than hindrance." He waved carelessly, nearly nicking Mike, who had regained his feet and was muttering to himself, scowling after Lafayette.

"Oh, hi, boss," Marv's voice called blurrily as Marv himself staggered from a side path to fall in beside O'Leary. "I give Percy a bum steer," he confided. "Tole him you could turn yourself into a big bird, and all. Sure you don't wanta try it?" His tone was wheedling. Lafayette ignored the suggestion and forged ahead along the poorly defined trail.

Chapter Six

    As O'Leary rounded a sharp turn in the rude path, he heard voices ahead—high pitched, almost squeaky voices:

"... only got a lousy one-percent droppage allowance."

"... three jumps and a slide outside our A-O Zone, and how we're gonna get back—"

"Never mind all that, Squirrely, I'm in charge o' this detail," a deeper voice cut in. "Hold it. We're closing fast."

Lafayette and Marv ducked aside into the concealment of a mass of foliage. At first he thought it was Trog: a stocky little man in worn leathers, carrying an immense backpack and wearing a jaunty red cap adorned with a bedraggled white owl's feather, appeared on the path ahead. He was frowningly studying a compass, which he shook repeatedly in an irritated manner.

"Damn that know-all Pinchcraft," he muttered. "I told him he was weak on theory on this one. 'Don't give it a thought, Roy,' he says to me. 'I personally guarantee the tagalong out to six parameters, anyway.' Nuts and bolts! According to this thing, we're practically falling over him right now—and all I see is more o' this lousy poison-ivy patch!"

"Sprawnroyal!" O'Leary cried and burst forth squarely in the little man's path. The dwarf recoiled; then, seeing Lafayette's face, grinned from one over-sized ear to the other and advanced to embrace him.

"Slim O'Leary, as I live and breathe!" he gasped. Then, turning to his companions who now formed a huddle like a cluster of gargoyles, "Boys, meet my old pal Sir Lafayette, which he's a right guy even if he is built like a beanpole." He gave Lafayette an abashed look. "Sorry, Slim, you know it ain't like me to, like, draw attention to a fella's build and all. I know there's some might think us boys from Ajax were a little on the sawed-off side our own selfs. Glad to see you, Slim! But what are you doing in this neck o' the woods? Meet the boys: Squirrely, Casper, and Rugadoon—Security Section, you know."

O'Leary shook three calloused hands and asked how things were back at the Ajax Novelty Works.

"Slow," Roy admitted gravely. "Frankly, Slim, we ain't never really what ya might say recovered from the trimming Prince Krupkin gave us on the Glass Tree job. Which reminds me—" He slapped pockets, found and extracted a small note pad which he rifled, then applied a stubby forefinger to a well-scribbled page.

"Slim, you remember old Flimbert, our security boss. Well, he's got a bee in his bonnet you still got equipment issued on a short-turn trial basis. He's nuts, I told him so myself. I remember when you turned in the two-man rug and the blackout cloak and all. Still, Flimbert says we're spose to bring you in. Pretty silly, eh?"

"Not really," Lafayette admitted. "It seems I advertently failed to turn in the flat-walker—left it in an inside pocket of a garment I don't wear much."

"Oh, no sweat, Slim. Hand it over and we'll be on the way." Roy studied the compasslike device in his hand. "This thing is still giving us a bum steer," he said. "According to this, I'm face-to-face with Commercial Enemy Number One, Slim, and there's nobody here but you." Sprawnroyal scratched his head, his lumpy features registering deep puzzlement. He turned to his friends. "Well boys, I'm stumped," he admitted. "Any ideas?"

"Sure, Roy," Squirrely replied promptly. "Put the arm on this old pal of yours, and we can be back in time for late chow."

"What, me pinch my own old comrade?" Roy demurred in a shocked tone.

"Actually," Lafayette said, "the idea isn't wholly reprehensible, Roy; I could use some chow myself—and frankly, I'd like to get out of this silly 'mission' I'm supposed to be on."

"That's very reasonable of you, Slim," Roy said. "Better a cosy cell back at the plant than this wilderness, eh? Let's go." He turned to Casper. "How's it look, Cas old boy?"

Casper shook his head dolefully. "Still can't get a reading, Roy," he reported glumly. "We must be outa emergency range, too." He pocketed the instrument he had been holding in his hand, its dials all frozen at null reading.

Roy turned to Lafayette. "We got a little problem area here, Slim," he said sorrowfully. "We shifted out with the new Mark II phase coordinator, a tagalong, you know. Spose to stick like a burr. Brand-new model. Frankly, the Mark I had bugs, and now it looks like maybe the Mark II ain't much better. Shifted us out OK, but now it acts like it don't wanta work—like, no power—and it drawing direct from the Primary grid, too. Don't figger."

"Things are screwy all over," Lafayette replied. "I was just sitting in the garden with Daphne—you remember Daphne—and suddenly we were here, and I haven't seen her since."

"Tough," Roy commiserated. "Swell looker, too, if you like 'em that high—and I know you do. Built, too. Well, why not look around for her. She probably just went back inside the palace, eh?"

"There's no palace," Lafayette reported. "Just ruins. Except for the tower—"

"That's it!" Roy cut in. "We duck up to the old lab and get Central on the hook."

"No go." Lafayette shook his head. "It's guarded by two or more sets of morons that are afraid to go near it and won't let anybody inside."

"This ain't good, Slim," Roy conceded. "When I seen you, I figgered we were home safe, but if you're as lost as we are . . ."

"Same here," Lafayette agreed. "I assumed you could use one of those neat Ajax gadgets you fellows manufacture and get me out of here—but I can't really leave until I've found Daph, and I've already lost track of Aphasia I, the locus I last saw her in. This is Aphasia II."

"Have you tried focusing the old psychical energies, like you usta?" Roy cut in eagerly. "Maybe you could get back and get word to HQ to work up a Mark III and get us outa here."

"I've pulled off a few small tricks," Lafayette said. "I *think*. They could have been coincidences. But I can give it a try."

"Atta boy," Sprawnroyal said enthusiastically, clapping O'Leary on the back. "Go to it, kid, which me and the boys will wait right here for the relief party." He paused, frowning thoughtfully. "While you're there, maybe you could pass the word to Chief Pratwick that this Duke Whateveritis is as good as cuffed. As soon as we know we got a route outa here, we'll close in on him."

"Wait a minute," Lafayette interrupted. "What was that name again? Duke who?"

"Lessee." Roy pulled at his chin. "Kind of a screwy name: I guess I don't remember exactly. But the boys back at the lab have pinned enough on him to keep him on the treadmill for the next two glacial epochs."

"It wouldn't be Duke Bother-Be-Damned, I suppose," O'Leary offered.

"That's it! How'd you know, Slim? Lemme guess: you're on the same job, which is how you come to be out here outside o' your regular jurisdiction, like. No offence: we can use all the help we can get.''

''Hold it,'' Lafayette cut in. ''I wasn't sent here to nail this duke; that's something a local boss who calls himself General Frodolkin dreamed up. I'm supposed to lay this Duke Bother-Be-Damned by the heels, single-handed, and I don't even know where to find him.''

''Frodolkin, huh? Seems to me like I heard the name.'' Roy got out his notebook and ran through it quickly. ''Yep, here it is: '. . . a mythical figure known in many loci, regarded by some scholars as a per-sonification of the antisocial impulse!''

''This one's real,'' Lafayette corrected. ''He's a me-dium-tall cutthroat wearing a beatup Artesian uni-form.''

''Artesian, eh?'' Roy looked thoughtful. ''From your old stamping ground, eh, Slim? Maybe he came along when you switched lines.''

''I doubt it,'' Lafayette replied. ''First there was an even raunchier character named Trog. While I was in the Tower, Frodolkin ran him off, apparently.''

''I heard that, Al!'' the familiar voice of Trog cried from the underbrush. ''Get them hands up, all you guys!'' Trog swaggered into view, a gang of unshaven louts twice his height at his heels. He halted at the sight of Roy and his entourage.

''Well, if it ain't my old pal, Sprawnie hisself,'' he declaimed, striding forward to offer a calloused palm to the astonished Ajax rep, who jumped back.

''You!'' Roy exclaimed. ''Troglouse III! A deserter! Grab him, boys!'' As the three little men leaped to seize the other little man, the latter's troops stepped in and laid about them with knouts, driving them back. Lafayette grabbed the club from the hands of one of the attackers and laid it across its owner's head; then the world exploded in white light. The light faded to a featureless gray. ''Not again,'' Lafayette groaned, get-ting to his feet long enough to collapse into the chair Frumpkin had occupied on his last ghostly dream-visit. Then Daphne approached out of dimness, carrying a bulldog pipe in one hand, a pair of outrageously beaded scarlet slippers in the other. She came close, hardly glancing at O'Leary. He started up, calling her name. She seemed not to hear, but looked around in a confused way.

"If you're looking for Frumpkin, Daph, he just stepped out," O'Leary said harshly. "What's the matter? Why won't you look at me?" Lafayette caught a glimpse of a tear on her cheek as she turned away. Then the dimness deepened into full dark, and Lafayette was sitting up, muttering her name and shaking his head to clear it. An unshaved lout loomed before him and swung a hamlike fist. Thereafter, Trog's men quickly surrounded their diminutive chief, holding Squirrely, Roy, Casper, and Rugadoon at bay.

"I guess *we'll* do all the grabbing that's gonna be done around here," Trog yelled when order had been restored. He eyed O'Leary sourly where he lay on the grass, his head still spinning.

"Whatta you doin' loose, Al?" he inquired aggrievedly. "I tole Marv to lock you in the slammer."

"He did, milord, he did," Lafayette reassured the irate fellow. "But I got bored, so I left."

"And all the time you had a meet set up with this bunch of spoilsports," Trog accused.

"No, we just happened to meet here on the trail," Lafayette corrected.

"I don't believe in coincidences," Trog declared, looking around defiantly. His eye fixed on Roy. "How about it, Sprawnie, do you say you just happened to meet this character by accident?"

"Well," Roy said reluctantly. "Not entirely. You see, we were following a new Mark II tagalong, and it led us right to him."

"Ha!" Trog barked. "The way I remember the Mark I, it had more bugs than a four-bit flop. Old Doc Pinchcraft goofed on that one!"

"Right," Roy agreed, "but the Mark II is a great improvement."

"You small-timers still scratching a living working

for rubes like old Krupkin?" Trog inquired genially.

"Only as a sideline," Roy corrected. "We've recently entered into a wide-scope contract with a personage of vast importance, like they say, to handle state security. That's why we're here, actually—on a bum lay, it looks like. We were after the Number One Public Enemy of all times, and all we found was Slim here, which he's a nice kid," he added in a lower, more confidential tone. "Only he ain't got the brains to be Big Time."

"Don't tell *me* about the fabled Allegorus," Trog huffed. "I'm the one nailed him coming outa his tower, ain't I? So he belongs to me. You boys'll hafta find yourselfs another pigeon."

O'Leary was taking deep breaths to clear his head. He was only half-feigning semiconsciousness now, meanwhile listening to the dispute between the two diminutive men.

". . . big shot around here!" Trog was declaring.

"I heard some fellow named Frodolkin had thrown you out of office," Roy countered.

"That crum-bum!" Trog snarled. "After I set things to rights again, I'll string him up by his heels and esplain the arrow of his ways to him with the cat-o'-nine-tails—two teams working in relays. He'll be worry he ever *seen* this place."

"Trog," Roy said in a more kindly tone, "do you ever regret the way you sold out Ajax and made off with classified materials?"

"Naw," Trog said firmly. "Anyways, I never made off with no secret stuff, nor no plans and specs neither."

"Then, how'd you get here, three octaves outside your own A-O zone?"

"It was screwy," Trog said. "I was onna trail, headin' for a big time in Port Miasma, and all of a sudden I run smack into a swamp where no swamp oughta be."

Lafayette's attention wandered, and he dropped off into a sound sleep. It seemed hours later when Sprawnroyal's hoarse voice at close range penetrated his lazy dreams of ease and comfort back home in Artesia:

"... you're too big to lug, Slim. So, come on, wake up now while we got a chanct, and let's check this out. This could be the break we been waiting for."

O'Leary opened his eyes and winced at the throb in his skull. He fingered a lump the size of a walnut above his ear. Slowly, he got to his feet. Trog, trussed from neck to ankles in stout new hemp rope, lay beside a small campfire. Around it Squirrely, Casper, and Rugadoon, bruised but cheerful, sat eating enthusiastically from small cans.

"I had a nice talk with old Trog, here," Roy told Lafayette comfortably. "I think maybe we gotta way outa this mess after all." He paused to hand Lafayette two of the small cans from his bulky backpack. "Better chow down now, Slim," he suggested. "Once we get moving, there won't be no time."

"What are you going to do?" Lafayette asked, dipping into a can of swamp-pheasant fricassee. "Good," he commented.

"Right; what we figger is a man on a tough field job needs class eats to keep up the old morale," Roy confided. "Now, you know how to triangulate, Slim, check out what parts of a locus match up with your baseline, and calibrate how far out you are, locus-wise, from where you was at when you begun."

"I've never done the calculations," Lafayette replied, "but I understand the principle. For example, we can figure Aphasia II is very close to Aphasia I, where Daphne's lost, on the basis of the similarities in the landscape, plus personnel. Trog, for example."

Roy shook his head. "Trog's a bad example, Slim. This here's the *same* Trog you run into before, not a analog. But you're right; you're still in the same A-range as where you lost Daphne at. But where's *that* at? Huh? How close are we to the Artesia range? That's a little tougher; we got to fall back on topography. Like, in Artesia, you got a desert, a dry lake bed, west o' town. Then in Melange, it's still a lake, and farther in the same direction, just in the next range, you got a bay, a arm o' the sea: that's Colby Corners and all, your old home town before you came to Artesia. So here we got a saltwater swamp. Looks like a little tectonic activity has pushed up a ridge and cut the bay off, and here it's partly drained. In Melange it's turned into a freshwater lake: The swamp never formed because the ridge wasn't that high there; so with the springs at the bottom, plus rainfall, you got a lake. In Artesia, it drained and there was a spillway open in the ridge, so it went dry and you got a desert. The swamp here puts us off on a tangent to our direct route back to the Artesia/Melange wide-range."

"How do we get back?" O'Leary cut in impatiently. "At least to Aphasia I, if not to Artesia?"

"There's things I can't tell you, Slim—security, you know," Roy said apologetically. "Your best bet is still the old psychical energies. Casper's got the emergency gear in his pack, which we ain't allowed to use it except in case of what they call a 'dire emergency.' But don't worry: If we hafta pull the chain, we'll get back to you ASAP, and whip you outa here. So why don't you just go ahead and give it a try? It'll be tricky, you being outside your primary range this time and all. But what the heck: Maybe you can do it. Good luck, and I'll see you back at Ajax which we'll hoist a few in memory o' this contretemps, which we'll have a good laugh when it's over."

"Yes, but what about Daphne?" Lafayette countered.

"One thing at a time, Slim." Roy fell silent, cocking his head. "On your feet, boys," he ordered quietly. "You can come too, Slim," he added. "Listen, they're tryna sneak up on us. Hear that?"

As a twig cracked loudly, the small foursome shouldered packs and disappeared into the surrounding underbrush. Lafayette picked up a club dropped during the brief battle with Trog's bodyguard and waited, watching the spot whence the sounds had emanated, as the twilight deepened.

• • •

"Hi, Al," Marv's voice broke the stillness. He pushed into view, brushing twigs and leaf mold from his tattered garments.

"I been laying low, waiting for a chanst to duck in and rescue ya and all," he confided. "I guess now's the time, huh, while them little devils is out of sight."

Lafayette handed Marv the second can of food. "Have some lunch," he said. "The little fellows are friends of mine," he went on. "But that doesn't make your rescue efforts any less appreciated."

"Oh." Marv looked crestfallen. "They looked pretty rough and tough," he explained. "And the way they turned the tables and cleaned up on Fred and Lump-Lump and Omar was what ya might say impressive."

"A natural mistake," Lafayette agreed. "But now we have to hurry up and catch up with them. They're my only link to Artesia and Aphasia One."

"Sure, Chief," Marv acceded, finishing his can of food. He looked at the label doubtfully before tossing it aside.

"No littering," Lafayette said severely. "But with the whole kingdom in ruins, I don't suppose it really matters."

"Sure, boss," Marv said complacently. "By the way, I never had peaner butter with olives before." He belched comfortably. "Wondered what it was. Pretty good at that. O' course, hungry as I was, boiled harness woulda tasted good."

Lafayette led the way down the path, expecting to catch sight of the pack-laden Ajax crew at the first bend. But rounding the turn, he saw only more path stretching ahead into deep shade. He accelerated his pace, his feet slipping on the damp soil underfoot. Marv, at his heels, complained.

"Fer crine inta yer homemade soup, Chief, we can't keep up no gallop like this. Take it easy."

Lafayette ignored him, intent on closing the gap. There were puddles in the path now. Through gaps in the foliage pressing close on the tunnellike path, Lafayette caught glimpses of moonlight reflected on water. At the same time, the path underfoot had grown steadily soggier. He splashed on, Marv trailing at a distance.

An hour later, winded, he sat on a stump to wait for Marv to catch up, wheezing and holding his short ribs.

"Cripes, Mine Fewher," Marv complained. "I think I busted sumpin'. I got a side-ache like a mule kicked me. Okay if we rest awhile, bwana?"

"We've lost them, Marv," Lafayette said bleakly. "I was a fool not to follow at once. They probably scattered, now that I think of it, and in this jungle we'll never find a sign of them."

Marv sighed with relief as he flopped down full-length on the soggy path. "In that case, sahib, we can take it easy," he commented and at once began to snore.

O'Leary envied the simple fellow; he closed his eyes, experienced a moment of disorientation, and was back in the big gray room. He heard Frumpkin's angry voice:

". . . tell you what to do. I've explained the consequences, you little idiot! If you'd any sense, you'd leap at my generous offer!"

There was a sudden flurry, and Daphne darted past his chair; before he could get to his feet, she was gone. Lafayette dropped back into the padded seat, which suddenly seemed harder than before. He squirmed, failed to find a comfortable position, then realized he was sitting on a rotting stump, his feet cold and wet.

Chapter Seven

Dusk had deepened the gloom of the shaded path to pitch-darkness; Marv awoke, fighting off an imaginary attack by spooks.

"Geeze, Al, am I glad to see *you*!" he cried as soon as he had dispersed his phantom foes. "I dreamed I was back inna Dread Tower, onney I was lost, like. Couldn't find my way out, and these here ghosts was coming at me from all directions; wanted something, but I couldn't figger out what."

"That's all right, Marv," Lafayette soothed the excited fellow. "It was just a dream. I had one, too. But the fix we're in is real. Since we can't expect any help now in getting back to semi-civilization, we have to do something effective at once, before things get any worse."

"Sure, Cap'n," Marv agreed absently. "Onney if we go back the way we come, we'll run into old Froddie; and if we keep going, we'll be into quicksand and stuff pretty soon. We're in the swamp, you know."

"I'm going to have to try the old psychical energies again, I guess," O'Leary said grimly. "This time it *has* to work, because I'm all out of alternatives. Just be quiet for a moment while I concentrate. And I thought the path skirted the swamp."

At first Lafayette concentrated on his luxurious

palace suite in Artesia, vividly envisioning the marble floors, the view of the gardens from the wide windows, the closet with his hundred-odd elegant costumes, the big, wide bed. . . .

His thoughts strayed to Daphne—dear, brave, loyal, delightful little Daphne. Where was she now, poor kid? Lost in some dismal swamp like this, or maybe dying of thirst in a desert in some locus where the swamp had drained? Or was she really hanging around in the spooky gray room he kept having visions of, waiting on Frumpy? Impossible, he decided. Loyal little Daphne would never consent to be anybody's handmaiden.

Lafayette pulled himself together. "Concentrate," Professor Schimmerkopf had urged—and he had done it before, so he could do it again. The suppressor that Central had once focused on him had long since been lifted. He remembered the time in the jail-cell back at Colby Corners when he had accidently shifted back there, under stress—but he had gotten back to Artesia by concentrating all his psychical energies.

The grayness closed in, and Daphne was standing a few feet away in front of the big chair where Frumpkin lolled at ease.

"This nonsense has gone on long enough," the Man in Black was saying. "And I've decided—" He got to his feet and paused, looking puzzled. Then he turned to face O'Leary squarely, and at once showed his teeth in a snarl of rage.

"Look here, you!" he muttered, then coughed, as if attempting to conceal the byplay from Daphne, who was looking at him wonderingly.

"You've lied to me!" she said as sharply as that dulcet voice could sound. "And that means you're not quite as self-confident as you seem. Good-bye!" She turned and had gone two steps when a pair of armed bruisers appeared and seized her arms. Lafayette jumped to her assistance and met an invisible cushion which bounced him back, while Frumpkin's eyes seemed to burn into him like laser beams.

"Hey, Al, look out!" Marv yelled as he jumped up and splashed for cover. A beam of brilliant white light lanced out from above, whence also emanated a sudden din resembling a rock truck on a steep grade, afflicted with the grandfather of all slapping fan-belts. A miniature whirlwind whipped the treetops, then swirled muddy leaf mold and other vegetable debris into Lafayette's face.

"It's only a chopper, Marv," Lafayette called, but his nervous ally was gone.

"You down there," a PA-amplified voice boomed out. "Stand fast! I got authorization to shoot." The rattle of a machine gun sounded, emphasizing the point by making confetti of a swatch of foliage and churning mud into froth only a few feet distant from the tree trunk behind which Lafayette had groped his way. Moments later, a man in a bundlesome combat suit, helmeted and goggled, appeared in midair, climbing down a flexible-link ladder. He dropped the last few feet and swiveled smartly to cover O'Leary's tree with a weapon of discouragingly effective appearance. Clearing his eyes of debris at last, Lafayette blinked, but the commando failed to disappear.

"Don't shoot, I'm harmless," O'Leary croaked, emerging. The armed man reslung his automatic weapon and drew a bulky revolver.

"Take it easy, chum," he said in a hard voice. "I'm Sergeant Dubose, state cops. I'm going to put the cuffs on you and then we're going for a little ride. Come over this way nice and slow."

"What's the charge, Sarge?" Lafayette asked, immediately regretting his choice of words.

"This ain't no joke, slowpoke," the sergeant returned.

"Look," O'Leary essayed desperately, "this is some kind of ridiculous mistake. I was just out for an evening constitutional, and—"

"This here whole area east of the mine is off limits to all personnel, dopey," the noncom cut him off. "If you din't see it on the tube, you shoulda read the signs—and that bob-warr you cut mighta give you a hint, too." The sergeant unclipped a microphone from his belt and muttered into it. The copter moved off.

"I didn't see any barbed wire, and I don't watch the tube," Lafayette countered in the abrupt silence.

"Tell it to the judge, Moe," the cop said wearily as he fetched his cuffs around from his hip-pocket region. "Just don't try nothing. So far all we got on you is a small federal rap for aggravated trespass." He beckoned, and Lafayette stepped forward and extended his wrists, which were at once encircled with cold steel which closed with a decisive click. The cop spun O'Leary and prodded him.

"Right back this way, pal, and we'll give you a nice ride in the whirlybird."

Lafayette started off obediently, then shied at a sudden sound from the brush as a dimly visible Marv burst from cover to barrel into the cop, knocking him down. Marv caught the pistol and aimed it at the fallen policeman's head.

"I'll hold this sucker, Al, while you beat it," Marv grunted. "I never seen a rod like this one before, but I can tell which end of it the bad news comes out of."

"Marv, wait," Lafayette yelled, "don't spoil things! We're marooned in the middle of a swamp, and this is our way out, so just give the sergeant back his gun he dropped and let's go quietly." He extended a hand to assist Dubose to his feet, muttering and slapping at the mud on the uniform.

"Al, wait!" Marv keened. "You don't mean to go off with this here magician which he come in a dragon! It might come down and eat all of us!"

"Don't be silly, Marv," O'Leary said. "It's just a helicopter."

"Don't care what you call it, I seen it sitting right there in thin air, with that eye shining down. It seen us, all right—and here it comes back!"

O'Leary hooked Marv's ankle with his toe as the latter turned to bolt back into the swamp. Marv hit with an elaborate splash as the copter's rotor beat the air directly above with a deafening *whap! whap!*

"Lemme go!" Marv screamed. "I can hear it flappin' its wings! It's gonna strike any second!" He leaped up convulsively as the ladder struck the mulch a foot from his head. Dubose hauled him to his feet.

"Up," he snapped. "I'll leave yer hands free till we're inside." He released O'Leary's hands as well, ordering both men up the ladder. Lafayette rubbed his cold-stiffened hands briskly to restore circulation.

Marv complied, moaning. O'Leary followed, mounting up into the warm glow from the open canopy while an ice-cold tornado beat down at them, causing the flexible metal-link ladder to buck and sway until the weight of Sergeant Dubose at the bottom stabilized it.

A fat-faced cop in the pilot's seat eyed the new arrivals over his shoulder, a dubious expression on his meaty features.

"What you two bums think yer gonna complish in the Little Dismal this time o' night?" he inquired without interest. "Anyways, the comet hit a good five mile west of where we're at now."

"What comet?" Lafayette asked. "We didn't know about any comet; we were just out for a stroll."

"Sure, and I'm waiting for a elevator," the pilot returned cynically. "What comet, eh? How many comets you think hit here to Colby County lately?"

"Colby County?" Lafayette echoed. "Oh, no!"

"Don't go knocking the county," the cop commanded. "Finest little county in this end o' the state."

"How far are we from Colby Corners?" Lafayette asked.

"Oh, you mean the ghost town. Where you fellows from, anyways? Reckon even a tourist oughta know where the Corners is at. 'Bout six mile north," he concluded. "Closed anyway, this time o' night."

"What do you mean, 'ghost town'?" Lafayette demanded. "The last time I saw it, it was a thriving community, with a high-school team rated third in the state."

"You must be older'n you look, young feller," the cop commented as Dubose arrived and settled himself, unlimbering his cuffs.

"Hey, Al," Marv said weakly as the copter lifted suddenly, banking off steeply in a climbing turn. "Now! Nows the time to do one o' your swell tricks."

"Quiet, you!" Dubose barked; and to Lafayette, "Any tricks, Bub, and I'm gonna hafta start rememberin'."

It was almost dawn. Warm and dry in a cosy cell at County Jail, Lafayette and Marv sat disconsolately on their Spartan bunks, watching the pinkening of the rectangle of sky defined by the small high barred window.

"Don't worry, Marv," Lafayette said encouragingly to his cellmate, whose expression suggested that he was on death row at Sing Sing, rather than in a provincial drunk-tank. Marv moaned.

"I dunno if General Frodolkin even could bust me outa this dump," he said, "even if he knew these magicians had one of his best boys locked up here."

"We're not in Aphasia any longer," Lafayette told his cellmate. "And that's good in a way; I mean, I'm responsible. I was trying to shift us back to Artesia, and my mind wandered; I got to thinking about the old days when I happened to slip back to Colby Corners and wound up in jail. Now I'm back there again, and bumrapped again. Sorry to get you mixed up in this, Marv, but we'll get out somehow. Let's consider the situation."

"The situation, wise guy," said a heavy voice over the other side of the barred door, "is you dummies don't never seem to learn nothing."

Lafayette looked up to see a strange face peering in at him. Or, corrected himself, a face not precisely strange, but only half-familiar.

"Belarius!" Lafayette cried, coming to his feet. The face at the door recoiled as O'Leary approached.

"Where's Frumpkin, your old sidekick?" O'Leary demanded. "I've got an idea he's holding Daphne somewhere against her will—at least I hope it's against her will!"

The newcomer, who Lafayette realized wasn't Belarius at all, but merely a look-alike, this one half-shaved and with acne scars, paused in his retreat to look distastefully at O'Leary.

"Look," Lafayette said desperately, "I know we

haven't always gotten along, but let's let bygones be bygones; get us out of here."

"I don't know whom you think I am," the Belarius-like stranger replied coldly. "But let me set you straight: I'm Sheriff George B. Tode, and I run a clean administration, and it's about time you chiselers learnt that."

"Not 'whom,'" Lafayette said severely. "After the verb 'to be' the nominative case is used: 'I don't know *who* you think I am,'" he quoted.

"I know durn well whom you are," the sheriff came back. "You're the latest in the series of Light-Fingered Looies Jukes has been sending in here to try and get a piece o' the comet, so's to embarrass me."

"To try *to* get a piece of the comet," O'Leary corrected. "What comet?"

"First and only one to hit here in Colby County," the cop said. "Don't play dumber'n what you already are."

"You can leave my IQ out of this, you half-witted flatfoot!" O'Leary retorted hotly.

"Nix, Al," Marv hissed. "You were gonna get this feller to get us out o' here, remember?" Then he addressed the sheriff: "Ya gotta excuse my pal," he explained. "He's got problems, you know, upstairs." Marv tapped his unkempt head to make his meaning clear. "But he ain't a bad guy, except when he turns inta a bird or something. *Then* he can get mean. But if you was to just kind of let us outa this here dungeon, you could get on his good side, and he might fix you up with a solid gold bathtub or like that."

"You tryna bribe me, sucker?" Sheriff Tode demanded. He looked both ways and pressed his face closer to the bars. "Did you say 'bathtub'?"

"Whatever you like," Marv assured him. "If you prefer buckets o' emrals and rubies and ten-dollar bills, Al, he can—" Marv broke off as Lafayette jabbed him in the side with an elbow, at the same time easing him away from the door.

"Marv was just kidding around, Sheriff," he said. "He doesn't have any gold bathtubs on him—or even any buckets. Of course, he might turn up the odd sawbuck you boys missed when you cleaned us out."

"I never missed no sawbuck," Tode replied hotly. "When I shake a feller down, I don't miss nothing. Hey, where you going?" He concluded, as Lafayette, easing sideways, passed from the officer's field of vision.

Or almost nothing, Lafayette told himself, checking his secret pocket for the flat-walker, finding it still safely tucked away. *Not that he'd have known it was important, even if he'd found it,* he reflected.

The sheriff was now bawling for someone named Cecil, turning after each yell to order Lafayette to stand ". . . whur I can see ye!" Marv eyed Lafayette anxiously while making soothing sounds directed to the suspicious sheriff.

"It's all right, Shurf," Marv reassured the cop. "Old Al's kinda shy is all. He's right here a-hiding in the corner. No need to do nothing hasty, Shurf, sir."

Cecil arrived, looming six inches over his chief's considerable bulk. "What's up, boss? These here jailbirds try something funny?"

"One of 'em's hiding, Cease," Tode explained. "Says he's shy, but I don't like it, a feller just kind of sliding sideways out o' sight whilst I'm talking to him. Ain't respecful."

"Durn right, Shurf," Cease replied eagerly. "Just leave me in there to take a few minutes to teach 'em a few manners, Colby County style."

"No need, Mr. Cecil, sir," Marv cried. "We got more manners'n we can use now, don't we, Al?" He looked imploringly toward O'Leary who, flat-walker in hand, was facing the masonry wall.

"Take it easy, Marv," Lafayette said reasonably. "I'll be back for you in a few minutes." As he activated the Ajax device, he heard the rattle of a key, and from the corner of his eye saw the heavy steel-barred door swing in, slightly obscured by a haze which thickened to an opaque blackness shot through with tiny darting lights—random high-speed cosmic rays striking the retina, as Sprawnroyal had once explained.

As from a great distance, O'Leary heard Cecil's

bellow. "Hey, Shurf, one of these crud-bums has busted out!"

The light-shot darkness lightened to watery gray, and through an open doorway O'Leary saw the Man in Black speaking urgently to a coarse-looking middle-aged woman, though his words were inaudible. Lafayette approached, looked into the vast, dim room he had seen before. Far away across a faded pseudo-oriental carpet, Daphne—he was almost sure—stood beside a bric-a-brac-cluttered end table, her shoulders slumped dejectedly. Then she looked up: It *was* Daphne. Lafayette started through the door, encountered an impalpable resistance against which he lunged in vain. Frumpkin looked up at O'Leary, at once dismissed the frumpy woman, and started toward him. Daphne hurried forward to come up behind Frumpkin.

"Clobber him, Daph!" O'Leary wished frantically. But Daphne stopped and spoke quietly:

"You promised, milord." Frumpkin whirled and snarled something at her. As Lafayette tried desperately to push through the barrier, the pale light faded to impenetrable darkness and profound silence. He pressed forward—and the barrier melted.

Then the darkness cleared and he was looking at a brown-painted concrete-block wall with a tattered and fly-specked poster exhorting the viewer to reelect 'Hoppy' Tode as Sheriff of Colby County—a document, Lafayette reflected, which, though unprepossessing, had apparently proven effective. Then he noticed the sheriff himself standing a few feet away, staring through the barred door through which Cecil's complaint was still issuing:

". . . let one of these here sneak thiefs break outa our jail! Jukes ain't going to like it, Shurf, and you gotta election coming up!"

Tode turned casually, then started violently at the sight of O'Leary standing nearly at his elbow. He tugged his hogleg from its holster and aimed it at Lafayette's face.

"Jist you hold it right there, feller!" he yelled. Then through the bars to Cecil:

"It's OK, Cease, I got the skunk! Get out here and get the cuffs on him! Then we got to find out where the secret tunnel is at. Where is it at, boy?" He switched his attention from Cecil to Lafayette. "You gonna tell me polite, or has Cease got to loosen you up?" He cocked the pistol. "You can have it hard or you can have it easy; up to you, wise guy." He raised his voice. "Snap it up, Cease, my trigger finger is getting twitchy!"

Lafayette shrank back against the wall, speaking soothingly to Tode as the pistol's bore seemed to expand to the size of a tunnel.

"Here, you," Tode yelled. "Don't go pulling no tricks on *me,* you low-down!" The detonation of the .44 was deafening, but the slug hissed past Lafayette's ear, smacked the wall, and whined off into the distance. The light-shot darkness was closing in again. Disoriented in the sudden gloom, O'Leary took a step and stumbled; then he seemed to be falling freely, end-over-end. He yelled, but heard no sound. His breathing was getting labored. Slowly, orientation returned; he groped with his feet, felt a springy surface, and took a tentative step. He seemed for a moment to glimpse the gray room, then lunged forward—or in some direction—tripped, and fell headlong into glaring light and a half-familiar odor of office supplies and duplicating fluid. The floor was smooth and cold, regulation asphalt tile in nine-inch squares, pale gray with pink and yellow flecks, he saw as his eyes reluctantly focused.

"Oh, brother," a dispirited female voice said from somewhere above: O'Leary lifted his head and saw a desk with a telephone, in- and out-baskets, and behind it a severely handsome woman of middle age, eyeing him sharply.

"Another nine-oh-two," she complained. "Why do all the hard-luck cases have to phase in here in Reception?" She was jabbing vigorously at a button set in a small console beside the desk.

"Just keep calm; a realignment team will be here in a moment," she said rapidly to O'Leary, jabbing even more urgently. As Lafayette was getting shakily to his feet, the doors across the gray-floored room burst open and an unperturbed medical type in starched whites came through, manipulating a hypodermic to expel air and totally ignoring O'Leary to address the woman:

"I assume, Miss Gorch, that you have some adequate reason for calling me away from a staff meeting with Class Four emergency signal." His eyes wandered to Lafayette.

"Who's this fellow, Mary-Ann? I suppose he's something to do with your disaster alert?"

"Damn right, Clyde," Miss Gorch replied, coming to her feet. "That last nut-case one of you big-domes accidentally shifted into HQ from some kind of orgy in a classified locus tried to attack me before I could even get his grab number! I'm taking no chances with this one!"

"Calmly, my dear girl, calmly," the official said, moving to confront Lafayette directly.

"I'll be calm when this rapist is in irons," Mary-Ann snapped.

"Wait a minute," O'Leary cut into the conversation. "I don't know who you think I am or what you claim I've done, but the fact is I'm Lafayette O'Leary, and I'm the victim of a whole series of disasters I had nothing to do with."

The man in white dismissed this with a wave of his hand. "Take him, men," he ordered; and his two aides sprang to grab Lafayette's arms and twist them into complicated come-along holds.

"Wait!" Lafayette yelled. "Don't do anything hasty! If you'll take a minute to check your records, you'll find I'm a legitimate part-time agent of Central!" He paused. "This *is* Central, isn't it?" he demanded. The man in white wagged his head solemnly.

"By no means, fellow. You are now at Prime, impelled here by our irresistible Come Hither device. Now it remains merely to assess the full impact of your guilt, so as equitably to assign penance." He turned on his heel and strode away, shied violently as the uncouth figure of Sheriff 'Hoppy' Tode materialized in his path. The two musclemen released Lafayette's arms and leapt to their chief's side.

"It's an invasion!" Clyde barked. "I've been expecting this! Archie, sound the alarm!" He thrust the smaller of the two guards toward the door as the other put a hammerlock on Tode, who struggled to no avail. The .44 was back in its holster. He pointed a shaky finger at O'Leary.

"That man's my prizner!" he yelled. "Hadda shoot him, and he up and vanished. I ain't had a drop! Turned into smoke and went out, sure as I'm standing here. . . ." He paused, looking puzzled. "But *am* I standing here? Whereat am I anyways?"

"*Where* am I," Lafayette corrected sharply. "I told you before. And 'anyway,' without the *s,* is modern Artesian usage."

"How do *I* know where you're at, boy?" Tode shouted toward O'Leary. "I don't know where I'm at my ownself! Now," he went on in a carefully controlled tone, addressing Clyde:

"You look like a responsible individual, sir. So I hope you can see you got no call to sic these here fellers onto me, which I'm a duly elected peace officer. This here feller"—he nodded toward O'Leary—"he's the one you want. Only I got first call; had him right in my jail and he snuck out and—and after that it gets kindy hazy. But I'm still shurf and he's still my prizner."

"I fear Prime's jurisdiction overrides all petty claims," Clyde countered coldly. "Now, how did you get here?"

He turned to Miss Gorch. "What's his grab number?" he demanded impatiently. "And what is your explanation for initiating a retrieval not on the master schedule?"

"Don't look at me, Clyde," Mary-Ann returned hotly. "I had nothing to do with bringing these clowns in here. Must be your Come Hither field was tuned a little too wide."

"Rather than imputing slovenly technique to your superiors, my girl," Clyde cut in icily, "you'd best busy yourself getting your voucher files in order for investigation. This incident could create a detectable imbalance in the energy budget."

Lafayette took advantage of the internecine wrangle to ease toward the door, reached it, and slid through to find himself in a long corridor which he at once saw was the precise analog of a similiar passage at Central which he had once visited briefly. If the parallel held, he should find the office of the Chief of Operations behind one of these doors. He flattened himself against the wall as Clyde and his bodyguard burst through the door at a run. Neither man looked to the side, but hurried past only inches away.

"Where's he gone? He's got to be here!" Clyde yelled, sprinting ahead.

"Wait a minute, Chief," the attendant wheezed, slowing. "He couldn'ta got clear that fast! Are you sure he come this way? Maybe he done another shift."

"Nonetheless, we must give chase!" Clyde threw the words over his shoulder.

As the two pounded off along the carpeted corridor, yelling, Lafayette eased along to the first door on the right and opened it a crack to peer in. At once a booming voice cried:

"There you are at last! Messenger service is a disgrace! What's kept you, boy?" Lafayette slid inside the small office to confront a large, irate executive type with a mane of bushy gray hair and an expression of apoplectic fury.

"I'm not a messenger," Lafayette gasped. "I just need to get a few things cleared up. They sent me to you, said you'd know, if anybody would."

The seated man's expression softened slightly. "What's all that commotion outside?" he inquired offhandedly. "How's a Chief of Logistics to function in this bedlam?"

"Beats me," Lafayette conceded, sinking unbidden into a leather chair. "I'm Sir Lafayette O'Leary," he proceeded. "I've had a bad time of it, what with one or another set of barbarians determined to do me in. Something's up—I don't know what; but the Ajax crack investigation team is onto it, and a fellow named Allegorus is involved. That's about all I've managed to find out; and Daphne's lost somewhere along the line—

some renegade named Frumpkin's got her, I think—and the more I try to find her, the farther away I get. Judging from the swamp in Colby County, I'm well outside my usual widerange. I seem to be shifting loci spontaneously—so what can you do to help me?''

"Why should I help you, sir?" the Chief of Logistics inquired blandly. "Outside my interest cluster entirely. The chap you want is Belarius, over in Ops. I'm Zoriel, Supply."

"I've met Belarius V," Lafayette put in desperately, "and he tried to kidnap me. He and this other bureaucrat named Frumpkin. He's no help."

Zoriel frowned. "If Belarius tried to put the arm on you, he doubtless had a reason," he mused, pressing a button on his desk-top. "So perhaps we'd best just have him in on this."

"And now Sheriff Tode's doing it, too," Lafayette added. "Popped right into Prime here, and he's never even so much as heard of focusing the Psychical Energies, I'd be willing to bet. Things are coming apart." O'Leary rose to his feet to emphasize his point. "This is an emergency," he declared feelingly. "And it's time for someone in a position of responsibility to slow down and listen to me, and then take some affirmative action!''

"Calmly, Sir Lafayette—I trust I got your style right? Calmly, we'll just get Belarius in here and get to the bottom of all this nonsense."

"Look," Lafayette said desperately, "I'm no theoretician, but I know that when basic geological features like the bay at Colby Corners turns into a swamp, something is drastically wrong. Even back in Aphasia I, the weather was different—it seemed very close to Artesia, otherwise, except for some kind of barbarian invasion, but it was pouring rain in Artesia; and not a drop in Aphasia. So that must have been a bigger jump than I thought at first. Then this whole string of loci: I've been popping along from one to another, everytime I . . ." He paused, looking thoughtful, then took the flatwalker from his pocket and examined it closely. It seemed, he noticed, to be vibrating minutely;

the faintest of buzzes was audible when he held it to his ear.

"At least twice I did a major shift when I used this gadget," he told Zoriel. "Funny; it never had that effect before." Then he noticed that the faint buzz was modulated into speech.

"Chidler ovigex, raf tras spintern," Lafayette heard clearly, followed by a moment of silence. "Repeat," the tiny voice resumed. "This device is under emergency recall. It must be returned to Ajax at once. DO NOT USE. Repeat: *Chidler ovigex, raf tras spintern,* uh, that's, 'This device is under IEC.' Bring it in at once. An Ajax rep is standing by at your local field office. Repeat, *Zum vix orobalt, insham totrus bewhif groat. Raf tras spintern. Onfrac: raf trass spoit."*

"Great," Lafayette murmured half-aloud. "It's declaring an emergency in some unknown tongue." He looked appealingly at Zoriel. "Do you have a translator handy?" he inquired hopefully.

"See here, young fellow," Zoriel replied sharply. "I don't think I like your having that thing in your possession, whatever it is. You'd better hand it over to me for safekeeping."

"Sorry," Lafayette said. "You're not authorized. I have to turn it in to the Ajax field office at once. It said so."

"In that case," Zoriel said coldly. "I shall be forced to place you under restraint." He opened a drawer and took out a flat, deadly looking handgun. "I hope you're not going to be difficult," he said distastefully.

"Don't count on it," Lafayette said bitterly. "I'm getting a little tired of being placed in custody for no reason." As he spoke he noted a renewed buzzing from the flat-walker. He held it to his ear. "OK, I heard that, O'Leary," the tiny voice said. Lafayette remembered belatedly that all Ajax devices included emergency two-way communications capability. "I have you on my 'A-list,'" the gadget chirped, "so I'll send somebody around to assist you in turning in the recalled item, IAW Section Nine."

"I'm keeping it," Lafayette told Zoriel. "It's mine, and I'm doing no harm; just trying to find Daphne and go home. So forget the tough stuff and be civilized. After all, this is Prime, not some barbarian HQ in the jungle."

"Not Prime, lad, but Supreme Headquarters itself! And you'll find SHQ is not lightly to be penetrated by nobodies such as yourself."

"I didn't penetrate your lousy HQ," Lafayette yelled. "I was yanked in here against my will by some quack named Clyde, with a Come Hither field!"

"Ah, doubtless you refer to Professor Doctor Anschluss," Zoriel said soothingly. "If the professor saw fit to bring you here, no doubt he had an excellent reason." Zoriel rose and came around the big desk. "In the meanwhile," he added, "you'll hand over that, er, item, which is producing a category-blue indication on my E-stress sensor." He showed Lafayette the compasslike instrument he was holding in his left hand, while pointing the gun with his right. Lafayette saw the needle was well into the blue range marked HIGHLY IMPROBABLE.

"I can't help that," he said between his teeth. "This whole crazy situation is improbable. Nobody just goes bouncing across the loci like the ball on a roulette wheel."

The door burst open behind Lafayette.

"There you are, you jailbird," Sheriff Tode's raucous voice yelled. "Ain't nobody ever broke from me, and it ain't gonna start now!" Lafayette turned in time to see Tode's large hand descending, clamplike, toward his shoulder. He ducked aside and Tode followed, planting himself between Lafayette and the door, barring his way, then advancing.

Still holding the flat-walker in working position, Lafayette stood his ground. Tode's bulk pressed against him—then the pressure was gone, and with it light and sound, except for a bewildering display of the high-speed particles, like those he had observed before while passing through solid matter. But they were whirling in dizzying patterns now, concentrated immediately in front of O'Leary's wide-open eyes. The nucleus of the speeding lights widened, engulfed him.

. . . Let this feller get past me again, Boss Jukes ain't gonna like it none a-tall. Where'd he go to? I had him right here, and—hey, what's goin' on? Can't hardly think straight . . . dizzy. Better do like Boss said and call fer help. . . .

Carefully disentangling himself from Sheriff Tode's confused thoughts, Lafayette made a determined effort to orient himself; then took a precise step sideways, felt his foot slip, experienced a momentary vertigo, then opened his eyes to dimness. He had a view of Frumpkin's back as the latter stood before a large and complex instrument panel where colored lights blinked excitedly. Frumpkin spun around, then recoiled as he saw O'Leary.

"How?" he croaked. "Deal: Just explain how you can broach a Type Nine force-bubble at will, and I'll . . . well, I'll go easy on you."

"It's how I'll go on you you'd better be worrying about," Lafayette countered grimly. "Get away from that board."

"But," Frumpkin protested, "this is unthinkable. I happen to know you were relegated to nonrealization some time ago! You *can't* be here!"

"Too bad," O'Leary replied, and started across toward the cowering Man in Black, who turned and scuttled away behind the big panel. Lafayette peered around the corner of the massive equipment cabinet, saw nothing except a tangle of rudely cut cables and a stretch of dusty floor. He turned back to the big room. Light glared, dazzling him. He tottered; hands caught his arms, not restraining him, but easing him down into a chair.

"Take it easy, Al," the familiar voice of Sprawnroyal urged gently. "You had a bad experience there, stuck in half-phase for six weeks and all, but we got you out OK. So just take a minute to get it together before we debrief you."

"Roy," Lafayette said urgently. "Where did it go? A

big gray room full of fog. That's where he's keeping her. What do you mean 'six weeks'? It hasn't been more than twenty-four hours since this whole crazy thing started. And I've only got forty-eight more to get Daphne out of Aphasia II before it disappears!''

"Easy, boy," Roy soothed. "We'll take it one step at a time. First, we have to extricate your ego-gestalt from Mr. Tode's—that's a delicate procedure. You should never have merged with him, Slim. I know you were under pressure. Still, it was a lousy idea."

"It wasn't an idea," Lafayette returned in a silent yell which echoed in blackness. "It was an accident. I walked through a man once before with that infernal device of yours and nothing happened; how was I supposed to know it was dangerous? Anyway, *he* walked into *me*. I was standing still."

". . . just another few days," Roy was saying in a tone of controlled patience. "I assure you I'm as uncomfortable as yourself."

"Who said anything about comfort?" O'Leary demanded. "Just get me out of this moron's skull!''

"Who you callin a moe-roan?" Tode's heavy thought pattern cut across O'Leary's demands. *"Sure is a funny kinda dream to be havin' and I ain't touched a drop all the day."*

Gradually, Lafayette was becoming more able to ignore the sheriff's elemental conceptualizations. A dim, sourceless light became visible, but it revealed nothing. So far as Lafayette could see, he was alone in a vast, empty space suffused with an eerie glow which emanated from the space itself. Abruptly, he was overwhelmed with a bleak loneliness.

"Hey, Roy, where are you?" he called; as before, no sound was to be heard. He tried to draw a deep breath to reassure himself that he was breathing—but nothing happened. Still, he reflected, suppressing panic, he was quite comfortable, physically. He assessed his bodily sensations, but was unable to decide whether he was standing, sitting, or reclining. He had no idea which way was up. He tried a swimming motion, and was rewarded with a sensation of darting swiftly ahead—but with no fixed point of reference, no actual motion was apparent.

". . . Slim, I told you to stay put!" Roy's faint voice seemed to ring, echoing, all about him. "If I lose my fix—hey! Where are you at?"

"Over here," Lafayette called silently, feeling a sudden apprehension. "Don't go away, Roy," he added. "You're my only contact with . . . whatever I was in contact with."

Chapter Eight

"Swell," O'Leary told himself half an hour —or half a lifetime—later. He had been resting quietly, waiting, making no furthur move; and still he hung suspended in the featureless glow which he knew was characteristic of half-phase, the anomalous pseudo-space between the loci of actualization. He was lost as he had never been lost before. Perhaps, if he sculled back the way he had come in his swift fish-dart . . . But Roy had said to stay put before he had faded out. Maybe he was still in the vicinity, but keeping quiet.

"Oh, Roy!" Lafayette shouted, and this time he heard an echo, faint and distant. Encouraged, he tried again. This time it was the hoarse voice of Sheriff Tode he heard:

"Whunder whut that feller meant about six weeks? Ain't got no six weeks to waste; got a 'lection comin' up."

The voice, O'Leary realized with relief, was no longer coming from within his own personal mind-volume. It was close, but external. Somehow he had unmerged himself from the irate peace officer.

"That's a start," he told himself. "Maybe Roy's working on it."

"Looky here, feller," Tode's voice spoke from what

seemed to be a point approximately half an inch from Lafayette's left eye. "Let's make us a gentleman's agreement, like they say: You lay off the tricks and come on out whur I can see ye, and I'll put in a good word about your cooperation and all at the trial."

"Where are you, Sheriff?" Lafayette inquired desperately. "I can't see you—just hear you."

"Why, I'm right here, settin' on this here fancy settee, just like the feller told me. Said he'd be right back, but I got a feelin' I been tooken. By the way, feller, where have you got to? Hear ya but cain't see ya nowheres."

"That's too complicated to explain, Sheriff. Just sit tight and hope for the best," O'Leary said silently.

At that point Lafayette became aware of the distant mutter of voices, distinct from Tode's hoarse croak, near at hand; more like people arguing in the next room, he decided. He tried a move toward the sound, a flick of the tail which sent him gliding from the deep shadow under the lily pads out into the dazzling, diffuse glare of open water—or open *something,* he corrected, noting that his gills were pumping nicely, sluicing cool, oxygen-laden *something* over the absorptive membranes.

"—told you it's a ghost bogie on number seven," an aggrieved voice said loudly from across the room.

"And I said you better check the Manual; this could be a type nineteen, for all *we* know," someone answered sharply.

"Fruits and nuts. It's just another dumb exercise they forgot to put in the OD book."

"Just humor me, Fred: run a six-oh-two on it. Please? Pretty please wit' sugar on?"

The pellucid something dimmed, grew thicker.

Lafayette waved his limbs slowly until the now rapidly jelling medium immobilized him. He made a mighty effort, managed to thrust with his pectoral fins. Cracks opened across the solid medium in which he was suspended like a fly in amber.

"Got something here!" Fred's voice yelled. "Les, maybe you better get off a Class One after all: don't know if the field's gonna hold!"

"I'm way ahead of ya, Fred; got a net team on the way already."

"Seems OK now." Fred said more calmly. "Or maybe I lost it; don't feel nothing now. . . ."

Lafayette tried a tentative flick of the tail, was rewarded by a stab of pain from somewhere around the dorsal-fin area; he relaxed and the pain subsided, then became a steady pressure, tugging him in some undefinable direction. For a moment he went along, then made a sudden resolution: time to use the Psychical Energies.

He concentrated on the face of Daphne, her dark eyes and snub nose, her sweet lips and the delicate curve of her cheekbones. The lustrous dark hair. . . .

" 'Through the black of night, I gotta go where you are, ' " he hummed to himself. " 'And no place can be too far, where you are. Ain't no chains can bind me, if you live I'll find thee. Love is calling me. I gotta go where you are . . .' "

"Lafayette?" Daphne's voice said uncertainly. O'Leary squinted through the gloom. It clarified into the familiar dimness of the gray room. Daphne was nowhere to be seen. Lafayette saw a door across the room, went to it, past big chairs arranged in conversational groups, from one of which a conversation was emanating:

". . . too good of a offer to turn down," a harsh female voice was saying.

"Ain't saying it wasn't," a meaty male voice replied. "Only what guarantee we got?"

"You have my word," a voice that sounded like Marv's put in. "Hurry up," he added.

"Looky here," Meaty-Voice started, "we got— ouch! Don't go doing nothing like that feller! All's I said was—"

Lafayette reached the door, found it locked. Only then did he realize that he was no longer limited to swimming through gray Jello. He paused, considering: He no longer felt the pressure of the dim-glowing substance in which he was trapped. He thrust hard, burst through a membrane and lay gasping on a shaggy surface which, he realized, was a grassy bank sloping down to a mirror surface marred by ripples.

"Got him!" the gigantic voice of Les boomed out from far above.

"What is it?" Fred inquired in Olympian tones. "How'd it get into our Y-field anyway?"

"Probably one o' *them*," Les replied. "Just got a little too tricky for his own good. Let's get it up under the light and check it out."

The pain stabbed in Lafayette's back; he uttered a choked yell as the giant hook jerked him upward into blinding light where two large, homely faces peered down at him.

"Hooked from the outside," Les's voice said, issuing from the face on the left, the whiskery one. That meant the round face with warts belonged to Fred.

"Fred," Lafayette gasped, "Les. Help! I'm an innocent victim, not one of *them*."

"Les," Fred said casually. "Did you hear this thing say sumpin'?"

"Don't be silly," Les replied. "How could I of? Only folks can talk. Let's open it up and see what makes it tick."

Lafayette caught only a glimpse of a polished, razor-edged scalpel poised over him before the light winked out and he was back in pitch darkness. He waited, but no blow fell. He slept.

Chapter Nine

O'Leary woke slowly from vague dreams of strolling in the palace gardens at Artesia City. Reluctantly he became aware that he was lying on his side on what felt very much like a bed. Hard and rather lumpy, but still a bed. Fine! Maybe someone had finally dropped a net over him and carted him off to the booby hatch to start his cure. He moved tentatively: no stab of pain from his back, he noted with relief. He tried a leg, felt it respond. No more fins; that was good news. Obviously the shrinks had some effective techniques going for them nowadays. He'd only been in the pest house for a few hours and already he was thinking clearly, his hallucinations gone.

He opened his eyes to dim light and a tall woman standing beside the narrow cot.

"No more mischief now, sir," she said in a cool, melodious voice. "I'm Doctor Smith, and I want to help you."

"That's fine, Doctor," Lafayette replied briskly, sitting up. The woman at once bent to rearrange his pillows to support him in a half-erect position. "Please don't exert yourself, sir," she said in a no-nonsense tone. "And actually I must ask you to do nothing at all for the present; don't even think. The debriefing team will be along in a moment to wire you up and set things to rights.''

"Wire me up?'' Lafayette echoed vaguely. ''I don't think I like the sound of that.''

"Please, sir—''

"My name's Lafayette,'' he stated, feeling a vague impulse to stabilize the situation. ''I've had a bad time of it, but I'm better now, I think. Is Daphne OK? Is she here?''

"I'm sorry, sir. The DB team will handle all your queries. You may sleep a little now, and they'll be here.'' Then she was gone with a rustle of starched whites.

Let's hold it right here, O'Leary said sternly to himself. *This has gone far enough. They've been herding me along like a sheep to the slaughter. I haven't been just wandering around at will,* he told himself with dawning comprehension. *Someone's been manipulating me— and the time has come to break the cycle!* He rose from the Spartan hospital bed and discovered he was clad only in a threadbare purple pajama bottom. There was a steel locker against the wall. Inside, Lafayette found his once splendid court suit, sadly worn and stained but freshly cleaned and pressed. He at once checked the trick pocket. The flat-walker was still in place.

"But that's what's been messing me up,'' he said aloud. ''Every time I used it, I got in deeper; so I won't touch it again until I'm back at Ajax—or an Ajax field station.'' With that decision, he felt a surge of confidence. ''Now I can start unraveling this mess,'' he told himself. 'It's still not too late to rescue Daphne. But I've got no time to waste.''

He dressed quickly, then went to a window and looked down on a city street bathed in afternoon sunlight, lined with cars parked by shops bearing signs announcing Giant Sales and Discounts up to 70%, and Your Credit's Good. For the first time in years, Lafayette remembered his old life in Colby Corners as a junior draftsman at the foundry, living on a diet of

Tend-R Nood-L soup, sardines, and crackers, and salt-water taffy, his sole indulgence—except for his scientific work, of course. And that was what was needed now, he realized with sudden insight. The mundane bustle in the street below seemed to him to restore a correct perspective to the mad jumble of events of the last day or so. Now, before committing himself to another move, it would be well to sum up, to reexamine affairs in the cold, precise light of the scientific method. First, as he had already concluded, it was clear that he had been manipulated, herded along from one blunder to the next. But for what purpose? That point would have to await furthur clarification. Basically, the thing that had been nagging at the back of his mind was the problem of energy imbalance. Formerly, in simply shifting himself by means of the Psychical Energies from one locus to an adjacent one, the transfer of energy had been slight, and as had been explained to him by Nicodaeus, the equation had been balanced by an equivalent displacement of inorganic matter at scattered points. Thus, when he had first changed loci from Colby Corners to Artesia, a number of small items equal in mass to his own one hundred thirty-eight pounds had, quite unknown to him or to anyone, slipped across from Artesia to the Corners, causing some Artesian housewife, perhaps, to wonder what had become of her antique ginger jar, while some ragpicker in Colby Corners had come upon a perfectly good cannister marked GINGER in an ash-can on his regular route. A loose stone on an Artesian road might have disappeared when no one was looking and just as unobtrusively appeared on the potholed tarmac of the Springs Road. So that part—as had been explained to him at length by Nicodaeus on the latter's last visit to Adoranne's court—was rational enough. But these shift-overs he'd been making lately to loci well outside his home widerange involved massive energy demands across wide stretches of E-space. That fact, in turn, implied that someone, somewhere, for some reason, was supplying the required energies. Question: who? Also, why, how, etcetera, Lafayette reflected in frustration. His fingers, idly exploring his pocket, encountered the angular shape of the flat-walker. Only slowly, and with a sense of shock, did he realize what he was fingering; with sudden awe, he brought out the waferlike device and studied it carefully, as if he had never seen it before. It looked like nothing more than a rectangel of bluish plastic embossed with wavy lines. Could this thing actually enable one to pass through solid matter? Again, whence the energy supply? It was too silly, he decided, and checked an impulse to toss it into the immaculate wastebasket beside the window. Had he been hallucinating? The question shook him. Some people *did* hallucinate, and if he were one of them, where did the imaginary begin? With Zoriel, or with Doctor Anschluss and the waspish Miss Gorch, or earlier, with Shurf Tode and Cease? Or the gray room that kept popping up? Or was it Frodolkin and his troops who had initiated the nonobjective phase of his mental life? Or Lord Trog—or Allegorus, the mysterious visitant to the tower? Or did it go farther back, to Artesia itself, to Adoranne and Alain, and Lod, the two-headed giant, or even to Daphne—dear, loyal, lovely Daphne? No! he almost yelled aloud. His bride of ten years was no figment: of that he was sure. But where was she now? Why had she been taken from him? Where was the gray room?

The pattern of his manipulation was far from clear, but a few points could be fixed firmly: He had drifted progressively farther from the Artesian locus. Aphasia I was a recognizable analog, Aphasia II not much different. Then, in the swamp, his attempt to find Artesia had misfired, placing him, along with Marv, in an alternate version of Colby Corners, in some ways much like his old home town but grossly different at the geological level—which meant a massive shift indeed. Then the disembodied passage through half-phase, to emerge at Prime, no doubt of another order of reality entirely, quite outside the purview of Central. Then, once again he had made use of the flat-walker. . . . How clear it was, now that he was pausing to consider matters in

depth, that the seemingly innocuous device, outré
though it was, was at the bottom of most of his trouble.
He put it back in its pocket, fully resolved not to use it
again. That last time, he recalled with a shudder, had
almost finished him: thinking he was a fish—but not
exactly a fish, merely some life form indigenous to half-
phase, existing weightless and intangible in the void between worlds, a subjective experience which his mind
had automatically rationalized by concluding that he
was immersed in a featureless fluid like a fish in water.
But somehow, by sheer luck, perhaps, he had been recovered from that eerie environment, too. He remembered the descending scalpel, Fred's immense face, then
—nothing, until he woke here, in this hospitallike room,
with the view of a sane and normal street in the late
spring sunshine.

And now, he told himself firmly, *now I'm taking
over. I'm not going to be herded anymore, not going to
take any more sudden desperate measures. Not even
going to try to focus the Psychical Energies,* moments at
which, he abruptly realized, he was peculiarly suscep-
tible to manipulation. And he would definitely not mess
with the flat-walker. Except, he hedged, perhaps to use
it to communicate with Ajax.

The decision made, he turned from the window to
ponder for a moment his next move—a move he must be
quite certain was entirely his own idea, made at his own
volition and not under some pressure, subtle or gross.

OK, he agreed firmly. *That brings me to the question
of what to do now. What do they expect me to do, want
me to do? They've left me alone and ambulatory, with
my clothes handy. And I'll bet the door is conveniently
unlocked. So, they think I'll do a bolt for freedom—but
I'll fool 'em. This time I'll play it smart: I'm staying.*

At that moment, the door to the big room opened and
Doctor Smith appeared, carrying a tray rather awkwardly. Lafayette caught a whiff of poached egg and
over-boiled coffee.

"It's time for your lunch, Mr. O'Leary," the woman

said in a tone in which he could read no fell intent. She showed no surprise at seeing him up and dressed.

"No, thanks," he said casually. "Not hungry. By the way, what town is this?"

"Why, the Institute is at Caney, Kansas," she replied glibly.

"Why?" Lafayette asked bluntly. "Why did you bring me to Caney, Kansas?"

"You were found, Mr. O'Leary, nearly dead of exposure and alcohol, in an alley only a block east of the Institute. A kindly passerby brought you here, since it was the nearest facility."

"I've never been in Kansas in my life," Lafayette stated more firmly than his certainty warranted. "And I don't drink—just a nice wine with dinner, perhaps, or a cold beer on a hot afternoon."

"Nevertheless, your body shows the ravages of advanced alcoholism," the doctor rebutted equally firmly.

"Uh, where's the men's room?" Lafayette blurted.

"You'll find a facility through that door," she said, pointing to a brown-painted panel Lafayette had not previously noticed. She put the tray on a table and came closer to Lafayette. "Seven P.M. at the YW," she breathed in his ear, and turned away before he could see her expression.

"Thanks, Doc," Lafayette said with a show of casualness. He went to the undersize door and opened it. A glance inside revealed the usual plumbing. He went in and closed the door.

"OK," he told himself. "She expects me to break out of here—probably through the window." He eyed the small square unglazed opening through which a brick wall opposite was visible. " 'Seven P.M. at the Y,' " he echoed silently. "She must think I'm the original sucker —and why shouldn't she? I've taken every cue, so far— went along like a puppet on strings. But no more. So, I'll just kill a few minutes here and see what they try next."

This decided, he felt a sense of accomplishment which he recognized as out of proportion to his actual achievement. He determined to take it easy, resort to no desperate measures, and to look for the unexpected opportunity. Meanwhile, it wouldn't hurt to take a peek out that window to check on the lay of the land. He pushed a dusty crate into position under the window, climbed up, and looked out at a narrow slice of street visible between corroded red bricks on the left and a slant of heavily tarred roof on the right. An intersection was partly visible, and a drug store on the corner. A dusty old Buick was parked on the side street, and a man stood leaning on it, his arms folded. The man was Marv. Lafayette blinked and looked again; there was no doubt of it. Old Marv, here, in this far-out locus! How had he managed it? He was dressed in an anonymous suit and seemed quite at home, gnawing a toothpick and idly gazing up toward Lafayette's vantage point. Marv's head jerked in a mild double take. He was looking Lafayette squarely in the eyes. He came away from the car, swiftly consulted his wristwatch, glanced around him, and returned his gaze to O'Leary. He raised a hand and gestured a furtive greeting. Lafayette ducked back, climbed quickly down, and without hesitation thrust open the door and was back in the big airy room with the narrow bed and faintly steaming tray on the table. Dr. Smith was gone.

"Clever," Lafayette conceded. "Just when I'd decided to play it my own way, they spring Marv on me, and I nearly took the bait. It would have been an easy drop from that window to the ledge, then to the adjacent roof, and no doubt all the way down I'd've found a wide-open route. But I'm *not* taking it. So they'll have to think up another one. But who is this 'they' I'm blaming everything on? Sounds remarkably like paranoia. I'd better be careful what I think even." He went across to the door the doctor had used; as he neared it he heard voices on the other side:

". . . careful. A shock at this point, and all our careful work could be undone. He's in a delicate condition, you must remember, balanced on a knife-edge."

"Sure, I know all that—but we can't just sit on the

case. You know as well as I do he'll expect expeditious action."

"Of course, Mel, and the first step is to get him out of here to a safe place; so let's do it."

Then the latch rattled and the door opened, causing Lafayette to step quickly aside. A man whom Lafayette had never before seen came through at a brisk pace. He paused to turn and look incuriously at O'Leary.

"You're all ready," he commented. "Good. We're a bit early, but no matter."

The other man busied himself closing the door, and it was some moments before Lafayette caught a clear look at his warty face, which he recognized at once as that of Fred, one of the two giant faces from the hallucination about being hooked like a fish.

"It's good to see a familiar face, Fred," Lafayette said glibly. "There are a few points I wish you'd clear up for me. First, where was I when you and Les found me?"

Fred gave Lafayette an astonished look, then turned to his colleague: "Hasn't this subject received initial conditioning?"

"Well, as to that . . ." Mel hesitated. "You recall this is a special case, referred in by Number One personally."

"Say, fellows, if you'll excuse me," Lafayette cut in heedlessly. "I think I'd better see to my tropical fish. See you soon. Ta." He jostled past Fred, still hovering in the doorway and set off briskly down a long, well-lit corridor.

"One moment, there!" Fred's authoritative voice rang out belatedly. Lafayette ignored it and went through a door on the left marked 'Private. No Entry,' and found himself at the top of a steep flight of gray concrete steps with a rusted handrail improvised of two-inch I.D. galvanized pipe. He went down three steps at a time until he heard feet on the landing he had just vacated, accompanied by Fred's hoarse cry: "Stop, there!"

As O'Leary grabbed the newel to whirl around the

next turn, he felt a sudden vertigo, as if he had spun around and around. . . .

The gray room again, Lafayette realized in frustration. Still, perhaps it was as good a hidey-hole as any—if he was really here and not just dreaming. He tried a step forward, found the faded rug normally firm underfoot. Neither Frumpkin nor Daphne was in sight. The big panel was off to the right, a trifle dim through the curiously semi-opaque air. He went to it and on impulse threw a large knife-switch marked MAIN STAGE ON OFF. As it slammed home, the dimness seemed to flicker for a moment, and at once Frumpkin's hoarse voice rang out. "No! Get away from that!"

Quickly, Lafayette opened and closed other switches at random, noting no effect other than a busy blinking among the idiot lights on the panel.

"Look here," Frumpkin said more calmly, from near at hand now. "I'll . . . make a concession," he offered. "Stop now and there's no great mischief done, except perhaps for a few relatively minor astronomical oddities, the odd meteor, that sort of thing. Stop your sabotage at once; and I shall arrange for a retroaction in the case of Henriette. What say? Is it a gentleman's agreement?"

O'Leary glanced around at the renegade, looking haggard now, his once immaculate uniform dusty and rumpled.

"I don't know any Henriette," Lafayette said coldly, "and I wouldn't make a deal with you anyway. I don't trust you, you slimy little toad."

"Very well! Beverly, then, or Androgorre, or possibly Cynthia; whatever you choose to call her: the female upon whom you've anchored your defense, as young fellows will do. You're a fool. She sold you out at once when I mentioned the furs and jewels and other trifles she'd possess as a willing collaborator. Don't be a fool, O'Leary! Throw in with me and end this needless contest! There's plenty for us both in all the worlds of if!"

"If you knew how silly you sounded," Lafayette told Frumpkin, "you'd blush purple. Now bring Daphne here, right now, or I'll have to close the big one marked "PROGRAM DUMP."

"Certainly, lad, whatever you say; but she'll be disappointed, just you watch! Kindly just step back from the panel a trifle. And why here? You'll be trapped."

O'Leary put a hand on the DUMP switch. "Get going," he ordered. "You've got ten seconds."

"No! I mean, of course!" Frumpkin gabbled. "But it will take at least half a minute! Do nothing hasty, Mr. O'Leary!" Frumpkin backed away, still gibbering, then turned and ran, disappearing in the dimness. The room seemed to tilt, then began to slide sideways. Lafayette clung to a convenient post as the room whirled around him. Now he was leaping down narrow concrete steps, feeling dizzy; he staggered, caught himself, went on, down, down, into dusty daylight.

Chapter Ten

    Lafayette reached another landing and whirled through a wire-glass door into a narrow foyer with elevator doors. *I'll ask all the questions later,* he promised himself, and punched a button at random; a moment later feet clattered hastily past the door behind him; then the door to his left whooshed open and Lafayette stepped in among fat ladies and a spidery old fellow carrying a paper-wrapped package.

    "Come on, ain't got all the day," the old boy said in a ratchety voice.

    "Sorry I'm late, sir," Lafayette replied diffidently. "Want me to take over now?" He eased the big flat package from the oldster's hands and glanced at the address:

    Global Presentation, A.G., 113 Bayberry Bldg, Suite B. Attn: Dr. Glovewelt.

    "Say, that's square of you, fellow," the elderly courier cried, exercising his arm in exaggerated mime of severe cramping. "Goes on *my* ticket, o' course," he added. "After all, I'm the one signed for it."

    "Hurry back and tell 'em you were mugged in the park," Lafayette suggested. "Just in case."

    "Hey," the septuagenarian protested. "You *will* exercise due care and all like it says, won't you, fella?"

"Count on me, Pop," Lafayette reassured him; as the car stopped and the doors jolted open, he extracted himself from the plump matrons and headed for the door marked 'Fire Stair—Emergency Only.'

After an interminable descent, Lafayette saw the glow of daylight below and soon reached a littered floor with a big blue cold-drink machine, and stepped out into a narrow alley. He turned right and quickly emerged on the street he had seen from his room. Marv was no longer in sight, but Lafayette went across anyway and meandered casually to the corner where he had seen his erstwhile comrade. He found nothing but a candy-bar wrapper to indicate that anyone had loitered there. His eye was caught by a neon sign reading COLD BEER glowing in a dusty window across the narrow street. He started across, adroitly dodging a cab which took an abrupt right turn, nearly grazing his shins, and pushed through the heavy plate-glass door into a dim interior redolent of generations of slopped-over beers. He took a table and two deep breaths before a large man in an apron like a four-master's tops'l over an expansive paunch bellied up to the table, shifted a toothpick in a meaty face, and said,

"You want sumpin'?"

"Why, no," Lafayette said seriously. "Actually I just stepped in to get out of the blizzard." He had dumped his package on the table before him. Now he stripped off the tape and tore away the brown wrapper, exposing an inner wrapping, removed that and was looking at a stack of fourteen-by-twenty-two glossies. The top print, in gaudy color, showed an ornately decorated interior, all red-and-white marble and gold wainscoting. He shuddered and examined the figures in the foreground. One, standing in advance of the others, was undoubtedly Frumpkin, in black no longer. He was wearing a species of brocaded toga, somewhere between a pope's robes and Roman senator's bedsheet. To his left was Daphne, looking relatively drably clad in a gown of shimmering silver. The others were strangers, except for a fellow who looked remarkably like Marv occupying a pew for one, raised above floor level in the background.

The other prints showed other angles of the same ceremony, except for the last, which showed a gold-uniformed Frumpkin standing in a stiff Napoleon pose amid the ruins of what seemed to be the same rococo hall.

The big man was still hovering. He shot a glance at the translucent window with **COLD BEER** on it, and muttered. "Wise guy, hah? I got a good mind to throw you right back out in your own snowdrift, crum-bum, you get smart with me, which I own this here dump." He reached for O'Leary's collar with a hairy arm bigger than most peoples' leg. Lafayette dodged casually, fixed a steely gaze on the red-rimmed eyes of the owner-bouncer.

"Raf tras spintern," he said distinctly. *"Raf tras spoit."*

The big fellow checked his grab and rearranged the salt and pepper shakers and paper napkin dispenser instead. "Whyn't you say so?" he demanded, then straightened up, looking over O'Leary's head. "Sorry, sir. Been on-station too long, I guess. Kinda forgot the routine. You wanna wait right here, I'll have a contact man here in a sec." He backed away from the Presence, then fled.

"I see you and Special Ed are old pals," a chipper feminine voice spoke up at O'Leary's ear. He jumped, then turned to see a small dark-haired girl with a neat figure in a tight electric-blue dress. She had a pretty face, marred by an excess of eyelash goo and an oversize slash of gore-red lip rouge. She took the seat opposite him and dumped a wicker handbag the size of a small suitcase on the table, shoving the photographs aside.

"Hi," she went on breathlessly. "I'm Mickey Jo. You sure put the fear into old Ed, all right. Who are ya? Ain't seen you around here before, I don't think."

"Actually," O'Leary said carefully, assessing this new player moved onto the board, "I've never been here before."

"New on the job?" Mickey Jo frowned in sympathetic inquiry.

"Not *on* the job," Lafayette replied. "Just trying to find Daphne and go home."

"What's Daphne?" the girl asked.

"Not 'what,' " Lafayette corrected. " 'Who.' She's a very beautiful young woman, and my wife."

"If that's a hint to me to take off," Mickey Jo said regretfully, "I get it. Just sat down to rest the dogs, anyway. Well, nice meeting you, Mr. . . . ."

"Brown," he supplied. "Lafayette Brown. *Sir* Lafayette Brown in fact. Don't go. I wasn't hinting. I never hint. I come right out and say things."

Mickey Jo hesitated. "If you're sure . . ."

"I'm sure," Lafayette stated firmly, realizing he meant it. "Frankly, I'm lonely. Stay and talk to me. Have a drink?"

The girl tossed her head half-defiantly, half-decisively. She resumed her seat and at once emitted a short, piercing whistle, directed at the proprietor still hovering in the background. He hurried over.

"Draw two, Ed," Mickey Jo ordered crisply. "The *real* stuff, not that Milwaukee soda water."

"Well, Mick, you know I always serve nothin' but the best to my prime customers," Ed said in a hurt tone. He made a ritual dab at the tabletop with a gray rag and departed at a trot, to return at once with two sudsy schooners.

"Now," Mickey Jo said comfortably, "tell me all about this Daphne dame—excuse me—your wife, I mean. I suppose she's one o' these classy broads which she don't ever let nothing slip—or slip past, eh, sir?"

"Just call me Laff," Lafayette said tonelessly. "You remind me of a girl who used to call me that."

"Laugh? That's a heck of a name, no offense," the girl commented between drags on her tankard. O'Leary tried his beer and found it to be an excellent, nutty brew. He took a long, healing gulp and his morale improved at once. Outside, he noticed, it was almost twilight.

"Daphne and I were sitting in the palace garden, just

chatting about old times," Lafayette began his recital, "and I happened to be looking at the stars; noticed if you changed things a little the so-called Great Bear would look a lot like a unicorn or something. So . . ." he paused. "So I just twiddled with it a little, without any intention whatever of tampering, you understand—and the next thing I knew we were in the middle of a cloudburst. We ran for it—and somehow got separated. I mean, there was only one door she could have gone through, and it led nowhere—or only to the stairs to the Dread Tower, I mean. I went up and ran into a couple of sharpies from Central, who tried to kidnap me. But I forgot: before that, I was grabbed by a couple of thugs named Marv and Omar and dragged into the presence of Lord Trog. He told me I was in Aphasia and nobody had seen Daphne. And the palace was in ruins. You see, it was *almost* Artesia; just the same, except nothing was the same—if you know what I mean."

"I'm sorry, Laugh, I don't—see what you mean, I mean," Mickey Jo responded. "It sounds like you been hit on the dome once too often, maybe. So let's forget all that, and just talk about *us*."

" 'Us'?" Lafayette echoed wonderingly. "What about us? I just met you, I hardly know you—"

"And all I know about *you*," Mickey Jo cut in, "is you got a chipped knob. But what the hell, the night is young, like they say, and so are we—so why be choosy? You can buy me a nice dinner in a first-class restaurant, and we'll go from there."

"I don't know if I have any cash," Lafayette said doubtfully, patting pockets. He brought out a crumpled Artesian ten spot, a corroded copper coin, some gray lint, and the flat-walker.

". . . repeat, OK, Slim?" its tiny voice peeped, even fainter now. "You're way overdue at the field office. You get that address OK? One two eight South Canal, one flight up. Over to you, Slim."

"Uh, one two eight South Canal," Lafayette repeated dully. "I never heard of it. But I'll try to get there ASAP."

"*South* Canal?" Mickey Jo repeated in a dismayed

tone. "You sure you don't mean *East* Canal? And whatdaya mean, you never heard of it? It was you mentioned it. All I said was—"

"I know," Lafayette said quickly. "I was just sort of thinking aloud, only I wasn't thinking. I mean—"

"Skip it, Laugh." Mickey Jo patted O'Leary's hand with a hard little palm. "We don't want to go and get you all mixed up again. Let's just go chow down." She rose quickly, and Lafayette was again impressed by her neat little body. He got to his feet and glanced toward Special Ed, busy behind the bar.

"What about the, uh . . . tab?" O'Leary muttered.

"Don't kid me, Laugh," the girl said, tugging at his arm. "I know all you guys got unlimited expense accounts. So does Ed; know, I mean." She pulled at Lafayette's arm; he followed, and in a moment they were outside in chill evening air, on a gritty sidewalk beside a pitch-black street. The moonlight glowed pinkish-white on the upper stories of the facades opposite.

"Just a minute, Mickey Jo," O'Leary said, hesitating before starting across. "You seem to know more about things than I do. Do you know where the gray room is? I have to find it; that's where Frumpkin hangs out, and he seems to be holding Daphne there, and—"

"Who's this Frumpkin?" the girl cut in. "I don't know anything about the Gray Room—lousy name for a restaurant; let's go to the Schnitzel Haus over on Central."

"It's not a restaurant: this is serious," Lafayette corrected.

"If it's so serious, why don't you just go over there and break it up?" Mickey Jo asked reasonably. "After all, it's *your* wife with the guy."

"It's not like that. And anyway, I don't know where it is."

"Then, how do you know they're shacked up there?" the girl wanted to know.

"I saw them—lots of times—only it's not what you're implying. He's holding her there against her will."

"If you saw the place, you oughta remember where it's at," Mickey Jo stated with finality.

"Where it *is*," Lafayette corrected automatically. "I have no idea where it is, otherwise I'd get there as fast as I could. Poor little Daph. . . ."

"What's he got, chains on her, ropes, kinky stuff like that?" Mickey Jo demanded.

"Why, no, she's wearing a simple white dinner gown, very elegant."

"Then what makes you say he's holding her there? Maybe she likes a fellow provides her with elegant dinner gowns."

"You don't get it at all," Lafayette complained. "Who do you work for? Who do you think I am?"

"My immediate chief is Mel Grunge," Mickey Jo said, "if it's any of your business. He's assistant chief, Information Services—pretty big shot. And I think you're a poor boob named Laugh, which your marbles is a little scrambled—which don't mean we can't put on the feed bag together. Maybe we'll run into Daphne and her boyfriend." She tugged at Lafayette's arm.

He resisted. "It's not *like* that!" he objected. "He's not her boyfriend!"

Mickey Jo looked at him sympathetically. "They say the husband is always the last to know," she murmured. "But, what the hell, two can play at the game. I'll try and keep yer mind off the whole thing."

"Try *to* keep my mind off," O'Leary corrected tonelessly.

"That's what I said. Come on."

"Wait," Lafayette objected. "Do you know where the Y is ? And what time is it?"

"You want the YM or the YW? The C or the J? The YMCA's about two blocks north, and it's six-thirty. Why?"

"She said 'Seven P.M. at the Y,' " Lafayette told her.

"Oh. 'She,' huh? I got a idea you don't mean this Daphne dame—I mean Mrs. Laugh."

"No. Docter Smith. She's rather severe-looking, but not bad. But that has nothing to do with it."

"So, you already got a date, Laugh? Whyn't you say so? Hey, did you want them pictures you had? You left 'em on the table. You're a deeper one than you look, I guess, Laugh. Well, it was nice knowing ya, kid. So long. Mickey Jo Obtulicz ain't a gal to break up nothing you got going. Good luck, and thanks for the beer."

"Wait! I haven't asked you—" Lafayette started.

"I know," the girl cut him off. "But it's A-OK, Laugh. I din't mean to butt in on nothing."

There was a scrape of shoe-leather from the darkness ahead; then a vague form took shape, moving directly toward them. Mickey Jo yelped in alarm and clutched O'Leary's arm.

"It's cool, lady," a blurry voice came from the darkness. "How's it, Sir Al? Glad to see ya, an' all, you bet." Then the mysterious figure was directly in front of O'Leary.

"It's me, Marv, your old pal," Marv said. "Doncha know me, Al? After all we been through." Marv's calloused hands clutched at O'Leary as if afraid of losing him. Lafayette disengaged gently and turned to the girl.

"Nothing to fear, Mickey Jo," he said. "This is my friend Marv I told you about."

"Al, where you been? How'd you get here?" Marv moaned. "When you done that neat sneak, right troo the wall an all, I thought our troubles was over. But you never came back, and old Cease come inta the cell to work me over and left the door open, so I clobbered him good and took off. Only some guys said they was some kind o' Feds grab me and quiz me plenty. I got lots to tell you—"

"Later, Marv," O'Leary said soothingly. "I'm sorry about ducking out on you, but I got lost—I'm *still* lost. This place seems a lot like Colby Corners, so maybe we're closer to home than I thought."

"Al!" Marv cut in. "You mean you don't know? You poor guy, you got a awful shock coming."

"Don't know what?" Lafayette asked, absent-mindedly encircling Mickey Jo's slim waist and hugging her gently.

"C'mere," Marv said soberly, tugging at O'Leary's arm. He followed as Marv led him off a few steps to the intersection, where the pink moonlight gleamed across the worn brick street unimpeded. His face pale in the wan light, Marv looked at O'Leary earnestly. "Now, easy, pal: Just turn slow and look up."

O'Leary complied, squeezing Mickey Jo's hand, which somehow he still held. She returned the pressure. Glancing up casually, Lafayette allowed his gaze to drift to the bright orb of the full moon. He gasped, tried to speak, but uttered only a croak.

"My God!" he managed at last. "Mickey Jo, look at it! Look at the moon!"

"Sure, I see it, Laugh. Purty. Romanticlike. But you got a late date, remember?"

"Romantic my eye!" Lafayette yelled. "It's falling! Ye Gods, look at it! You can see every crater—it can't be more than a hundred thousand miles away! Doesn't anybody care? Isn't anybody doing anything about it?" As he spoke, he was hastily measuring it with his thumbnail held at arm's length. Nearly a full degree, he decided.

"Easy, Al," Marv said. "It ain't exactly fallin; it's already fell. I mean she's spiraling in real slow, about half a mile a year, they say, and pretty soon it'll hit Roche's Limit and *then* we'll see some fireworks!"

"But it can't, Marv!" Lafayette protested. "That's the moon! It's been gradually receding for five billion years; it can't just turn around and start coming in!"

"I guess it can if it gets a big enough push from a near-miss by a hundred-mile planetoid. Happened back in the Cretaceous, they say; had something to do with killing off a lot o' big critters they call deenersoors or like that. Not to worry: we still got another fifty thousand years, about, before she breaks up; and then look out."

"Do you realize what this means?" O'Leary groaned. "We're in a totally different manifold of loci from Artesia and all the old familiar places! I'll never get back! I'll never find Daphne!"

"Don't take it so hard, Sugar," Mickey Jo said in a

mtter-of-fact tone. "After all, it ain't *your* fault."

"But that's just it! It *is* my fault," Lafayette moaned.
"If only I hadn't started messing around with the constellations, this would never have happened!"

"That's what they call delusions of grandeur, Sir
Laugh," Mickey Jo protested. "Like calling yourself
'Sir,' only on a more ambitious scale. Better cool it.
Come on, Marv, let's get him in offa the street before
somebody hears him and calls for the nut squad."

═══Chapter Eleven═══

After straining to keep the grossly swollen moon in sight for as long as possible, Lafayette at length submitted to being led off along the dark street; then there were lights, people—ordinary-looking, well-dressed folk who seemed to take little notice of an apparent drunk being led along the sidewalk by his friends. Then they were tugging him through a revolving door, which thumped him on the back and propelled him into warmth, quiet music, the babble of table-chatter and the clink of dishes, and a heavenly aroma of roast beef, fried onions, fresh-baked bread and newly ground coffee. At once, O'Leary found himself taking an interest; he hadn't noticed how hungry he was until that moment. A head waiter appeared, impersonally obsequious.

"Table for three," Lafayette said briskly. "In a quiet corner where we can't hear the kitchen or the combo."

Moments later, the trio was seated at a cozy table agleam with white linen, polished silver, and sparkling glass. A waiter materialized and took their orders.

"Marv," O'Leary said to his whiskery companion. "How did you find me?"

"I never," Marv said quickly. "You found *me*. I was just standing there, and you come up and—"

"I know that, Marv," Lafayette cut him off. "But how did you happen to be on the corner for me to find?"

"I had a hard day," Marv complained. "Shot at, roughed up, throwed in the slammer—and they stuck needles in me, some kinda dope; made me groggy. But I done a sneak and beat it. Din't know where to go; just taking a, like, break when ya come along."

"What about you, Mickey Jo?" Lafayette transferred his attention to the girl. "Why did you come in as soon as I sat down?"

"Laugh," she replied seriously, "what were them pitchers you had? Looked like somebody getting coronated or something."

"Ask Marv," Lafayette replied. "He was in one of them."

The girl looked at Marv. "That's right," she acknowledged. "It must have been a big affair, Marv; tell me about it. How did you happen to be there?"

"Don't know whacha mean," Marv muttered. "What pitchers you talking about?"

"They were addressed to 'Global Presentations,' in the Bayberry Building. Ever heard of it?"

"Not me," Marv dismissed the subject. "How'd you get these here pitchers, Al?"

"I'm afraid I stole 'em," O'Leary admitted.

"Cheese," Marv exclaimed softly. "A straight-up guy like you, Al, it ain't like you to steal nothing. What'd you do with the loot?"

"I'm afraid I left it at Special Ed's," Lafayette said.

"Spose he turns you in?" Marv speculated.

"Don't be silly," Mickey Jo put in. "Ed's no stoolie, and anyway, how'd he know they was stole?"

"Uh-oh," Marv said, his eyes on the entry behind Lafayette and Mickey Jo. "Looks like Ed finked."

O'Leary turned as if casually and saw three harness bulls shouldering through the door, eyes alert, hands on pistol butts. They hurried across to a table in a far corner, bent in earnest consultation with a plain-looking gray-haired woman. After a brief conference, the three

cops made their way to the kitchen doors and passed
from view.

"Some rich dame who didn't like the service, eh?"
Marv cracked. Then their waiter arrived with a bustle.

"This is the life," Lafayette said, inhaling expansively over a bowl of meaty soup which he knew was a
mere hint of delights to come. "Relaxing in a cozy
eatery with an old pal and a pretty girl: that's what I
should be doing, not being chased all over a dozen continua by an assortment of shady characters. That last
pair: Fred, from the fishpond, and his boss Mel. They
had big plans for me. Well, I've broken the pattern at
last, and already things are looking up. Marv, I was
really surprised when I looked out that window and saw
you, of all people, in this strange place. And you seemed
to expect me: you looked right at me."

"Never seen you, Al," Marv grated. "Just looking
around, like; then I got fed up and taken off; and then I
got to thinking maybe I better stick around a little
longer, so I come back. After all, the message was pretty
clear: corner of Main and Sioux, at five pee-em
sharp—"

"What message?" Lafayette cut in. "Maybe I'm not
as clear as I thought if somebody knew I'd be there."

"You know, Al, *your* message," Marv said around a
mouthful of soup.

"I didn't send any message," Lafayette said between
spoonfuls.

"Sure, you know," Marv urged. "When I come outa
the dungeon after I clobbered old Cease, I seen it right
away. Old Shurf was gone, so I didn't have him to con-
tend with and all. Stuck on the wall, right where a
feller'd see it: a arrer pointing at the wall and right
under it, FOLLOW ME was wrote, kind of shaky,
which I guess you was in a hurry. I never knowed what it
meant, but I give it a try—and I fell right through that
solid wall!" Marv shook his head wonderingly. "Then I
thought I was a bird, sailing troo the air, like. After a
while I landed in some kind of hospital, like, and they

worked me over until I got loose—and here I am. Uh, I forgot, the old lady in the hospital slips me the word you'd be on this here corner. So I come over and see nothing of you, Al, but like I said, I waited around, and here you are!"

"It seems to me, Marv," Lafayette said offhandedly, "that for a fellow from a simple, unspoiled locus like Aphasia, you take all this pretty calmly—even the city here. Even though it's only a hick town like Colby Corners, it must be a lot bigger than anything you ever saw back in Aphasia."

"I dunno," Marv replied, equally casually. "I been around some, you know, Al."

"That message bothers me," Lafayette confessed. "It means somebody's still one jump ahead of me."

"Unless he's lying," Mickey Jo said sweetly. Marv's head jerked. "Hey," he said weakly. "Who you calling a liar?"

"I just said 'if,' " Mickey Jo asserted soothingly.

"Never mind; Sheriff Tode might have left that sign on the wall," O'Leary commented. "I didn't. Apparently Tode went through the same soft spot you did. I ran into him later, at Prime HQ."

"I don't get it," Mickey Jo put in. "You guys talk like walking through a wall is routine."

"Somehow," Lafayette hazarded, "using the flat-walker must have left a temporary permeable area in the wall. I don't know if that's usual, or not. I guess I should have found out a little more about the gadgets from Ajax before I used them—and that reminds me: Ajax gave me an address on Canal—but I didn't show up. Instead, I met Mickey Jo," Lafayette said, smiling at the girl. "And I'm really glad I did. But I wanted to ask you: Who did you think I was? You apparently assumed I was somebody you more or less expected, asked me about the job I was on, assumed I knew the bartender, and had an expense account, and so on. Who did you think I was?"

Mickey Jo looked at him helplessly. "I don't think we should discuss that in public, do you, sir?" she said in a strained voice quite different from her usual carefree tones.

"There's nobody here but Marv," O'Leary replied comfortingly.

"And by the way, why did the Ajax rep you mentioned tell you to go to Canal?" the girl asked, looking around as if she expected to see the answer to her question closing in from all sides.

"I assume there'll be an Ajax contact there," Lafayette admitted doubtfully. "But to heck with that, for now. First, let's enjoy our dinner."

"She's right, Al," Marv put in. "How you gonna find this Daphne dame if you don't make contact?"

"I'm perfectly willing—" Lafayette began, but was cut off as the side wall of the spacious room burst inward, propelled by a wall of water which churned tables, chairs, and patrons together as it thundered toward the little group in the quiet corner. Lafayette felt his ears pop and quickly employed the Valsalva maneuver to equalize pressure. Marv was on his feet, yelling. Mickey Jo fell against Lafayette, her face next to his. It was a long, chaos-filled moment before he realized she was saying something:

"Use the flat-walker. *Raf trass spoit.*"

He fumbled the Ajax device from his pocket even as the foaming flood engulfed him. He put it to his mouth, said, "Ajax—emergency! Get me out of here!" before he choked on a mouthful of muddy water. Through the translucent gray-green swirl, he saw a rectangle of gray light, struck out for it, slid easily into open air, and lay gasping on the faded carpet. Frumpkin came up out of his chair with a yelp of surprise and stood over Lafayette, looking down at him balefully.

"You're spoiling everything," he said mournfully. "Now I'll have to relocate my Prime Vault."

"I've heard of that," Lafayette said, coughing. "It blew up."

Frumpkin waved that away. "Not really. Just a small Schrödinger collapse; a diversionary tactic, you see. That was while I was still vulnerable, when Belarius attached himself to me—or so he thought.''

"Where is this place?" Lafayette demanded. He got to his feet and looked about for a window, but the long, dim expanses of wallpaper were unperforated except for the door behind him.

"Ah, that *is* a question, eh, my lad?" Frumpkin said unctuously. "I fear you'll have to come to terms, Lafayette. Unless you put an end to your resistance, I fear you shall never find the headquarters."

"What resistance?" Lafayette demanded. "All I want to do is get back home with Daphne and go on having a swell life."

"Precisely. Your conceptualizations of the swell life are no longer viable, Lafayette. You must accept the new order—willingly."

O'Leary rounded on him truculently. "If your 'new order' means I'm supposed to like being kidnapped, thrown in dungeons, kicked from pillar to post, and kept in the dark about what's going on, you can forget it. Just call Daphne in, and we'll leave quietly."

Frumpkin snapped his fingers, and at once Daphne rose from the depths of a nearby overstuffed chair and came to stand before Frumpkin, seeming not to see O'Leary.

"Are you ill-treated, my dear?" Frumpkin asked her silkily.

She shook her head. "No, but that's not the point."

"Ah, the point, actually, is survival, eh, Dame Edith?" Frumpkin prompted. He turned to Lafayette. "As you can see, this young lady, by any name, is quite content."

"Daphne!" Lafayette cried; he took a step toward her but was thrown back by an invisible but resilient barrier; then the light faded abruptly.

═══Chapter Twelve═══

They lay on a long shingle not of sand but of finely granulated particles of the harder substances of which the streets and buildings of the city had been constituted. Before them stretched the breeze-ruffled surface of a broad lake; behind, an expanse gf grayish-black mud from which the steel framework of a former building thrust up, debris clotted on it. A late-model Auburn roadster lay on its side nearby, partially buried under a jackdaw's nest of broken lumber. No people were in sight, but in the far distance a few lights glowed, and somewhat closer a wisp of smoke rose almost vertically into the tranquil evening sky. Overhead, the bloated moon showed a tracery of red lines across its mottled face.

Lafayette was the first to sit up, his mind filled with the confused recollection of the gray room and Daphne, so close—then an interminable struggle in churning water, fighting upward toward dim light. He looked closely at Mickey Jo, lying unconscious beside him, her electric-blue dress sodden and clinging. Beyond, Marv raised himself on an elbow.

"Why'd ya hafta go and do *that*, Al?" he inquired in an aggrieved tone.

"I didn't do anything," Lafayette replied. "I was just

about to try that crabmeat salad. It looked awful good.''

"I et mine," Marv commented. "It was plenty OK, onney I wisht I'd of had time to try a bite of that steak, too.''

"There's smoke over there," Lafayette said, pointing. "Let's go over. There must be some food left somewhere in the ruins.''

"I dunno," Marv countered. "What if they got guns?''

"I didn't propose to attack them," Lafayette said.

"Marv," Mickey Jo spoke up feebly. "Why don't *you* go? We'll wait here. No use in all of us getting kilt.''

"Well, if you ain't a square-deal little . . .'' Marv's voice faded to a mumble. He got to his feet, slapping at the mud adhering to his soaked garments. He looked at O'Leary, who was looking at the girl, who was holding a small automatic pistol aimed steadily at Marv's head.

"Go on," she said harshly. "Git!''

"Now, wait just a minute," O'Leary objected. "There's no need for anything like that, Mickey Jo. I don't mind going with him.''

"You're staying right here, O'Leary," she grated past clenched teeth. "You're both covered.''

"You know my name!" O'Leary gasped. "Look here, Mickey Jo, it's about time for you to tell me what your game is. Who are you, really?''

"I got no game, O'Leary, I just do like the man says. I'm a Group III agent in the PSS. Play it nice, now, and you won't get hurt, as far as I know. They just want to reason with you.''

"Who's 'they'?" Lafayette demanded, sidling to the left. The gun at once shifted aim by a few degrees to remain aimed between the two men.

"They're the Emergency Research Committee," the girl said. She was sitting up now, her wet hair strung across her face, from which the paint was gone, leaving her a remarkably wholesome-looking young woman.

"Sure. Now explain the explanation," Lafayette suggested. "And don't throw in a lot of weird names and places I never heard of."

"Some things just ain't simple," Mickey Jo answered. "But I'll try. After the disruption bomb on Nuke City, they slapped on Full Class One Security; then the Prime Vault blew, and we knew we were in deep trouble. That was in October. Before the TRAN meters blew out, they registered a force-seven anomaly. Got it so far?"

"No," Lafayette said. "But go on. Where does Belarius IV fit into the picture?"

"Nowhere. He was in the metering vault when it blew. But what do you know about the big shot?"

"He survived," Lafayette said. "He and another sharpy named Frumpkin. But that's enough double-talk. Let's get down to detail. How do you know my name? Even Marv here only knows me as Allegorus, a crazy idea he got just because he met me in the Dread Tower, as his bunch call it." Lafayette glanced at Marv, now fifty feet away and moving off slowly.

"You know what an entropic disjunction is, Mr. O'Leary?" Mickey Jo inquired coldly.

"Sort of," Lafayette admitted, "to the extent that the term is self-explanatory. But the idea is a paradox. So, it doesn't mean anything."

"When the entire mass of galaxy is expelled from its natural entropic lamina," Mickey Jo said in a tone of exhausted patience, "all kinds of anomalies are generated. The last time it happened, fifteen billion years ago, matter came into existence spontaneously at the tertiary level, where it had no business being at all. That's what's known as the Big Bang."

"What's that got to do with anything?" Lafayette demanded hotly.

"Everything," Mickey Jo returned firmly. "All this is the direct result of that unique event."

"But, if it ever happened, it was fifteen or twenty billion years ago," Lafayette protested. "I've only been around for thirty-three."

"And no matter how far back or forward we travel along the temporal axis," the girl said, "the Bang's always twenty gigayears off. That's the temporal diameter of this manifold. The entire cosmos naturally had to re-adjust to accommodate the new mass. All else follows."

"But what's all that got to do with *me*?" Lafayette yelled. "I was just sitting quietly in the garden . . ."

"Figure, Laugh," Mickey Jo put in. "Everything shifts one parameter, right? Now, you figure the spatial distance of the Event, plug in one hundred eighty-six thousand miles is equal to a second, and a couple finagle factors like the cosmological constant, and whata ya got? Three hundred years displacement is what. So, of course some compensation is required."

"What kind of compensation could that be?" Lafayette wondered aloud. "All that, if it ever happened, was still maybe twenty billion years ago. What can anyone do *now* to influence that?"

"Time is a convenient fiction," Mickey Jo said flatly. "A billion years or a billionth of a second: What's the difference, really? They're both just ideas, existing only in the mind."

"Maybe," Lafayette replied. "The question still stands."

"There are two choices," Mickey Jo said crisply. "It can be all at once, or distributed over the whole reality manifold."

"And . . .?" Lafayette prompted.

"And somebody is busy redistributing it," Mickey Jo finished. "We thought it was you," she added. "But I guess that idea was just grabbing at a straw."

"Who's 'they'?" Lafayette demanded. "I'm getting very weary of the impersonal 'they,' and calling them a committee doesn't help. And who are you, and what were you doing in the beer joint?"

"I'm just who I said I am," Mickey Jo retorted. "I work part-time out of Supreme HQ, and I was at Special Ed's dump to meet you."

"What's the survey?" O'Leary asked. "And don't tell me it's the executive wing of the Council or something. Just skip ahead. I don't need all the intermediate obfuscations."

"*Some*body has to keep an eye on things," Mickey Jo

said in tones of exasperated patience. "After all, if every little entropic vortex generated over a low probability area were allowed to gather energy until it became a full-scale probability storm, the entire cosmos would remain in a state of chaos."

"So this Supreme HQ has appointed itself Boss of All," Lafayette deduced without approval. "But they've gotten too big for their swivel chairs when they start bouncing a law-abiding Artesian nobleman around like a mouse in a washing machine."

"That's purely incidental, O'Leary," Mickey Jo said, waving the idea aside with a shooing motion of her hand. "In fact when your presence was discovered I was dispatched here to enlist your cooperation in a scheme devised by the Technical Council to try to divert the main thrust of the entropic surge off into a manifold of unevolved continua. Will you help?"

"Why me?" Lafayette demanded. "What can I do?"

"Hey, Al," Marv's distant voice echoed across the mud-flat. "Come on, I can see sumpin'."

"Ignore him," Mickey Jo rapped. "As for what you can do, it seems somehow you are the focal point of certain gigantic forces, over which in some curious fashion you are able to exercise some influence. We want you to employ that ability in the interest of restoring order to the Manifold."

"How would I do that?" Lafayette inquired. Marv was on his way back now, waving his arms and shouting:

"Hunnerts of 'em! Got some heavy equipment. Camped out around that old building yonder! Better try a sneak-up after dark." He arrived, panting. "Don't think they seen me. We needa get outa sight, find some cover."

"Why?" Lafayette demanded. "Why assume they're hostile?"

"Got a whole bunch o' guys hung up by the neck," Marv explained.

"Maybe they've just got a hanging judge," O'Leary suggested. "We could use some Law and Order." He looked around at the seemingly endless mud-flat which surrounded the lake and stretched to the horizon on all sides, interrupted only by a low knoll beyond the ruined building. The sun was low in a sky heavy with clouds the color of used dishwater. The gusty breeze was cool, and his wet clothes were clammy.

"We need to find some shelter, whether we're hiding or not," he commented. "Come on, Mickey Jo, let's take a walk." He offered the girl a hand, which she ignored.

"And you'd better give me the gun," he added. She fished it out from her sodden décolletage and handed it over silently. As he dropped it in his pocket, Lafayette noticed it was not a common slug-throwing pistol. He leaned to grasp Mickey Jo's arm and hauled her to her feet. Marv fell in on her other side, and they set off across the mud, their feet squelching at each step. Lafayette looked back: their footprints filled with water as soon as they were made.

"An inch of rain and we'll be swimming," he commented.

"Ain't seen no rain in years," Marv commented.

"Nonsense," Lafayette replied. "It was raining cats and dogs the evening we met. That's why Daph and I had to run for it."

"No rain outa clouds like them," Mickey Jo remarked. "Gotta have vertical structure to squeeze the rain out."

"Oh, Al?" Marv called, pausing and falling a pace behind. "Talk to ya a minute?" Lafayette glanced at him. He was mouthing words with grotesque facial distortions.

'Gotta get ridda the dame,' Lafayette interpreted.

"Go ahead, Mickey Jo," he told the girl. "I'll catch up."

"Ever occur to you I might hafta take a leak too?" she demanded in an irascible tone, but she went on ahead.

"Don't trust that little broad," Marv said hoarsely. "We gotta ditch her, Al; she's some kinda fink. We can lose her easy, come dark."

"You seem to stick to me like a burr to tweed," Lafayette said. "Why? It isn't sheer affection, I feel sure."

Marv looked at Lafayette blankly for a moment; then, as if at a decision, his expression firmed to a look of shrewd determination.

"I'll level with you, milord," he grated. "You seem like a right guy, and you stuck up for me when you didn't hafta. So I'll lay it all out. I'm a agent of Prime. My assignment is to stay with you. That's taken some doing, too, I can tell you, pal."

"Why?" Lafayette inquired casually.

" 'Cause that's my orders," Marv replied.

"Sure, but why the orders?" Lafayette persisted.

"Look, Al, I'm just a plain guy, see? I got the job because I happena pick a big shot's kid outa the way of a runaway rail-wagon. I don't unnerstan half I know about entropic disjunctions and Schrödinger Functions, and—"

"Collapsed ones," Lafayette put in. "Somebody said that," he added vaguely. "Go on."

"What we got here is a classic worst-case analysis," Marv stated. "Course, I dunno what that is, but it don't sound good. And we're into what ya call 'nondeterministic polymonial complete' problems, too. Tie that, will ya?"

"According to Ramsey," O'Leary said dully, "total disorder is impossible."

"Maybe: I don't hear about this Ramsey," Marv said. "But we're close, I can tell you that. And we're tryna hold it short of the edge. We don't want to let any more temporal anomalies sneak in, and that's where you come in, Al."

"I had nothing to do with it, I tell you!" Lafayette snapped. "I'm as much a victim as you are—maybe more; at least you've got some kind of official status. Mickey Jo, too."

"I don't trust that broad," Marv said. "Like I said, Al; she's working some kind of a angle."

"She's a duly accredited agent of Supreme HQ," O'Leary said. "She's got you outranked."

"Maybe, maybe not," Marv grunted. "That's a point for the philosophers. Meanwhile, let's you and me kinda do a fast fade, and leave her go on into town alone."

"Fade where?" Lafayette inquired. "The landscape is as flat as a pool table in all directions."

"In the wrecked car," Marv suggested, nudging Lafayette in the direction of the overturned roadster half-buried in mud and sand. When they were close enough for Lafayette to see the chrome-plated cranks on the cherry-red dash for opening the headlight covers, a sound from the hulk brought them to an abrupt halt.

"Somebody in there," Marv said.

"Or hiding behind it," Lafayette suggested.

A blurry voice contradicted him. "Never hid from no wight in my life, by my halidom!" Then a bulky, menacing figure rose from behind the long hood of the formerly elegant vehicle.

"Just catching a little rest is all," the deep voice went on. "Spot of bother, damned tidal wave washed me right off the king's highroad. But bother be damned! I'll find the scamps responsible for broaching the dam and see them hanged on the windy tree for nights full nine!"

Lafayette took a hesitant step forward. "Uh, sir," he began, at which the mud-coated, bulletlike head of the stranger turned as if noticing him for the first time.

"Are you Duke Bother-Be-Damned, by any chance?" Lafayette blurted.

"By no chance, sirrah, but by proof of single combat!" His Grace roared, groping for the hilt of an over-sized sword. "But bide thee until I get this damned muck out of me eyes," he added more calmly, "and I'll prove it on your person."

"That won't be necessary, Your Grace," Lafayette said. Then to Marv, "We're back on the track; this is the chap I was setting out to find when everything got confusing."

"I be no 'chap,' " the duke bellowed. "You sought me, did you? You'll rue the day you found me, wittol!" The mud-coated nobleman took a step back and at once toppled sideways with a splash that sent a sheet of mud across the scarlet lacquer of the fender, spattering both Lafayette and Marv. The latter slapped at the mud globules sliding down his soaked trench coat, and turned away.

"Come on, Al," he urged. "I guess we'll just hafta go in right in plain sight and take our chances."

"Wait," Lafayette countered. He squelched around past the crushed radiator shell of the Auburn and stooped to lend a hand to the fallen duke, who lay on his back, his arms and legs moving aimlessly like an overturned beetle. Lafayette caught one hand: the duke's grip, though slippery, was powerful. Lafayette winced even as he heaved backward, and was rewarded with a sudden lessening of the load as the duke sat up with a loud sucking sound.

"Again!" the nobleman commanded, as he strove without success to raise his seat from the grip of the mud.

"Get your feet under you," Lafayette suggested. The big man complied and in a moment was standing, towering over Lafayette's two meters by at least half a foot.

"You have our thanks, Sir Knight," the featureless head said, brushing a forearm across the muddy brow with a metallic clank.

"You're wearing armor," Lafayette guessed aloud. "No wonder you're so heavy."

"Aye," the armored duke agreed. "In these parlous times you pretty near gotta. Woods are full of brigands which they'd assault the very bitch that bore them, onney the woods is gone now." He waved a hand. "Useta be fine country for the chase of hart and boar," he commented sadly. "Then the big flood come and ain't never went down." He eyed O'Leary doubtfully. "Who're you?" he demanded abruptly. "Never seen you before, nor your squire yonder neither." The duke's hand had wandered to the muddy hilt of the six-foot broadsword slung at his side. "If you be the warlock that brought the doom on all Aphasia," he rumbled, "dire shall be thy fate."

"Not me, Duke," Lafayette said briskly. "Actually I was caught in the flood myself. Did you say 'Aphasia'?"

"Art a warlock, then?" Duke Bother-Be-Damned growled. "The waters rose these three hundred winters since. No living Christian man could have seen that day. Speak! Dost claim mastery of the black art?"

"Only a few card tricks," Lafayette explained apologetically.

"Card magic, eh? Meseems I've a pack of pasteboards back at my ducal seat; necromancy is illegal, of course, but in a good cause I'd wink my eye and reward you of my largesse as well. Come along, fellow. I'll send a troop of menials along for the car." He turned and set off without awaiting O'Leary's assent, then halted suddenly and turned ponderously.

"If ye be a creature of the infamous Trog," he barked, "be assured I'll lay the rascal by the heels ere he knows of your treachery."

"You know Trog?" Lafayette gasped. "That's wonderful; it means I really *am* back in Aphasia—not the same locus where I lost Daphne, of course—that disappeared several days ago by now, I suppose, if Belarius wasn't lying."

"See here, fellow," the Duke said heartily. "Though thy wits be scrambled somewhat, tis manifest, still thou had'st the wit to rally to my side, rather than having at me in cowardly fashion when I lay entrapped in the muck yonder. So I graciously extend my hand in friendship, be ye ever so base of birth."

• "I'm Sir Lafayette O'Leary," Lafayette said stiffly, accepting the duke's muddy hand. "And once rightful king of Artesia, withal."

"Oh. OK, no offence," the duke replied. "Leary, huh? Whereat is it? Never heard of the demesne."

"Not 'whereat,'" Lafayette corrected automatically. "*Where* is it? In the course of a lifetime you waste enough breath to deliver a three-hour speech, just putting in that redundant 'at.'"

"Don't ast *me* whereat it is," Bother-Be-Damned returned defiantly. "It was *you* brung it up. Me, I never hearn tell on it. Must be small potatoes." The matter thus disposed of, the duke turned away and resumed his march, not precisely toward the distant smoke, Lafayette noted as he followed. A hundred yards off to the left, Marv was standing, undecided, shading his eyes to watch Lafayette's progress. Then he shook his head, appeared to speak briefly into his clenched fist, and set off on an intercept course. Mickey Jo was nowhere in sight.

"By the way, Your Grace," Lafayette addressed his new acquaintance, "I'm looking for a gray room, very large, dim-lit, with a carpet and a bunch of big soft chairs. Do you happen to know of such a room?"

"Avaunt thee," Bother replied in a tone of dismissal. "I've rich chambers in plenty in my ducal seat, or anyways I *did* have before the tidal wave. Looks like it musta knocked it flat. Too bad."

"It would take a very large building to have a room of that size in it," Lafayette added hopefully.

"My castle is the largest in the province," the duke assured O'Leary. "Or was, since meseems tis gone, now."

"I have to find it," O'Leary went on. "You see, that's where this skunk named Frumpkin hangs out—and he's got Daphne."

"Unlucky in love, eh, lad?" Bother commented cheerfully. "Well, it's happened to doughtier fighters than you, Sir Lafayette; best to forget the baggage and find another."

"But she's my wife," Lafayette protested. "And I love her. I don't want some other baggage—and besides, she's not happy; I can tell, even though she said he treats her OK."

"Pity and all that," the duke said. "This Frumpkin, now, what sort of wight is he? Stout of arm and back, with a goodly company of men-at-arms about him?"

"Nothing like that," O'Leary corrected. "He's an ordinary-looking creep, and he's always alone, except when he's with Daphne—he calls her Dame Edith."

"Then trounce the rascal soundly, whip the wench for her impertinence, and proceed to matters of importance," Bother advised.

Slogging along at the heels of the duke, O'Leary half-listened as the nobleman recounted the multifarious deeds of infamy with which he, a humane and sensitive fellow, had been beset, most of which atrocities he laid at the doorstep of one Trog. ". . . or 'Lord Trog,' as the upstart styles himself," Bother sneered.

"I've met him," O'Leary put in; "a runty little fellow, all whiskers and fleas, surrounded by cutthroats thirsting for an innocent victim to turn over to the PPS."

"What? Trog runty?" Bother yelled. "Art daft in sooth, Sir Knight! He's a very clothes-pole of a man clad always in scented silks and satin, a dandified degenerate of the worst stripe!"

"Maybe he's grown since I saw him," Lafayette hazarded.

"Bah!" the duke barked. "But what of the upstart? Art his minion?"

"Not me." Lafayette reassured the armored duke. "I'm nobody's minion. I'm on my own."

"Indeed? Then t'were well you cast your lot with the forces of good, against evil and chaos. And eftsoons, methinks." The duke paused both in his speech and his stride to lower the vizor of his great helm, revealing a battered and scarred visage which glowered at O'Leary, and past him at Marv.

"Red Bull!" Lafayette gasped. "Am I glad to see you! I'm so lost I thought I'd never see a familiar face again! Let's get busy and figure out how to get off this mud-flat and back to Artesia!"

The duke thus addressed took a step back and drew his well-honed sword halfway from its mud-coated sheath.

"Avaunt thee, sirrah!" he barked. "It mislikes me not to hold converse with one who is manifestly afflicted of Oompah; still, I'll not outrage the proprieties by beheading thee if thou'll but cease thy frenzies!

Thinks't me a gentleman cow, eh? Aroint thee!''

"Don't be silly, Red Bull," O'Leary replied calmly.
"You know very well I can lick you. Remember that
time in the alley under the city walls, just before I went
out into the desert? *That* time Princess Adoranne was
missing—this time it's Daphne. She's lost somewhere
back in Aphasia, unless Aphasia's already dissolved
back into nonrealization. Come on! We always had
good luck as a team—except maybe the time I turned
into Zorro, and that wasn't your fault!"

"You pretend, fellow, to be my boon companion?"
the duke bellowed. "You rave! No doubt thy keeper
waits thee even now, among the huts yonder. But be
calm: I'll not reveal thy secrets! But in sooth t'were well
to make oblique approach, the beadles to avoid."

"What difference will it make what route we take?"
O'Leary countered. "We have to come in across open
mud no matter which way we go."

"True, but under cover of darkness, we can creep
close ere we're discovered to the watch."

"Hey, Al," Marv called, crossing the last few feet to
rejoin the party. "Innerdooce me to this here feller,
OK?" he proposed, eyeing the duke's six-foot-plus
stature, impressive even in its coating of mud, which
was beginning to dry now and to flake off in large
chunks, revealing the polished steel beneath.

"Certainly, Marv," O'Leary acceded. "Your
Grace," he addressed the duke, "permit me to intro-
duce my fellow refugee, Marv: We've been through
thick and thin together. Marv, His Grace, Duke Bother-
Be-Damned."

"Hi, Grace," Marv responded dubiously.

"Not my real name," the duke muttered, "merely an
eke-name given me by the common herd. But you may
call me 'Bother,' and you will." He extended his un-
mailed hand, which Marv took hesitantly.

"OK, pal, whatever you say," the latter said quickly.
He gave the hand a quick grip and dropped it, then took
up a position half behind O'Leary.

"Say, Al," he muttered. "If this guy is some kinda

dook, he must be the big shot around here, right? So maybe we oughta get in solid with him, and maybe stay offa the gallows, like.''

"Good thinking, Marv," O'Leary agreed. "I've already cemented relations, and we're on our way into town, if that's what it is, to straighten things out. Funny thing, Marv: Your old friend Trog, or someone else with the same name, seems to be at the bottom of the problem here.''

Staying a pace behind O'Leary as he forged on in the wake of the Duke, Marv shook his head. "Don't figure, Al. No one guy coulda caused a mess like *this*." He waved a hand at the sweep of soggy clay. "Especially old Trog. He's what you call a congenital psychopathic inferior. No more brains'n a grasshopper. Sits around and gives dumb orders, is all he can do. Like sending me and Omar off to the dungeon, and all.''

"Still, it's interesting that he's here," O'Leary pointed out. "So, we must not be as far from Aphasia as it seemed. Another thing, the duke is an alterego of an old pal of mine known as the Red Bull—which independently suggests we're not far from Artesia.''

"Beats me," Marv muttered. "All they told me was stay close, and report when I get a chanst.''

"How do you report?" O'Leary wanted to know.

"There's this contact," Marv replied. "He's spose to get in touch.''

"Listen carefully, Marv," Lafayette said. "Does *'raf trass spoit'* mean anything to you?''

"You're dang right," Marv said. "That's what His Lordship useta yell whenever anything din't go right.''

"You mean Trog?" Lafayette pressed the point.

"Old Troggie is right," Marv confirmed. "And now you say he's got a finger in this here mess, eh? We better have a talk with that little runt before it's too late.''

"Sure," O'Leary agreed. "We'll go see him and try to find out what's at the bottom of all this crazy business. He's the duke's worst enemy, but he'll probably be glad to send us on a secret mission.''

Ahead, a small crowd of ill-assorted survivors of

whatever had happened to the countryside had gathered to watch the advance of the three refugees across the glistening mud-flat. Spears, pitchforks, and clubs were among the articles with which they were prepared to welcome the newcomers. The sun was low now, staining the sky a bilious yellow which reflected from the wet surface like puddles of molten gold. The duke halted and spoke over his mailed shoulder:

"Withal, we'd best delay here until the light has gone." He paused to knock crusts of mud from his sword-hilt. "Once among the rabble," he went on in a conspiratorial tone, "you'll stand mute whilst I conduct negotiations." He growled, eyeing the group standing by the clapboard huts. In the glow of early evening, men and shacks alike were no more than black silhouettes against the lowering sky.

"It passeth all propriety that I, a royal duke, should skulk here, awaiting the pleasure of these churls!"

"Play it cool, Your Grace," Lafayette suggested. "There are too many of them for one to stand strictly on ceremony."

"Bah! Let not base caution wait upon my knightly valor!" Bother yelled and without furthur words, charged, sword brandished aloft. The squatters began hesitantly to close ranks, then abruptly scattered, retreating among the huts, where Bother made a desultory search accompanied by yells and whacks of his blade which brought a number of the ramshackle structures down in ruin. While the duke was thus occupied, O'Leary, with a quick word to Marv, moved off to one side and began a wide, curving approach which would bring him up at the rear of the settlement.

"Hey, Al," Marv called in a tone of distress, "wait up!" O'Leary turned to see his companion-in-distress struggling to his feet, coated with black muck except for the pale blob of his unshaven face, dim in the fading light.

"Smear a little mud on your face, Marv," Lafayette called softly, "and you'll be invisible." Marv complied. Even at a distance of two feet, he was but a dark bulk against darkness. At that moment, the duke's voice bellowed across the night.

"Very well, Sir Lafayette, you may emerge now. Sir Lafayette? Damme, where's the fellow got to? Come out at once, I say!"

"I'm right here," O'Leary called.

"Say, Al," Marv commented, "you're pretty well daubed your ownself. Prolly he can't see you. So now's our chanct."

"Chance," O'Leary corrected. "No *t*. Chance for what?"

"Art a warlock?" Bother demanded of the now near total darkness. "Hast the cloak of Darkness? Remember how I befriended you when you were a nameless vagabond. Come along, now, Sir Lafayette, we'll broach a keg to our comradeship."

"All of a sudden he wants to be pals," Marv commented. "Our chance to sneak in behind him and grab the best quarters in the local hostel," he went on as if there had been no interruption. "OK, Sir Al? Sir Al! Whereat are ya? Oh. I gotcha," he concluded as his wildly groping arms encountered O'Leary's shoulder.

"We may as well," Lafayette replied. "We haven't finished our dinner. Maybe we can get a nice haunch of venison and a stoup of ale and a bath and a bed. Let's go."

Chapter Thirteen

For the next quarter hour, while Bother hallooed in the distance and villagers roamed at random carrying dim yellowish lanterns, the two fugitives waded as silently as possible in a wide arc around the right end, coming up to the fringe of huts on the outskirts of the settlement without raising a halloo.

"Wait," O'Leary said, as they paused in the lee of the first shack. "It's time for me to make another try at focusing the Psychical Energies. This is just like the time I had to take refuge in the slums of Artesia City: I found an unprepossessing shed and sort of rearranged things to make it cosier. Just a minute." Marv assented silently. Lafayette cleared his mind of preconceptions and pictured the interior of the little structure as it would be revealed when he opened the door—a rudely nailed-up affair slung on rotted leather hinges.

Nothing fancy, he specified. *Just your standard Holiday Inn room, but with a counter-top fridge, well-stocked, and a hot plate.* As he held the image confidently in mind, Marv nudged him impatiently. . . . Or did the world jiggle ever so slightly? He brushed aside Marv's importunities, unsure.

Where was he? He seemed to have lost his place, thanks to Marv's interruption. Oh, yes, it was the room: a first-class USA-style motel. He envisioned it clearly and in detail; then the image faded, became misty and gray, and Frumpkin was there, working frantically at his oversize control panel. Without pausing to consider, O'Leary leaped, knocking the Man in Black away from the array of switches and instrument faces.

FLIP! The grand ballroom at Artesia, crowded with gorgeously gowned or uniformed people, among whom Lafayette recognized Lord Archie, an old ally. He called out to him and, FLIP! he was watching haggard people in gray rags, picking objects out of rubble.

FLIP! A star exploded in blackness. As the shock wave struck he was thrown back, back, tumbling end-over-end. He grabbed for support, felt a soft squishy surface underfoot. He concentrated on deducing which way was up.

"Hey, Al!" Marv's voice boomed out. "Where ya got to? You was going to fix us up with a flop, remember?"

"Don't bother me when I'm concentrating, Marv!" O'Leary hissed in annoyance, still dizzy from his wild ride through delirium. "Well, here goes." He tugged at the leather strap which served as door-handle, and a blackened slat fell away to flop into the ankle-deep mud. Through the slit thus opened light gleamed. Squinting, Lafayette peered through, saw wall-to-wall carpeting, the corners of two double beds, and a table-lamp which shed its warm glow on the flowered wall-paper.

"We're in, Marv," he said exultantly, and tugged at the door. This time it yielded. Pausing only to kick off his mud-laden boots, O'Leary stepped inside.

"Hold it right there, feller!" the familiar hoarse voice of Sheriff "Hoppy" Tode growled. "Been settin' up ever night fer a week, waitin' on you, boy. What taken you so long?"

" 'What took you so long,' " O'Leary corrected at once.

"Me?" Tode yelled indignantly. "Didn't I get on the job jest as soon's I got things straight with that Clyde feller? Been right here ever since they carried me here and told me how you'd be showin' up soon—and yer sidekick, too," he finished as Marv poked a wondering expression through the doorway. "Said to keep a eye on him; tricky, they said."

"Whom, I?" Marv said in a tone of wonder, edging away.

"Inside, you," Tode barked. "Got the both of ye; old Cease'll be glad o' *that,* I betcha." The sheriff motioned with the nickle-plated frontier-model hog-leg he carried.

After the two adventurers had placed their hands behind their heads as ordered, Tode frowned at their muddy footprints.

"Dern shame to mess up these here rugs," he said. "Strip whur you're at, and get in yonder and take a bath," he ordered. Marv complied at once, disappearing into the tiled bathroom.

"Fine," O'Leary agreed. "And while we're cleaning up, perhaps you could rustle up some bacon and eggs, or whatever's in the icebox. By the way, Sheriff, how did *you* get in here without getting muddy?" He dropped his clothes on top of the black mound of Marv's discarded garments.

"Tole you they carried me here. Some kind of seat on wheels it was, only it, like, flew or sumpin'. Beats me. One minute I was back at Headquarters, the next one here I was."

At the door, Lafayette paused to say, "By the way, Marv here is an agent of Central, Sheriff. If you're working for Prime now, that makes you colleagues of a sort, doesn't it?"

"Ain't been tole nothing about no jailbird bein' my boss," Tode replied shortly.

"I was really surprised to see you here, Sheriff," O'Leary said. "The last I saw you, Clyde's boy Archie was pulling your arms off. Then I heard your voice in the fog, wherever *that* was."

"When you taken and slipped out," Tode explained, "they forgot me and run after you. I started to ast the gal back o' the desk whereat I was and what the heck was going down; but she taken to yellin' her fool head off, so I taken a quick powder out the side door, and my-oh-my, wasn't them fellers excited! Taken me for

somebody named Alligator or like that. Started offerin'
me bribes if'n I'd let up. Couldn't figger it out. Then
some other big officials come in and told 'em something, and next thing I knew I was on the way here.
Thought that part about the fog and all was jest
dreamin'. After a while they come for me, and here I
am. Told me to nab you and I'd get a big ree-ward, and
a gold medal and a stay of execution. So I'm holdin'
you until somebody comes to take you off'n my
hands."

"That sounds so dreary," Lafayette said sympathetically. "Why not put the revolver away and sit
down? We're as innocent as yourself—and we have one
advantage."

"Oh, yeah? What would that be?" Tode inquired
cautiously.

"Would you like to go home?" O'Leary asked.

"Who, me?" the sheriff demanded, surprised. "Tell
you the truth, I don't even know whereat Colby City is.
Don't know nothin' about no mudflats noplace in the
county. Sure, I'd like to go home. How?"

Steaming gently, Marv tugged at O'Leary's sleeve.
"Next man," he said.

"Not now, Marv." Lafayette shook him off. "All we
have to do," he told the sheriff, "is find my old pal the
duke. He's from back home, or almost. We'll find out
what he knows, and then I've got a couple of other
ideas, too. Remember when I walked right through your
jail wall?"

"I been kinda wonderin' about that," Tode conceded. "You tellin' me you sure-nuff done that? Wasn't
no trick?"

"Right," Lafayette confirmed. "Now, put up the
gun and we'll stick together and break out of this."

In the taut silence that followed his proposal, there
was a quick tap at the door. Before anyone could respond, it opened and a mud-blackened figure stepped
through.

"Hi, fellas," Mickey Jo's voice said. "Say, you got a
shower-bath in here?" she cried in a delighted tone,
looking past Lafayette into the pale-green tiled cubicle.

"Come on, I'll race ya." Her sodden garments fell to the floor with a heavy thump, revealing a slim but well-rounded girlbody with muddy face, hands, and ankles. She thrust past O'Leary and Marv, who tried in vain to preserve the conventions by wrapping himself in the shower curtain.

"Don't bother, honey," Mickey Jo said. "I reckon I seen it all before." She stepped into the stall and disappeared in a deluge of hot water and soapsuds.

"Who's the gal?" Sheriff Tode asked weakly.

"Mickey Jo," O'Leary told him. "She's a Prime agent, like you."

"Jest part-time, is all," Tode reminded Lafayette. He holstered his weapon. "Reckon we better get started," he added. "You got any clothes to put on?" he inquired vaguely.

"In the closet," O'Leary improvised, mentally picturing a row of natty outfits in both his size and Marv's, plus an assortment of Western costumes for Mickey Jo. There was a faint *bump*, he thought—or was it a distant explosion?

There was a moment of disorientation; then the gray room was back. This time, O'Leary told himself, crouching behind the nearest chair, he'd play it a little smarter. No jumping out and yelling BOO! If he just laid low and listened . . . there were faint voices. Lafayette peeked out from behind the chair and saw Frumpkin clad in a wine-colored bathrope, deep in conversation with Special Ed and a paunchy, sly-faced fellow in a dowdy alpaca suit and worn cowboy boots.

". . . no danger of that; he's a simpleton," Frumpkin was saying.

"I dunno, Chief," Ed countered. "He made the take-out slicker'n owl-do, and I tole you he had them pitchers."

"He couldn't have," Frumpkin snapped. "You'd been sampling your stock again, Ed." He scribbled a note in a small pad and turned to the other man.

"Now, Chuck, I don't like your coming here like this without specific instructions," Frumpkin said in a sharp tone. The paunchy man threw up his hands.

"Don't go getting riled, boss. I cun't help it. I and the missus had just went out for a bite, and"—he paused to gulp—"and it jest happened. Makes me nervous." He looked around, failing to note O'Leary as he ducked back.

"No matter," Frumpkin dismissed the subject. "All can yet be retrieved. These aberrant inputs have kept me a bit off-balance, I'll admit. It's time to recalibrate. Just follow along, gentlemen."

Lafayette poked his head out to watch, and it struck a large gong which someone had put there while he wasn't looking. The clang echoed and reechoed, louder and softer, on and on. . . .

Sheriff Tode's meaty face seemed to be hanging disembodied before him. "Easy, Shurf," Lafayette said soothingly. "As soon as I can get the world slowed down to a slow whirl—or whirled slowed down to a world, I'll explain everything—except possibly the moose in the bedroom."

"You're a-foolin' me," Tode accused, but he turned and watched as O'Leary went to the closet door and opened it on precisely the gaudy wardrobe he had envisioned, plus a row of well-shined boots on a rack below.

"I can see somebody's been a-funnin' me," Tode remarked. O'Leary ignored the comment and invited Marv, now pink from a vigorous toweling, to pick out a suitable outfit for himself.

"Oh, boy," Marv purred appreciatively as he looked over a scarlet doorman's uniform with gold epaulets, but passed it up in favor of a powder-blue confection with silver braid and buttons. A drawer at one end of the closet supplied socks and undergarments.

The roar of the shower ceased, and Mickey Jo, a towel around her hair and another held carelessly before her, emerged and uttered a yelp of joy at sight of the closet.

"I always wanted one o' them cowgirl getups," she cried, "just like Dale used to wear." She hurried over and suited up while Marv struggled with his tie, lingering before the full-length mirror on the back of the closet door.

"Marv," Mickey Jo cooed, "I never dreamed you were so handsome! But how about a shave to go with it? Or do you want me to just shape it a little?"

O'Leary finished dressing in a well-fitted hussar's tunic and breeches, complete with nickle-plated helmet and sword-hilt, a costume selected for him by Mickey Jo, who had transferred the contents of his pockets to his new finery; there came a peremptory knock at the door, followed at once by a pounding as with a pistol-butt; then an authoritative voice yelled:

"Open up, you in there! Police business!"

"Why, fur as that goes, I'm a police orfiser myself," Sheriff Tode began as he opened the door, only to be thrust aside by a bulky fellow in greasy rags which may have been the remains of a regulation dark-blue city-cop suit. He looked from Mickey Jo to Marv to O'Leary, then planted his feet solidly before the latter and barked:

"You'd be the boy I want, I don't doubt. Are you coming quiet, or do I hafta cuff ya up?" He jingled a set of rusty bracelets at his belt and shifted his cigar butt to the other corner of his mouth.

"No need for force, Chief," Lafayette assured the intruder. "I'll come quietly. And perhaps you can tell me something about just what it is that's going on here."

"Don't count on it, rube," the cop snarled, whacking his palm with his billy club. "The rest o' you riffraff stay here," he added, eyeing Tode without approval. "I'll get to you later."

"Sir," Tode stated firmly. "I myself am Shurf Tode of Colby County. You may depend on my cooperation in any police matter."

"Happens the shire reeve's a close acquaintance o' mine," the cop growled, "and he's over to the ducal quarters right now tryna splain to His Grace how he happen to be in that lynch mob."

Trailed by Marv with Tode at his side while Mickey Jo disappeared into the bathroom, O'Leary followed the cop out into moonlit darkness along a catwalk improvised from debris. The catwalk protected his mirror-polished boots from the mud, from which at irregular intervals the ruins of former masonry buildings projected, vaguely visible by moonlight. The moon itself, Lafayette noted, had resumed its normal size. Studying the ragged rows of huts, Lafayette was struck by a thought: "Marv," he said quietly to the gaudily dressed Prime agent, "this used to be a city, and the shacks are lined up along the old streets. Do you think it could be Colby Corners? If it is, it means the Chantspell Mountains ought to be over there, to the west, but there's nothing there but those low hillocks. Somehow we're close to home, but an awful long way off, too."

"Beats me," Marv muttered. O'Leary now noticed up ahead a curiously rickety structure some fifty feet tall, with a solid-looking room at the top. He pointed it out to Marv. "As I figure it," he said, "That's just about where the Y is back in Colby Corners—and the palace, in Artesia."

"That don't look safe," Marv said, eyeing the fragile underpinnings of the top-heavy building. Ignoring the curious edifice, their guide turned in at a tumble-down affair he referred to grandly as the Palace of Justice, a collapsed building with one brick wall and two more of packing crates and tarpaper, roofed with a rotted tarpaulin. Only the top step of a wide flight projected above the mud level.

"Had a flood here, eh?" O'Leary hazarded.

"You could say that, wise guy," Lafayette's escort grunted. "Now, you ack nice in front of the Inspector, and I'll try to make it easy on you."

O'Leary looked around at the squatter's village of mean hovels linked, he could now see, by a network of catwalks of an extent that indicated more than a brief occupation of the site. A few drably clad people were in sight, apparently engaged in routine tasks.

"C'mon, feller," the cop urged from the step. "Ain't got no backlog in the courts anyways. Jedge's waitin' on ye." Tode hurried up the steps; Lafayette followed. Marv was nowhere to be seen. Tode forged ahead confidently.

They pushed through heavy oak doors with pieces of

billboard nailed over the broken plate-glass panels. Inside, Lafayette detected the stale odor of boredom, incompetence, bribery, treachery, and poor sanitation common to all such institutions of law-without-justice. He trailed Tode and the arresting officer to an inner pair of swinging oak doors and inside into a small theatrelike room where a middle-aged man with a plump and half-familiar face sat hunched in a black robe behind a lectern on a raised platform. The smack of the gavel made O'Leary jump.

"All right, Agent X-9," the presumed judge muttered, not quite looking at O'Leary's guard. "Case of the Supreme Authority versus O'Leary. Court is now in session." He looked vaguely at O'Leary. "Do you have anything to say before I pronounce sentence?"

After a moment of appalled silence, O'Leary burst out, "Damn right I do!" He stopped short as the gavel banged again.

"Looky here, boy," the judge said without heat. "No profanity in the court."

"Sorry about that," Lafayette said contritely. "But this is no trial! I don't even know what I'm accused of!"

"No matter; the rest of us do."

"Not me," Tode spoke up from behind O'Leary. "Him and me both, we're innercent is what we are."

"And," the judge went on, "you're not 'accused,' O'Leary; you're convicted."

"Of what?" O'Leary and Tode said together.

"Can you deny . . ." the judge said sternly, at the same time beckoning to a gaudily attired couple sitting in the front row of the sparse audience. They rose and bustled forward eagerly, skirting O'Leary to take up proprietary positions flanking the podium. "Uh, can you deny, as I was saying," the jurist continued, peering sharply at Lafayette, "that on the fourteenth instant—that would be yesterday—at approximately nine pee em, you did willfully disposess the plaintiffs, Chuck and Chick, of the motel accommodations which they had reserved, engaged, and paid for in advance, at a time they were briefly absent therefrom?"

"Well, not exactly," O'Leary responded dubiously.

"We're the Chick and Chuck of 'Chuckles with Chick and Chuck,' a clean family act which we're playing the Twilight Room of the Holiday Inn right here in Duluth," the male member of the duo of variety artists volunteered in the silence which followed O'Leary's statement. O'Leary recognized him as the paunchy man he had seen in the gray room. "Which we stepped out for a bite after we unpacked," Chuck went on, "and when we come back we couldn't find our room no place. Seemed like there was just a kinda open space where it shoulda been. Checked the number, too: skipped right from one thirteen to one seventeen. We didn't hardly know what to do. Then this cop feller came along, and here we are."

". . . and all our brand-new costumes in there, too," Chick mourned. "Most of 'em not even wore yet—and *he's* wearing one of 'em right now!" She pointed an indignant finger at Lafayette.

"So's *he*," Chuck added, aiming an accusatory digit at Marv, who had retired to a position behind Tode.

"Well," the judge growled, scowling at O'Leary. "I'm waiting. Can you make such denial? Remember, you're under oath."

"I am not!" Lafayette declared. "I just got here, and I don't know what's going on. I'm sorry about Chuck and Chick, but I can explain."

"Very well," the judge said agreeably. "Explain."

"I guess I can't exactly explain," Lafayette confessed. "But I didn't mean any harm. I mean, we were cold and wet and hungry, and I just thought it would be nice if we had a first-class motel room waiting for us."

"So you tooken ourn!" Chuck supplied. "Dern if I can see how you done it; must be one o' them new packaged-unit buildings like I seen onta the tube."

"So you admit taking the room," the judge recapped carefully, "but you plead necessity."

"I didn't take it on purpose," Lafayette protested. "I mean, it was like the time I wanted a bathtub, and I got one with Daphne in it. You see, when I seem to conjure up something out of thin air by focusing the Psychical Energies, I'm not really creating it; I'm just shifting it from another, nearby locus. So there was no malicious intent.''

''Now we're getting somewheres,'' the judge said in a satisfied tone. He motioned unobtrusively, and two uniformed bailiffs moved in to flank O'Leary closely. The judge was peering sharply at him. ''You confess freely and without duress, that you did willfully tamper with the entropic integrity of this locus, known and referred to hereafter as Alpha Nine-Two, Plane V-87, Fox 1-W.''

''Hey!'' O'Leary yelled. ''That's not far from Artesia, only Artesia's Fox 221-b! We're almost back! I guess we've been luckier than we thought,'' he added more calmly to Marv.

''I assume,'' the judge, whose name O'Leary belatedly saw lettered on a brass plate on the lecturn, was Grossfarb, continued implacably, ''that you are aware that this constitutes a gross violation of the GRC.''

''I never heard of it,'' Lafayette said. ''Or maybe Belarius mentioned it.''

''Ignorance of the law is no excuse, Bub,'' the judge returned coldly.

''Still, it goes to establish that my intent was innocent,'' Lafayette insisted.

Grossfarb turned pages before him. ''This whole matter is quite irregular,'' he grumped. ''I'd be tempted to throw it out, except for the fact that I have an Emergency Directive here, specifying that you're to be detained at all costs.'' He looked at O'Leary. ''You don't *look* dangerous,'' he conceded. ''Still, we all remember the Axe-handle Killer. He was only nine years of age and had an angelic appearance. Now, before I remand you to custody, I want to clear up a few minor points, just for my own satisfaction:

''Where is your probability engine hidden?''

''I don't know what that is,'' O'Leary replied with dignity. ''And I certainly don't own one.''

''No question of ownership,'' Judge Grossfarb corrected. '' 'Possession' is the word. Though I confess I don't see how you could transport and hide a fifty-ton unit, which is the minimum, I am assured by my advisers, required to dislocate an entire motel suite."

"It's ridiculous," O'Leary pointed out. "I arrived here on foot, not packing a Mack truck on my back."

"To be sure," Grossfarb murmured. "Still, I'm given no latitude in the matter. Bailiff—" he broke off as the courtroom doors were thrust open and a man dressed in immaculate black strode in, heading directly for the bench.

"Order!" Grossfarb barked weakly as the newcomer briefly flashed a bit of bright metal, then leaned on the podium and addressed the judge confidentially.

"It's irregular!" the latter said in protest, at which the Man in Black took out a folded document from an inner pocket and slapped it down in front of Grossfarb, who rose, looking flustered, and addressed the room:

"Jurisdiction in this case has been preempted by an overriding authority," he announced. "Bailiffs, pass custody of the prisoners"—he paused at a word from the Man in Black, then resumed—"prisoner, that is; the tall one; put the other fellow away until I've clarified the matter further. Turn this O'Leary over to His Excellency here. The present action is nol prossed." He sat looking frustrated.

Lafayette turned to speak to Marv, who was staring, open-mouthed, at the Man in Black standing by the bench in an attitude of patience stretched to the limit.

"Al, that there's the Man in Black!" he gasped. "He's as bad a spook as you are—I mean . . ."

"I recognize him," O'Leary said. "He's a big-shot Prime agent named Frumpkin. I wonder how he got here."

"Quite simply," Frumpkin spoke up. "I followed you, Sir Lafayette, and a merry chase it's been. Your resourcefulness has quite surprised me."

"What happened to Belarius?" Lafayette blurted.

"Alas, he was a trifle slow in his last transfer—from the laboratory, you'll recall. He fetched up somewhere in uncontrolled space-time, no doubt, poor chap. Another crime to be laid at your feet, fellow-me-lad."

"I had nothing to do with it," O'Leary rebutted.

Chapter Fourteen

"It is your contention," Frumpkin asked carefully, eyeing Lafayette keenly, "that you are a native of this desolate locus? That you are not guilty of unsanctioned shifting, that you have employed no probability device?"

"No," Lafayette replied stiffly. "That is *not* my contention. If you'd let me say something, I could tell you what my contention is."

"Say all you like, young fellow," Frumpkin acceded easily. "But I doubt you'll be able to say anything which will give the lie to the official recordings of your unexampled peregrinations." He tapped the papers he held in one hand. "It's all here, lad. I'm merely giving you an opportunity to demonstrate whatever vestigial sense of social responsibility you may possess, by speaking up manfully, to confess the part you've played in this gigantic crime."

"Speaking of crimes," Lafayette came back hotly. "What about kidnapping?"

"You wish to confess to a kidnapping?" Grossfarb put in gingerly.

"No. *He's* the kidnapper," O'Leary corrected, pointing at Frumpkin. "He's holding Daphne in a . . . place."

149

"What place?" Grossfarb demanded.

"Sort of a vague place," Lafayette explained. "A big, misty-gray room, full of easy chairs and a big control console."

"Where is this curious installation?" the judge asked patiently.

"That's what I want to know!" Lafayette yelled. "Look, make him tell you, and we can go there and free poor Daphne—or Dame Edith, or whatever name she goes by here!"

"This person employs an alias?" Grossfarb asked coldly.

"No—it's not really Daphne, maybe, just her alter ego in this locus."

The gavel banged like a pistol shot. "It is my duty to caution you, O'Leary, that what you say will be used against you," the judge stated implacably. "Tampering with interlocal weather is a serious violation of the GRC, as you doubtless know."

"Ask the prisoner," Frumpkin put in lazily, "if he has ever visited this curious place he speaks of, and if he has indeed seen evidence of any crime there."

"Not exactly," Lafayette conceded. "It's just that sometimes things go all wivery, and then I'm there—only sometimes I'm not really there; it's just sort of a vision."

"That's enough, O'Leary," Grossfarb said coldly. "You may step down."

"Don't forget the charge I brought, Your Honor," Frumpkin spoke up, intercepting O'Leary. "Perhaps you'd best throw yourself on the mercy of the court."

"For what?" Lafayette demanded.

"Look about you," Frumpkin suggested with a wave of his hand. "The entire landscape stands as mute testimony to your infamy. Look upon a dead world, Mr., er, that is, *Sir* Lafayette. Look and know that *you* are responsible."

"Why me?" Lafayette countered. "All I did was try to stay alive, while one disaster after another hit me. If you ask me, it's some of those sharpies at Prime who got things all messed up."

"Those sharpies at Prime," Frumpkin muttered, jotting a note. "I think you'll find perfect candor your best and only hope, Sir Lafayette."

"All right—but tell me one thing first: Is Daphne all right? Did she get away from Aphasia before it dissolved? I tried to find her, but I'd barely started when someone shanghied me off to some mixed-up locus where a phony sheriff locked me up for nothing!"

"But you didn't stay locked up, did you, my boy?" Frumpkin asked rhetorically. "You departed the locus by some means as yet unknown, causing an additional temporal anomaly of Class Three. Explain your innocence of *that,* sir, if you can." Frumpkin looked triumphant.

"I don't know anything about any temporal anomaly," O'Leary replied doggedly. "I did what I had to do to protect myself and my partner from a work-over with the rubber hoses. Anyway, what harm did it do? All it did was put me in another batch of trouble somewhere else."

"What harm?" Frumpkin echoed musingly. "Look about you, sir. You perceive a world in its deaththroes, its mountains eroded to mere hillocks, its seas distributed evenly over its leveled surface to an average depth of three inches. This"—he made a sweeping gesture—"is one of the few habitable patches. And it was the blue-green jewel in the crown of the Supreme!"

"That's ridiculous," Lafayette countered. "How could using an ordinary flat-walker one time cause all that?"

"Flat-walker, eh?" Frumpkin turned to look intently at Lafayette as if to detect any deviation from strict veracity. "Used it only once, you claim?"

"Oh, I may have used it a few times before that," O'Leary conceded vaguely. "But I haven't used it since. I had an idea it was having bad side effects."

"You call the abortion of the destiny of a galaxy a side effect?" Frumpkin barked. "Remember the folk wisdom which tells us that for lack of a valve core, a tire was lost; for want of a tire, a ground-car was lost; for want of a ground-car, an order was lost; for want of orders, an army was lost; for want of an army a war was lost; for want of a victory an empire was lost; for want of a government, a culture was lost; for lack of a culture, a planet was lost, etcetera, etcetera; a system, a galaxy with a great destiny—and at last that destiny was lost—and all for want of a valve core! From trivial causes mighty repercussions result!''

"Oh, you're talking about my little slip with the Great Bear—or the Great Unicorn, as it is now.''

"Tell me all about it, my lad,'' Frumpkin said silkily. "And perhaps a way may yet be found to obtain a reprieve for you.''

"It was unintentional,'' Lafayette protested. "I was only thinking 'what if'; I didn't really *try* to do anything.''

"So, you destroy a great galactic destiny without even trying,'' Frumpkin paraphrased in a sardonic tone. He took O'Leary's arm and led him aside a few feet, out of hearing of Marv and Tode who waited uncomfortably by the door, peering out along the shadowy corridor of the half-ruined building.

"Clearly,'' Frumpkin whispered hoarsely, "we've underestimated you, Sir Lafayette, with tragic results. However, it's not too late to salvage something from the wreckage. Work with me, my boy, and we shall yet stand alone together. I'm no glutton; I'll share with a worthy confederate—together, I say, on the pinnacle of the reconstituted Temple of Glory at Nuclear City, with *all* the worlds at our feet! With your mind alone, you said? Coupled with the entropic equipment at *my* disposal, nothing can stand against us!'' He thrust out a calloused but well-manicured hand, which O'Leary avoided.

"I have no ambition to rule any galaxies,'' he replied. "I just want to find Daphne and go home. Where is the gray room?''

"Greedy, eh? All or nothing at all for you, is it? But it won't do, O'Leary. Without my help, you haven't a chance; and I admit freely that without your native powers, my own victory is uncertain. But as reasonable men, surely we can resolve any points of contention to our mutual advantage. After all, the manifold is so unimaginably immense, no one can so much as conceive it, much less exploit all its potentialities for pleasure. I shall be content to be ostensibly the junior partner, unobtrusive to a fault. To you alone shall go the glory, the triumphal processions, the booze, the broads, the luxury goods, the great estates. I myself am a humble chap at heart. Give me one or two outlying galaxies of my own, and I'll be content to retire there in obscurity. I give you my word! The solemn word of a Council Member!"

"You've got me wrong," Lafayette persisted. "I'm not interested in parades or real estate: I want Daphne."

"And you shall have her, sir, be she never so cold to your attractions. She shall be placed at your feet—or in your bed, bound hand and foot, or however you desire her. She shall be your willing slave!"

"Who do you think you are?" O'Leary demanded hotly, "to be offering a countess who also happens to be my wife as a sort of door prize, as if she belonged to you?"

"She does, my lad, she does," Frumpkin returned coolly. "She and all else in this entire manifold of loci. You see, I invented her and all the rest. I, and I alone, evoked this reality phase from the infinity of the potential into realization! Who am I, you ask? Know, then, intrusive flea in the pelt of my high and mightiness, that I am the Supreme, creator and owner of this All! As such, I honor you by engaging you in personal converse."

"Why?" O'Leary demanded. "Why me?"

"Simply because you are the one intrusive element in all my worlds. You alone do not belong here, and great has been the annoyance of your presence. How dare you, petty creature, thrust your minimal ego, unwanted, into that which I created utterly?" Frumpkin had worked himself up into a state of pink-faced rage as he spoke. When he paused, Lafayette said:

"I *didn't* dare, if that's any consolation to you: I stumbled into this mess by accident."

"So . . ." Frumpkin mused, seeming mollified. "And yet, to do this, to cross over the energy barrier between my evocation and the rest of, shall we say 'natural,' creation, you must of necessity possess some secret the which you must divulge to me alone. I command you to speak of it to none other, on pain of pain, I mean on death of death; that is, on pain of death, death utter and final across all the worlds!" Frumpkin stood glaring at Lafayette and breathing heavily.

"That's easy," O'Leary replied insouciantly. "I can't divulge it to anybody. I don't know what you're talking about."

"Pah! You think thus easily to escape the full fruits of your inconceivable audacity?" Frumpkin spat, with plenty of spit.

"Beats me," Lafayette said offhandedly. "What are you talking about, anyway?"

Sheriff Tode's voice occluded Frumpkin's sputtering reply. "Somethin' funny going on in there, feller," he said casually, having come up beside Lafayette. "Big gray room, full of smoke, like. Weird-looking bunch in there—and I seen Cease—and that Doc feller was goin' to put me under arrest, and old Marv is givin' some kinda speech—and funny thing is, they're listenin'."

Ignoring Frumpkin's expostulations, Lafayette moved over to peer in through a ragged opening in the stained tarp which constituted the facade of the improvised structure. Inside, grouped incongruously in the center of the cavernous room, he saw Lord Trog, waist-high and whiskery, thrusting for position between the iron-clad bulk of Duke Bother-Be-Damned and the dumpy form of Mary Ann Gorch. Beyond, he glimpsed her boss Clyde, and Sergeant Dubose, minus his helicopter, as well as Fred and Les, all craning for a better view of Marv, who looked impressive in his scarlet doorman's outfit. He was standing on a box, haranguing them:

". . . do like I tole you. Everything's jake. I got him right here, and all you got to do is hang loose and I'll con him right in here into the grabfield just like I conned him alla way from the Big Muddy!"

"Sold out," Lafayette said mournfully to Tode, who nodded portentously. "Never did trust that Marv," he confided. "Too slick, had shifty eyes, and didja ever notice how his eyebrows grows right acrost, all in one piece, like? Sure signs o' the criminal type, never fails."

"Why did you wait until now to mention it?" O'Leary asked dazedly.

"Figgered he was yer sidekick; a feller don't like to hear nothing like that about his sidekick. Remines me: Old Cease is right in there listenin' hard, more'n he ever done when *I* was talkin'."

"Shhh," O'Leary whispered. "I want to hear the rest."

". . . all know yer jobs," Marv was reminding his listeners. "All we got to do is nail him and sit tight. And, you, Troglouse," he addressed the whiskery runt, "none o' yer tricks. This O'Leary, he claims his name is now, he's got more slick ones up his sleeve than *you* ever hearn on! Now, how about it, folks?" Marv returned his attention to the entire group. "Are we agreed we got to lay this here Allegorus by the heels, onct and fer all? Yeah!" His voice was briefly drowned by an enthusiastic yell from the crowd. "So, come on, let's go an get him!" Marv jumped down from his podium and bulled through the throng which fell in behind him and headed determinedly directly toward Lafayette.

"Better take cover for the nonce," Frumpkin said. "What's that he called you? But *you* can't—" he broke off and dashed down the steps just as Marv emerged, hand outstretched, crying,

"Al, baby, come on inside: I wancha to meet some swell folks here. They got a big welcome laid on fer us. Seems like we're some kinda celebrities, like, and all. By the way," he added, more casually, "grab that skunk." He pointed at the retreating figure of Frumpkin, who had abandoned the catwalk and was making for the rickety, top-heavy structure adjacent to the Palace of Justice. The eager beavers, among whom Lafayette noted Marv's old partner Omar, were hot on the heels of the Man in Black, but as they approached the open framework of battered timbers, their pace slackened and they stood silently in the mud and watched as Frumpkin splattered his way to a fragile-looking ladder and began a cautious ascent. Judge Grossfarb arrived on the scene and took charge:

"Now all you folks stand back there. Form up a circle, like, round this here spook-hole."

"Methinks yon Man in Black clambers to his doom indeed," the bass voice of Bother spoke up at O'Leary's elbow, sounding somewhat winded. "Aroint thee, Sir Lafayette," he went on, "tis a parlous day when gentlefolk are jostled by mean villeins in haste to their demise."

"I always wondered what 'aroint thee' means, Your Grace," Lafayette informed the duke. "Perhaps you'd be so kind as to tell me."

"Beats me, laddy-buck," Bother dismissed the query. "But in sooth it hath a right knightly ring to it. I always like to throw in a 'stap me,' or a 'zounds' now and then to impress the yokels. Makes 'em more tractable—or so my old papa tole me afore he croaked."

"Duke," Lafayette said earnestly. "We have to lay that Frumpkin by the heels. He's dangerously insane. He thinks he's God."

"Indeed? Why, the miscreant thinks to outrank me, it doth appear," Bother replied indignantly.

"It's even worse than that," O'Leary said. "He's out to conquer the world—or all the worlds."

"Forsooth, he be no man of war," the duke objected doggedly. "And of liegemen hath he none. And if he should win to the Demon Chamber yonder, and fall not from the scaffold, we'll see him no more; for he'll to the infernal regions instanter, and we'll be well rid of him."

"Your Grace," O'Leary addressed the armored duke solemnly. "We have need to speak in private to him. We can't let him escape. I'm going after him. Will you dare the Demon Chamber with me?''

The duke declined, pointing out that suicide by going voluntarily into the clutch of demons was not required by knightly honor. ''. . . And I urge you, Sir Lafayette, to stay your hand. Together we can yet bring order to this rabble scum, recoup my manor, and live out our days as befits noblemen.''

''Sorry,'' Lafayette said, starting to press his way through the rank of awed yokels gaping at Frumpkin's slow and unsteady progress upward toward his unthinkable doom.

''Hey, Al,'' Marv's voice came to O'Leary's ears over the babble of the crowd. ''Wait up; I'm coming.''

Lafayette turned to see his recent denouncer hurrying toward him, face aglow. He turned away, but a moment later Marv was at his side, excitedly recounting his experiences of the last few moments.

''I fooled 'em good, Al,'' he boasted. ''Got 'em all worked up on a wild-goose chase.''

''I heard,'' Lafayette told him tonelessly. ''And the wild goose is me. Thanks a lot.''

''You don't get it, Al,'' Marv protested. ''None of 'em don't know what you look like, so you're safe as can be, long's you don't let on. I hadda tell 'em sumpin'; they was about to string me up.''

''I don't suppose it matters,'' Lafayette conceded. ''I noticed they weren't paying me any attention. But that fellow on the ladder: he's the one we have to nail. I think he's at the bottom of this whole affair.''

''He's gettin' away,'' Marv stated, slowing. He pointed; Frumpkin had reached the relative security of a raftlike platform slung beneath the top-floor room, and was fumbling at something on its underside. Lafayette forged ahead, Marv complaining at his heels.

Reaching the ladder, which at close range looked even less dependable than from a distance, being crudely lashed-up of well-rotted lengths of scrap two-by-four, Lafayette started up without hesitation. Above, Frumpkin looked down at him, his pinched face pale in the shadow.

''Get back, fool!'' he croaked. ''You don't know the

potency of the forces with which you seek to meddle.''

"No, but I intend to find out, with your help,''
Lafayette returned, sounding more cheerful than he
felt. Only a dozen feet from Frumpkin now, he could
see a hinged panel set in the rough flooring between the
black and cobwebbed joists. Frumpkin returned his attention to his efforts to open the rusted hasps as Lafayette gained the narrow platform. He looked down. Marv
was at the base of the ladder, looking upward with an
unreadable expression on his meaty features.

"Better hold on a minute, Al,'' Marv called in a
cautious tone, as if he didn't want to overhear himself.
"Fella wants to see ya.''

"I can't guarantee anything, Marv,'' Lafayette replied. Off to his right, Frumpkin had succeeded in
raising the panel in the plank floor above him and was
starting through. For a moment O'Leary considered
using the flat-walker to present the megalomaniacal
Man in Black with a shock when he completed his climb
up into the sealed chamber.

Nope, he told himself firmly. *I decided to stop using
it, and I'm sticking with that decision.*

"Hey, you, feller, come on down here now,'' a beefy
voice called from below. Lafayette looked down, saw
the gross, hounds-tooth-check figure of Chuck glaring
up at him over the sights of a fat black automatic pistol
which he was holding with both hands in a position
which allowed O'Leary to see the rifling inside the
barrel.

"I'm sorry about your costumes, Chuck,'' Lafayette
improvised, "but it was an emergency. Would you mind
aiming that thing elsewhere? You couldn't want any
holes in your fancy suit, remember.''

The pistol came down. Chuck tried an ingratiating expression reminiscent of Dracula approaching a bared
throat.

"Guess you and me better talk,'' he said. "Never
mind about Ga—or Frumpkin I guess you call him. We
can see about him later on.''

"We'll talk, all right,'' O'Leary said hotly. "Start

with the gray room: Where is it? What were you doing there?''

"Never played no Gray Room, Mister," Chuck demurred. "Lousy name for a night spot, anyways."

"I saw you there," Lafayette charged. "You looked as if you were taking orders from Frumpkin. Where is it?"

"You claim you seen me there, you orter know where it's at," Chuck pointed out reasonably.

"Where it *is*," O'Leary corrected briefly. "I wasn't really there; I just *saw* it."

"Oh, you have visions do ye?" Chuck chortled. "Sorry, bub, I can't use no palm-reader in the act."

"Don't you go going soft, Charles," the harsh voice of Chick came from offside. Lafayette looked over his shoulder and saw the hard-faced woman, her wig awry, climbing to the scaffolding a few feet away. She gripped a small nickle-plated .735, aimed at Lafayette's right knee.

"Go on, git down there," the lady added. "And this corn-popper ain't much, but at this range it'd smart some."

=Chapter Fifteen=

Back on the ground, Lafayette went along apparently docilely when Chuck's pudgy but surprisingly powerful fingers clamped on his arm and urged him toward a nearly intact tent of an offensive ocher-pink color, with contrasting patches. Inside, in an odor of hot rubberized canvas, he accepted a seat on the edge of a folding director's chair with MINE lettered on its back. The showman took a position behind an unpainted board-and-orange-crate desk, the big .45 in front of him. Chick posted herself beside the fly, gun in hand.

"We're finely beginning to get a handle onta you, Mr. Whatever-Your-Name-Is," Chuck stated in the tone of a magistrate introducing a dull stretch on his calendar. "We know now we got to take you inta account. Leastways, Chief says so; and I'm a kump'ny man, so just you lay it out plain: What's your angle in this?"

"I have to find Daphne and get back home with her," Lafayette said tightly. "That's all. You can keep the rest."

"Don't go tellin' me what I can keep," Chuck instructed Lafayette coldly. "Don't get no idear you're in the saddle here; onney you got a couple tricks Chief wants to find out about, is all's kep you alive up to now; so spill it: How'd you tie in to the Prime Generator?"

"Never heard of it," Lafayette said.

"Now, don't go givin' us *that* old crap," Chick commanded in an irascible tone. "We ain't got all the mornin'."

"I thought it was afternoon," Lafayette said.

"Don't matter none," Chuck stated. "Mornin' or evenin', you're openin' up *now*."

"I would," O'Leary assured his captors, "if I knew what to tell you. All I know is, I don't know what's going on, and haven't, since I did that dumb trick with the tail of the Unicorn."

"Ain't no sich of a thang's a unnercorn, not in this whole lamina," Chuck cut in.

"Not a real unicorn," O'Leary explained. "The constellation, you know—the same one some people call Ursa Major, or the Great Wain."

"Now let's not get inta that level o' energy transfer," Chuck admonished. "Stick to plain old A-level stuff fer now. Chief'll wanna know all about the G-scale stuff later."

"I didn't do it intentionally," Lafayette explained. "I was just musing, sort of."

"Well, we ain't amused," Chick put in. "Come on, Charles, might's well take this feller on in to Field HQ; we ain't gonna get anyplace with him. Let's face it, we ain't got the education to ask the right questions."

"Guess yer right," Chuck conceded. "Jest figgered it'd be kind of a nice note in the old Performance Record if we could take Chief the whole story all wrapped up."

"Get us kilt or worse, tryna second-think old Chief," Chick stated bluntly.

"Quite right, my dear," Frumpkin's voice interrupted as the Man in Black strolled casually into the tent. "Actually," he went on, "I've decided to remain at this locus until I have all the facts from our Mr. O'Leary here. You two may go along now. I shall conduct the interrogation in my own way."

"*Tole* ya, Charles," Chick's metallic voice was informing her partner as they exited clumsily, Chuck muttering under his breath.

"Have no fear," Frumpkin said over his shoulder. "Your apprehension of this fellow will be noted in the record." Frumpkin turned casually toward the rude desk, but before he had taken a step toward it, O'Leary had reached him and taken a secure grip on the elegant official's neck.

"We'll talk, all right," Lafayette said. "But you'll be answering the questions. Start with that fiasco back in Nicodaeus' old lab: What were you and your sidekick Belarius V doing there? And why did you try to grab me? Where's Daphne?"

"Unhand me, Lafayette," Frumpkin ordered in a strained voice as he attempted to reach inside his well-tailored black tunic, a move which Lafayette countered by seizing the arm and bringing it up behind his would-be captor's back. Seeming to take no notice, Frumpkin continued: "You gain nothing by submitting my person to indignities, my lad. Inasmuch as I'm well aware you've not the necessary toughness of spirit to commit murder in cold blood, we may as well conduct ourselves as gentlemen."

"My blood could warm up," O'Leary informed his captive, "unless you tell me right now what's happened to Daphne." He increased pressure on both neck and arm, eliciting a sharp squeak from the no longer haughty Man in Black.

"Kindly accept my assurances that I know nothing of this Daphne persona to whom you allude," Frumpkin blurted, attempting to twist free of O'Leary's grip, which he accordingly tightened.

"Better not struggle," Lafayette advised the smaller man concernedly. "I don't like the sound of that shoulder joint."

"Oho," the hearty voice of Duke Bother-Be-Damned boomed in the entry. "I see you've the situation well in hand, Sir Lafayette. I encountered the curious pair calling themselves Chick of Chickenchuck and Chuck of

Chuckenchick, or the like. I managed to elicit from them the cause of their abrupt exit from this rude pavilion, and came hither at once, in the event you required my aid. But of course, 'twere footless. I am about to proceed now on the errand which was interrupted by the mishap to my fire-chariot, the which I hope will dispel this wretched enchantment. Wilt accompany me, Sir Lafayette? I'd fain have a true man at my side when I go to consult the dread witch-woman.''

"Sure, Bother, I'll come," Lafayette agreed, watching closely as Frumpkin, whom he had released, crept to the seat behind the desk, all trace of arrogance gone from his demeanor. He sat and began plucking at the papers scattered on the desk.

"Tis good," the duke commented cheerfully, "to see this popinjay's airs punctured. His manner was too pushy by half. Now," he continued, fixing a fierce-eyed gaze on the crestfallen Man in Black, "no mischief in my absence, mind. On my return I shall deal with your pretensions in mete fashion. Come, Sir Lafayette." He turned, and Lafayette followed him to the tent-fly and out into the watery sunlight.

"This witch-woman," O'Leary said, overtaking the big fellow, "this is the first I've heard of her. Who is she? Why do you want to see her?"

"How now? This province of Leary must indeed lie in the remote boondocks," Bother returned. "If you've heard naught of the fame of Henriette in the Hill, mistress of the Black Art."

"Yes, it's a long way from here," Lafayette conceded. "Do you really believe in magic?"

"How not?" the duke snorted. "Have I not seen the very world transformed before mine eyes?"

"Sure," O'Leary agreed. "So have I—lots of times; but that's different."

"Aye, as the great evil differs from the lesser," Bother proclaimed.

"No," Lafayette objected. "The difference is magic versus science." He went on to explain that a shift from one probability to another potentiality was accomplished by the manipulation of natural forces.

"Aye, with the help of the Evil One," the duke agreed, "as when by a potion of the poisonous love-apple steeped in the broth of nettle and thorn-of-rose a lady's love is obtained."

"That's not the same at all," O'Leary objected doggedly. "In the first place, that's nonsense; and in the second place, it doesn't work. Science works."

"And so had we best, lad!" Bother replied, giving O'Leary a hearty clap on the back with a mailed gauntlet which so emptied the latter's lungs that for some moments his attention was fully occupied with the effort to draw a wheezing breath.

He felt himself reeling, consciousness fading into grayness. A few feet away, Frumpkin was busily packing a gladstone bag with what appeared to be a mixture of iron rations and high-tech gadgets. The Man in Black looked up, shook his head impatiently, and snapped his bag shut. "See here," he barked. "Can't you see the futility of this persecution of me? I've made you a gentleman's offer; why not accept it, eh?"

"Where's Daphne?" O'Leary came back coldly.

"Back to that, eh?" Frumpkin inquired rhetorically. "I can assure you—"

"Don't bother," Lafayette cut him off. "Just call her out; I notice she comes on command," he added bitterly.

"That is not convenient, Lafayette," Frumpkin said with finality. "I'm in the midst of launching a significant new initiative," he explained, "and your interference now will not be tolerated."

"What are you going to do about it?" Lafayette challanged.

Frumpkin frowned at him thoughtfully, then smiled a wintry smile. "You shall see, in due course," he stated, turned away, and was gone. Lafayette spent a few minutes wandering among the big chairs, looking for the vanished agent, then went over to the control panel where a red light glowed over a dial calibrated in regular degrees from DUBIOUS to IRON-CLAD. On impulse, he closed a switch labeled RANDOM-INTRO. Needles jumped on the panel, and red and amber lights began to wink in phase. Frumpkin uttered a yell and his leap caught O'Leary off-guard. He staggered, caught himself, and found himself as out of breath as if he had run a mile. He staggered, unsure of where he was.

When he returned his attention to his immediate surroundings, he saw two large saddle horses approaching, led by a liveried groom along the narrow catwalk. The immaculately curried flanks of the great steeds were already mud-flecked.

"That's quite . . . a neat trick too," O'Leary observed with some difficulty.

"Nay, Sir Lafayette, I'll take no credit. I but employ my summoner"—he paused to show Lafayette a small hand-held intercom unit—"and give the appropriate instructions."

"Neat," Lafayette repeated, craning to get a better view of the device before the duke tucked it away in a pouch slung from his baldric. "But . . . where did they come from? I don't see any royal stables around here," he finished with a gasp and paused again to breathe.

"Trouble not thyself with trifles, Milord of Leary," Bother said solicitously, "but hast thou taken a quartan ague? I see you puff and wheeze like an aged chieftain in his dotage. Fear not, boy, Milady Henriette will have you fit in a trice. Good looker, too, tis rumored," he added. "Let's be off without ado!" He climbed aboard the nearest horse, a sturdy bay, with surprising agility, rejecting the aid of the groom who fell on his back in the mud, spurned by the ducal foot.

"You don't hafta overdo it, Inspector," the servitor muttered, getting up. "After all, we got a union, same as anybody else, and when this caper is over—" he broke off as Bother's mount, apparently accidentally, brushed him aside as the duke spurred forward.

"What was that?" O'Leary asked the confused lad as he rose for the second time from the muck.

"Tell ya," the groom said angrily, "some o' these spot-checkers get too big for their britches—ack like they was what they're spose to be—steada Civil Service like the rest of us." He shut up abruptly, then continued in a brighter tone, "Spirited mounts, sir knight. How's about if I just kinda hold the stirrup for ya?" He clung desperately to the reins as the big black reared, rebuffing O'Leary's first attempt to mount.

As the mud-coated groom, now looking like all the other residents of the village, tugged at his forelock and backed away, Lafayette called after him:

"Hey, wait a minute! What's your name? Who are you?"

"Sir, I hight Wryshanks, yclept Lard-Ass, 'prentice to the master of horse to His Ducal Grace, Lord Bother-Be-Damned."

"I mean *really*," Lafayette persisted. "When you're not on the job."

"Oh. Uh, Horace Ungerfelt, G.S.-3.5, on special TDY to AEDC."

"Working out of Prime?" Lafayette inquired casually.

"Nossir. I'm on detached duty direct out of Supreme HQ"

"Raf trass spoit?" O'Leary said clearly. Horace responded by snapping soggily to attention.

"Yessir. You can count on *me*, sir," he said in a tone of awe somewhat alleviated by a quick flick of the forefinger at the globule of mud quivering at the tip of his nose, a gesture which produced the clownlike effect of a pale nose on an otherwise mud-caked face.

"At ease, Lard-Ass," O'Leary said easily. "Now just who is this duke fellow, and what's his mission?"

"Inspector of Continua Second Grade Mobius," the groom replied promptly. "Out to nail down some designated Cosmic Enemy who's been overloading the potentiality grid at every level from local to extragalactic. Real menace. Tricky rascal. I even got a stopper tube to use on the devil if I get the chance." Horace patted his chest, where a breast pocket would be, under the coating of mud.

"Does this master criminal have a name?" O'Leary demanded.

"Oh, lot's of 'em. Goes by Sir Al, Slim, Sir Lafayette, Allegorus, and a couple other aliases. A tricky one, milord.''

''Wouldst waste time in gossip with a menial while high adventure waits us yonder?'' Bother's bass tones recalled Lafayette to the mission at hand. His horse started forward with a leap as the duke jerked at its bridle. Lafayette caught the reins, settled himself in the saddle, and spurred to overtake the duke, who had set off at full gallop, sending up sheets of mud which Lafayette tried with little success to duck. Coming up alongside the duke, he called:

''What's the hurry?''

''Legend has it the witch-woman will disappear one day, in a trice, as mysteriously as she appeared on that long-gone day,'' Bother yelled over his shoulder. ''We must not be late.''

''What long-gone day?'' O'Leary persisted.

''The same fell day when the great mud-flow engulfed my dukedom. She, poor creature, had clung for life to a floating pig-sty, and thus her devoir demands she honor my suit.''

''Does she really live in a hill?'' Lafayette cried over the thunder and splash of hooves. ''Is she really three hundred years old?''

''As near as may be in these parlous times,'' Bother called back. ''A great heap of rubble it be, caught round the ruin of a proud tower, a perch whence Henriette can oversee a vast sweep of territory. As for her age, I but recount the legend known to all.'' Having slowed to deliver this explanation, the duke spurred ahead again, and Lafayette held his mount neck-and-neck.

Chapter Sixteen

Perhaps an hour later, in full darkness, Lafayette and the duke dismounted within hailing distance of a cluster of lights which Bother assured O'Leary was the Place of the Hill. They went forward on foot, leading their mounts. Bother pointed to a dim, greenish glow emanating from a point perhaps seventy-five feet above the rest of the yellowish lights at ground level.

"Even there towers the Hill," he explained. "As well we leave the steeds here." He patted the neck of his big animal. "Poor brutes, tis but cruel to abandon them here without their expected grooming and fodder to wait in the dark until the locals find and butcher them. But there's naught else for it." He dropped his reins in the mud. The horse stood as if tethered. Lafayette followed suit, and the two set off in the intense darkness, locating obstacles by the simple expedient of falling over them, after which they assisted each other to rise with much puffing and many colorful oaths from the duke. They avoided the dim glow of glassless windows and soon reached the accumulation of litter which marked the tower's base. The drift slanted upward at a shallow angle to the more substantive heaped trash of the Hill proper, which rose nearly vertically into the night to where the pale green glow seemed to float disembodied.

"Damme!" the duke exclaimed, halting abruptly.

"There be a great beast here, the witch's guardian monster, I doubt not!" Even as he spoke, Lafayette heard a whorffling, slurpy sound and sensed the bulk of something large and low-built moving heavily to a position athwart their route, where it settled down with a muddy squelch and again whoffled.

"Faugh!" Bother snarled. "The beast reeks of the infernal regions!"

"Or of a pigsty," Lafayette suggested. "You said the witch arrived on one. There was one behind the palace, back in dear old Artesia, where the royal swine, Jemimah and George, used to produce vast numbers of piglets for the palace kitchens." As Lafayette spoke, the unseen beast made ploffy noises.

"The beast soundeth eager for his next meal," Bother said. "Stand back, my lad, and I'll try conclusions with it." Lafayette saw a faint glint of starlight on the blade of the ducal longsword as it cleared its sheath with an ominous *whoosh*.

"Wait!" O'Leary blurted, moving forward past the armed duke.

"George?" he called tentatively into the darkness, and was at once rewarded with renewed plobby, whoffling sounds. Lafayette advanced cautiously, sniffing the air.

"It *is* George!" he cried. "I'd know his brand of BO anywhere." A moment later, his outstretched hand encountered bristly hide, a large ear, then the moist snout of the great boar.

"He's tame," Lafayette assured Bother who, after briefly waving Lafayette back, had come up beside him. Lafayette patted the big head and scratched behind the gristly ears.

"I don't understand this, Duke," he said in a low tone. "This is George, no doubt about it. So we must not be as far from Artesia as it seemed."

"Thinkst thou we can safely pass by this monstrous beast?" Bother asked after he had felt his way all the way back to the pig's hindquarter. "In sooth, it hath the form of a great swine," he said doubtfully. "But an imp of hell can assume any form it listeth.''

"George won't bother us," Lafayette reassured his companion. "Come on." He forged ahead, encountering a steep rise which, by the feel of it, was composed of stumps, planks, mud, grasses, and assorted artifacts, all impacted into an impenetrable heap. He sought foot- and hand-holds, and started up. After a moment, Bother followed. George whoffled contentedly. A male voice hallooed not far away, and a moment later flaming torches were converging on the base of the mound, their orange light revealing the wild-eyed faces and tangled hair of those who bore them. Yells broke out.

"Stand whur ye be," a coarse voice commanded. "Sergeant-at-Arms," it went on in a lower tone, "ready yer arbalest to let fly when I give the word!"

Abruptly, George whoffled, a note of anger audible in his snorts. There were noises of sloppy movement below, and more yells, followed by sounds of hasty retreat. The torches, tossed aside, lay sputtering in the black mud, but afforded enough light to assist Lafayette in picking his way upward.

"Well done, George," Bother called down. "Methinks a knighthood is in store for the noble beast," he added, his pale unshaven face turned up to O'Leary who was a few feet in advance. "Press on, lad, there's naught to stay us now, and Sir George guardeth our flank right doughtily. They say there be a ledge near the top, whence we'll gain the door which leadeth into the bowels of the pile."

Lafayette, after a moment's rest, went on, soon gaining the ledge to which the duke had alerted him. It was barely a foot wide and unevenly surfaced with an improvisation of flattened tin cans. Bother clambered up beside him, puffing.

"Mayhap twere best I'd left my armor of proof below," he gasped. "I'm nigh undone, lad. Let us rest and take council here a moment."

"If the settlement back there is actually on the site of Colby Corners," O'Leary said, "this place is just about where Lod's castle was back in Artesia, and this pile must be the analog of the castle, which is actually the Las Vegas Hilton, which Lod had managed to shift onto Plane V-87.''

"I wot nothing of these mysteries, sir knight,'' Bother protested. "Work witchery if you must, but leave me retain my purity, OK?"

"Don't worry, Inspector,'' Lafayette reassured his ally. "I'm not up to witchery just now, only trying to dope out what we're up against.''

"I be up against a plank which formerly performed a useful function in an outhouse,'' Bother grumped, "judging by the aroma. I say let's up and seek the portal reputed to be here, ere I perish from these evil vapors.''

"Might as well,'' Lafayette agreed, and set off on hands and knees, the duke clanking behind him.

"You go in the other direction,'' Lafayette said over his shoulder. "That way we can cover it in half the time, assuming the ledge goes all the way around.'' Bother complied without comment. Feeling his way, Lafayette soon encountered a barrier of surprisingly regular iron bars. Investigating, he found that it was a thirty-inch-high railing, over which he climbed to find himself on a somewhat wider balcony.

Just then, the duke's hoarse voice spoke near at hand, and approaching. "No good, lad; this parlous ledge doth end abrupt but a few spans yonder. Twere a near thing, but by the help of the saints I retained my place, and—'' His account ended with a dull clunk as his helm collided with the railing.

"Climb over,'' Lafayette urged. "It's wider here.'' His hands groping along the wall encountered glass, small panes set neatly in a mullioned door. "Hey,'' he called in a low but excited tone to Bother, now hulking at his elbow, "it's a regular door! No garbage here. . . .'' He investigated, found an ornate wrought-iron latch, lifted it, and the door swung inward into darkness and the shriek of a female voice.

Lafayette blundered forward, uttering soothing words:

"There, there, take it easy, please, ma'am. No need for alarm. We're simply calling on the Lady Henriette in the Hill. Sorry to burst in on you, but it's dark out there, and we just sort of stumbled on the door."

After the first scream, the unseen female's response to the invasion of her lair was a barrage of small objects, thrown with surprising force and accuracy. Then a small and feminine voice said contritely:

"You startled me, sirrah, bursting in here in the dark into Her Ladyship's private withdrawing room, where even I, her faithful maid-of-all-work, am scarce allowed to dust. Forgive my fusillade if I did indeed score a hit upon thy persons. What manner of men be ye? One of ye, it seems, is made of metal, or so I judge by the clatter when my candlestick struck him."

"We're just ordinary fellows," Lafayette protested. "Of course the duke has his armor on, but that's only in case he has to do battle or something."

"Thou'lt find no battle here, sir knight," the now ladylike voice returned. "We be but two women, meaning harm to none." As she spoke, Lafayette could hear the sounds of flint on iron; then a spark glared, igniting a wick, and a bright flame glowed, flickering on a table-model cigarette lighter. It illuminated a shapely arm clad in gray cloth, leading up past a delightfully formed, though modest, bosum to a piquant face framed in golden-blond braid topped by a lacy cap.

"Adoranne!" O'Leary yelled. "That is, I mean, Your Highness! What in the world are you doing here" —he broke off as his gaze took in the spacious room behind her—"in Nicodaeus' old lab? And how did *it* get here? I had it figured the penthouse Frumpkin escaped into back in town was the lab!"

"Are you kidding, mister?" the girl returned. "Calling me 'Highness' . . . hmmp! Why make ye sport of a poor serving-wench? You look disreputable, sir, for all your finery, mud-splattered as you are. Is this a proper fashion in which to call on milady?"

"Sorry," Lafayette said hastily. "I guess you're not really Adoranne, just her analog in this locus. Still, it's a good sign that such a close analog exists here: it proves we're not really far from Artesia. You're as like Adoranne as Swinehild was, and Melange was practically next door to Artesia—''

"Don't get excited, feller," the girl said. "I'll see if she'll see you at this unholy hour. Don't hold your breath." She put the lighter on a handy tabletop and turned toward the door.

"Wait!" O'Leary blurted. "Before you go, tell us about yourself—and Lady Henriette. How you happen to be here, where you came from—everything. By the way, what's your name?"

"I'm known here as Betty Brassbraid, though that be not my true name. And I'll leave it to my mistress to tell you what she deems well to relate." She left the room with a swish of woolen skirts, her feet quick and light even in the heavy wooden clogs she wore. As the door closed behind her, Bother spoke up:

"Zounds, Sir Lafayette, what fell den of the Black Arts be this, in sooth?" He was looking around suspiciously at the black crackle-finish wall panels set with a bewildering array of dials, oscilloscopes and idiot lights, the arcane astrological symbols scribed on framed posters, the alembics and retorts on the marble-topped benches.

"Stap me!" the duke continued his plaint, "this be no canny place for Christian men. Mayhap, Sir Lafayette, twere best we repair to yon balcony, there to await Her Ladyship."

"It's just Nicodaeus' old lab, as I said," Lafayette reminded the knight. "It's a pretty weird mixture of science and superstition, I'll agree. See those little jars over there beside the electron microscope? Eye of newt and best mummy dust. But Nicodaeus was an Inspector of Continua, First Class. He'd been in some strange loci, and he picked up a lot of mutually exclusive ideas along the way." Lafayette was idly eyeing the gilded skeleton dangling from a wire suspended from a rafter lost in the shadows above.

"Funny thing," he mused, "back in Aphasia, the

bones were gone. Here, they're still in place. That probably has some heavy significance, if I were just sharp enough to figure it out. But every time I think I'm beginning to see a pattern, something like that pops up and proves I'm on the wrong track. If this room had been the one at the top of the scaffold back in town, as it should have been, I'd feel a lot better.''

"Meseems twere passing strange, Sir Lafayette," Bother commented, "that ye be not all of a-maze to find such a chamber here in a rubble-heap. But instead, ye talk calmly of stranger riddles still. Still, I'm but a simple man of war, knowing naught of these matters.''

"Don't kid me, Mobius, your groom told me you're an inspector yourself. It's time to drop the local persona and help me figure out what's happening before it happens."

"As to that," Bother said in a stiff tone, "doubtless you're aware that for me to divulge anything of a classified nature would be an LRC violation punishable by exile to uncontrolled space-time. Still, I shall do what I can to riddle me this curious circumstance. And a certain stable boy will rue the day he blabbed.''

"Sure," Lafayette said soothingly, "I don't want you to tell me any secrets. And go easy on the horse-boy; he was trying to do his job—looking for some master criminal.'' Lafayette paused to look interrogatively at Duke Bother-Be-Damned. "Do you have any leads?''

"Not I," Bother replied impatiently. "I'm no gumshoe, my vital energies to expend in pursuit of fugitives from justice who are in all probability no more criminal than the beadles who so assiduously persecute them. Bah! What interests me just now is the woman of mystery, yclept Henriette in the Hill." The duke took a few clanking steps as if about to begin pacing the floor, but he halted as the lighter flame sputtered and went out, leaving the spooky room in darkness.

"How now?" the duke muttered, the words accompanied by the familiar *swoosh* of his sword being drawn from its sheath. Lafayette heard grunts and whistling sounds of the blade cutting air as the duke executed a

few precautionary swipes at the surrounding emptiness.
"I mislike me this," the warrior grated. "What fell influence snuffed yon candle without human hand nearby?"

"It's probably just out of fluid," Lafayette said, and
groped his way to the table. He found the lighter, tried it
without any effect other than a colorful shower of
sparks, then dropped it to reassure the duke, who had
responded to the unexpected display with a selection of
colorful oaths and more swipes of the sword. Then a
crack of light gleamed as a side door opened and the
slim silhouette of a young woman appeared in the opening. She came in, followed closely by Betty, carrying a
lantern which showed the deep-blue cloak about Lady
Henriette's slim shoulders, then her piquant face and
her glossy black hair.

"Daphne!" O'Leary yelled and started around the
table toward her. Then, as the brunette beauty looked at
him wide-eyed, he checked himself. "Sorry," he said.
"I didn't mean to startle you, milady; for a moment I
assumed you were my wife, Daphne, but I suppose
you're just her analog in this locus, like the Lady Androgorre back in Melange, and for that matter Beverly
and Cynthia. But it's wonderful to see you anyway,
even if you aren't really Daphne."

"You speak strangely, sir," the Daphne-like woman
said stiffly, and was abruptly thrust aside by the Man in
Black, who had pushed past Betty and now stood block-
ing the doorway. He looked casually around and
nodded in satisfaction.

"Well done, my dear," he said silkily. "And now I
think the time has come for an end to meddling." He
looked sharply at O'Leary.

"As for you, sir, I've already indulged your pretence
of ignorance. Now let us down to business. What is it
you really want?"

"*Raf trass spoit,*" Lafayette said casually, watching
Frumpkin for his reaction, which was to stagger back a
step as if he had been struck. Then his look of amuse-

ment was replaced by one of determination.

"You wouldn't dare," he hissed.

"Would I not?" Lafayette countered in an indifferent tone. He moved casually around the central table, and across toward Frumpkin, who stood his ground, though looking nervous. Behind him, Lafayette could hear sounds of feminine weeping.

"You promised!" Betty Brassbraid's tearful voice charged, and Frumpkin half-turned to shake off her clutch at his arm. At that moment, O'Leary stepped in and administered a knuckle-first blow to Frumpkin's solar plexus, which caused him to double over, presenting to O'Leary an unimpeded access to his head and neck. Lafayette carefully took a stranglehold, his forearm locked across Frumpkin's throat and levering upward, causing the Man in Black to utter croaking sounds which prompted Betty to shriek:

"Don't do it *here,* sir! The blackguard deserves to die, I don't doubt, but—I can't watch." She fled into gray shadows.

With his left hand, Lafayette found the flat-walker in his jacket pocket where Mickey Jo had placed it only a few hours before, though, Lafayette reflected *en passant,* it seemed like days. Steadying himself against Frumpkin's frantic efforts to break the hold, Lafayette oriented the Ajax device properly and, for some reason closing his eyes, he stepped back against the stone partition and pressed his body against the wall. He felt the familiar sensation as of wet cardboard parting before him. He was aware of Frumpkin's frenzied efforts to escape, and applied enough pressure to lift the Man in Black to tiptoe. As Lafayette stepped back, Frumpkin's weight became a heavy drag. He wondered briefly if he were doing any irreversible damage to his captive's internal arrangements, but he thrust onward, eyes open now to the expected vista of utter blackness broken by only a few randomly darting points of varicolored light. Then the syrupy resistance was gone.

A dim gray light infiltrated the darkness. He had only a moment in which to see two large fellows coming toward him before, with a sudden lunge, Frumpkin broke from his grip. There was an explosion that hurled O'Leary down into hot blackness. He came to rest lying with his cheek against a carpet. He opened one eye and saw faded red-and-purple curlicues; then hard hands were hauling him to his feet.

"Fool!" Frumpkin said in a complacent tone. "Did you really imagine I'd permit you so easily to disrupt my plans?"

"I don't know anything about your dumb plans," Lafayette countered. The Man in Black stood before him, rocking casually on his heels, his torn and dusty uniform replaced by a crisp new one with gleaming gold braid.

"Your alibis will avail you naught," Frumpkin snapped. "My decision is made: In spite of certain minor inconveniences it will occasion me, I will now dissolve your entire troublesome Plane into unrealized status." He turned abruptly and went across to the big central panel. Lafayette kicked the closest knee, broke from the clutch of its owner, and in two jumps was at Frumpkin's side, catching the black-clad arm as it reached for a safe-wired switch. Before he could do more, a gust of opaque mist wafted across his vision. He thrust Frumpkin back and tried to push through the sudden gray mist. Unwittingly, he drew a breath as a hand caught his arm and drew him aside. As he came clear, he released his grip on Frumpkin, who collapsed facedown as O'Leary braced himself against the grip on his arm.

"Slim!" the hearty voice of Sprawnroyal, the Ajax rep, cried. "So you finely made it! Come on, hows about a good feed to start with, and then we can bring each other up to date!"

═══Chapter Seventeen═══

Feeling dazed, Lafayette looked around at a well-lit room with neutral walls and a tall window with a vista of forested hills and jagged peaks in the distance. He allowed himself to be led to a long refectory table and eased into a chair. Sprawnroyal ignored the prone form of the Man in Black.

"Easy, boys," Sprawnroyal advised the two small fellows who had done their best to steady O'Leary's beanpole physique while working at knee level. "He's been through a lot; lucky he finely won his way to the Static Point, which, by the way, Slim, how'd ya know whereat it was located at? Top secret info, you know."

"*Where* it was located," Lafayette started wearily, but abandoned the didactic impulse as hopeless. "I didn't know it was a Static Point, whatever that is," he told his diminutive friend. "I went along to call on an alleged witch named Henriette in the Hill, and her apartment turned out to be Nicodaeus' old lab, from back in Artesia. It seems Nicodaeus anchored it so well that it stays in place no matter what happens to the locus. Strange, too: I was sure the lab was going to be in an ill-fitting room at the top of a shaky-looking structure back in the town."

"Look, Slim," Sprawnroyal put in seriously, "we got

a real problem on our hands here. I tole you last I seen you, when I run into you out in the woods in one o' them hick loci: Some time back we took on a private security job for some kind o' local headman type name of Frodolkin, and pretty soon he come up with this Number-One-Public-Enemy-of-all-time deal, which we hadda go beating the bushes for him. And after we seen you, things really got rough. We got into some kinda swamp where the desert oughta be, and never did find this duke fellow.''

"That's just as well," Lafayette told the little man. "Bother's not a bad fellow; actually he's an agent working out of Prime. Why did you want him?"

"This Frodolkin character hands us a dossier on him that'd make the Murderin' Turk look like Baby Leroy. Seems he's out to break down the whole EQ, and let the whole plane slide off the deep end into unrealized spacetime. Nacherly, we hadda try and stop him, even if we din't have a contract, which we did have one. But like I says, we never seen the bum. We report in, and old Froddy gets all excited and says he's gonna do what he called a emergency dump on the whole level.

"That sounded bad, but it's just talk, we figger, and I and my boys get back onna job and pretty soon we're sort of swimming around like goldfish in a bowl, two guys watching us. After a while they pour us out on a cement slab, and we just about croak before we get straightened out and get it together, which we wasn't really goldfish, natch. And after a while we got used to breathing again and all, and then we found out we were *really* in the soup. We really gotta thank you, Slim. If it wouldn't of been for you giving us the old password from time to time, we'd prolly still be wading around in that swamp, or worse. But seems like every time we were really up against it, we picked you up again. . . . But I can tell you, Slim, you nearly slipped off the grid that one time, and we thought you were really a goner, and us too. But old *Raf trass spoit*''—Sprawnroyal broke off to glance cautiously about as he lowered his voice to speak the arcane words—"did the trick, and we homed back in on you. And now—here you are!''

"Right," Lafayette agreed. "But where *am* I? That's not Aphasia III out that window; there's hills and trees, and Aphasia III is all mud-flats."

"Cripes," Sprawnroyal muttered, as Lafayette went on to describe the bleak locus.

". . . And so," Lafayette concluded, "it seems she not only isn't Daphne, but she decoyed us here to turn us over to this Frumpkin, alias the Man in Black."

"Can't blame Daph for *that*," Sprawnroyal reassured Lafayette. "She's a true-blue dame if I ever seen one, even if she is twice too high, no offense." His lumpy face looked unaccustomedly solemn for a moment. "But it's this Frumpkin character that intrigues me." Sprawnroyal paused to glance toward the now quietly groaning man on the floor. "He claims he's manipulating the exocosm wholesale, eh? Prolly just a nut like you said, but the fact is, somebody's been monkeying around on a big scale—"

"I'm afraid I'm to blame," Lafayette said miserably. He went on to tell Sprawnroyal of his idle tinkering with the Great Unicorn. Sprawnroyal waved that aside. "Don't figure, Slim. The energy requirement alone—"

"Don't talk theory at me, Roy," Lafayette protested. "I'm talking about what happened. I goofed and I'm ready to take the blame."

"This Aphasia place is nothing but mud-flats, you say," Roy changed the subject. "Sounds like a whole lot o' geology has gone down. But the moon was back to its old size, eh? Looks like you switched planes that time."

"I must have," Lafayette agreed. "But where are we now? That looks like Melange out the window, and those peaks must be the Chantspells. How'd I get here? And since when is the Ajax plant next door to the lab?"

"Easy, Slim," Roy said, holding up a calloused hand. "You got here by a little Ajax device we call a Come Hither. When you used the flat-walker, that gave us a hard fix and we just yanked you in. About the Works bein' next door to old Nicodaeus' lab, it ain't, natch.

. . . We coulda retrieved you to any place we liked, so why not right here to the head office? You're right about Nicodaeus really anchoring his lab right. Tied it to the Prime Postulates, and can't nothing short of total dissolution shake that. Lucky thing, too: gives us a good access to an infinite series of loci across nine planes, and well into the next manifold.''

Frumpkin moaned and sat up on the floor, both hands carefully holding his head in place.

"I'll string yer innards out over an infinite series o' manifolds for this, you wretches!" he declared in a yell, rising to face O'Leary, who rose to confront him.

"Better quieten him down, boys," Sprawnroyal ordered his two handy men. They went briskly to the Man in Black, who shrank back with a yelp.

"Don't dare to lay hands on me, you miserable nits!" he commanded.

"No problem, Skinny," one of the sturdy little men said, and drawing a bright yellow, pen-sized tube from a clip at his belt, directed it at Frumpkin and released a jet of pink vapor.

"Ugh! Puce and lemon, a perfectly vile color combination," Frumpkin gasped as he sank to his haunches and squatted there, his face now on a level with the two Ajax men. His expression went vague.

"OK, Slim," Roy said to O'Leary. "One good sniff of Vox III and he's ready to tell us stuff he never even heard of before."

"I'd prefer to have him stick to what he *has* heard of," Lafayette protested.

"Just a like figger of speech, Slim," Roy reassured Lafayette easily. Lafayette followed Roy across to where the Man in Black squatted, and looked him directly in the face.

"What are you after, Frumpkin?" he demanded.

"You may address me as Sublime One," Frumpkin replied.

"And then again, I may not," Sprawnroyal replied, looking up to wink at Lafayette. "OK," he returned his attention to Frumpkin, "talk it up, Skin. What do you have to do with all this stuff that's been going on? Like running poor Slim ragged, and giving a hard time to I and my boys, and all?" Roy waved a stumpy arm to take in all the anomalies he had left unmentioned.

"To divulge what you suggest would be a gross violation of Cosmic Ultimate State Secrecy," Frumpkin replied in a grumpy tone.

"So, we pick up a little security violation, Skin," Roy returned briskly. "That's not as bad as *this* is it?" As he spoke he grasped Frumpkin's longish nose firmly between his knuckles and gave it a firm tweak. Frumpkin yelled and almost toppled. Roy hauled him up by the nose and said, "Talk it up, Skin. We got no time for games."

Frumpkin made muffled spluttering sounds and Roy tightened his grip. At once the Man in Black recoiled and said clearly:

"That did it, buster. You now occupy top spot on our personal hit list."

Roy adjusted his grasp on Frumpkin's now red nose and twisted it in the opposite direction. "You know, Skin, if that cartilage happens to get busted, you'll have a cauliflower nose; yer own old ma wouldn't reckernize ya." He twisted harder.

"Hurry up," he urged. "This is tough on a feller's knuckles."

"This isn't doing any good," O'Leary said unhappily. "He can't talk, anyway, when he's looking up his own nostrils."

"Slim," Roy said patiently, "you're a nice guy; that's yer problem: Yer too nice of a guy. With bums like Skin here, ya gotta squeeze. Maybe I'd have better luck with a ear at that—onney they break up awful easy." He shifted his grip to one of Frumpkin's generous ears. At once, the Man in Black yowled and blurted:

"All right, you nasty, ugly little monster! It wasn't *my* fault! If he hadn't continually interfered with me, I'd have never so much as known of his miserable existence!"

"My existence was far from miserable until you started tampering with it," O'Leary notified the irate Frumpkin, who glared at him and ground his teeth in fury.

"Aha! The technique of the Big Lie!" Frumpkin charged. "You, having had the temerity to seek to thwart my efforts to establish a New Reality, now charge *me* with the crime, directed against *your* petty person! Intolerable! You know perfectly well that it was you who initiated the series of antisocial acts aimed at destroying my life's great work!"

"Name one thing I did to bother you before you stuck your nose in my affairs," O'Leary challenged. "The first time I ever saw you, right here in this room, you handcuffed me and were all ready to kidnap me, when you panicked and ran."

"Panic? I?" Frumpkin echoed derisively. "Pooh. Are you attempting to maintain that you introduced no alternatives into the tranquil fabric of Reality during the years directly preceding the confrontation to which you refer?"

"I don't actually know what you're talking about," O'Leary started, "but—"

"He means the times you kind of did some unauthorized shifts, Slim," Roy put in. "Like when you come to Melange and changed Rudolfo's plans for Ajax —and Ajax Novelty is grateful, even if it did louse up Skin's plans, here."

"All I did was focus my Psychical Energies a few times," Lafayette protested. "And that one time, I messed with a gadget from the Probability Lab, accidentally almost. But I never heard of Frumpkin until after . . ." Lafayette paused to swallow. ". . . after I messed with the Great Unicorn," he finished lamely.

"Whatta ya talkin', ya messed with the Great Unicorn?" Roy challenged. "That's a constellation or something, right? How do you mess with a bunch of stars, some of 'em over a hundred miles away?"

"I didn't mean to," Lafayette explained. "I just happened to be looking at Ursa Major—that means the Big

Bear, or the Bigger Bear, to translate precisely—and it seemed to me like a dumb name. Bears don't have tails; it looked a lot more like a horse with a horn on its head. That was the only thing—I needed one more star for the tip of the horn—so there it was."

"Just a minute," Roy said, and went across to stare at a large star-chart pinned to the wall.

"Funny thing, Slim," he said, pointing. "This here chart has been here since Prince Krupkin's time anyways; here's the Great Unicorn, just as big as life. The star at the tip o' the horn is, uh, looks like a dim galaxy, Slim. NGC-51a, it says. A irregular galaxy of the Local Group."

"It wasn't there at first," Lafayette insisted. "Too bad I don't have a witness—"

"What about Daphne?" Sprawnroyal suggested. "You said she was with you."

"But I don't know where she is, Roy," O'Leary moaned. "I've been trying to pick up some trace of her, but it's no use. For a minute or two, I thought this Henriette was Daph, but she betrayed me, just lured me there to her place to turn me over to Frumpkin here." O'Leary prodded the black-clad leg of the red-nosed but still haughty Frumpkin, who responded with a cold smile.

"But, don't you understand, poor fool, the wench *was* indeed this Daphne of yours. But when I explained to her the consequences that would result if you were allowed to run loose any longer, she at once fell in with my plan."

"Prolly done it just to save you from something worst," Roy suggested sympathetically. "And maybe he tortured her—you can't expect a female to stand up to no PPS, even if she *is* over five foot high."

Lafayette groaned, "If even Daphne's against me, what's the use of going on?"

"Precisely, Lafayette," Frumpkin seconded eagerly. "Just relax now and let events take their course—and I'll still cut you in for a share."

"Maybe you oughta talk to the kid first before you go condemning her out of hand, like," Roy suggested.

"Sure, but how?" O'Leary returned. "She's not here. I should have brought her along, but I was pretty busy with Frumpkin here."

"Sure, Slim, nobody could fault you," Roy agreed. "But we could find her—or give it a try, anyways."

O'Leary turned to the little man gratefully. "Then you'll help me, Roy? With your Ajax gear we can get something done. Come on. Let's get started. We can truss Frumpkin up and leave Casper and Rugadoon to watch him."

"Sure." Roy gave quick instructions to his two helpers, who bustled off to procure ropes.

"Now," Roy said gravely, "we gotta figure our next move. How do we get back to Aphasia?"

"Easy," O'Leary assured him. "The room where I left her is just on the other side of the wall here. So—we use the flat-walker again and go back."

"Slim," Roy said, wagging his head heavily. "I guess I never tole you, but tryna use a one-man unit to merge two guys is risky. Fact is," he went on, turning to look at Frumpkin, still hunkered down on his haunches, watching blankly as Casper came back with a coil of fine white line, ". . . fact is, I'm surprised you got away with it that once without leaving old Skin's innards strung out in half-phase."

"Can't you rustle up another one?" Lafayette asked.

"That ain't too easy," Roy told him. "We had our problems here at Ajax too, Slim. This here trouble-maker"—he jerked a thumb at Frumpkin—"has put a crimp in operations. We managed to trace the interference to him before our energy tap was cut."

"He cut your energy tap?" O'Leary echoed in alarm. "That means you're out of business, for all practical purposes, according to what Flimbert told me about how you manage all your tricks."

"Bert always did have too big of a mouth," Roy said. "Anyways, you see how it is. Fact is," he added, "the only thing we can do, is I take the flat-walker and see what I can do on my own."

"Nonsense," O'Leary came back at once. "If only one of us can go, it'll be me. After all, Daphne's my wife."

"Sure," Sprawnroyal concurred, "and the whole future of Ajax is riding on us now, Slim—or on me, rather. I got to take some prompt and effective action, or all Melange will revert to unrealized status, and b'lieve me, Slim, that'll be a poor way to go."

"Struggle as you will, poor fools," Frumpkin contributed with a note of triumph, "you and your petty entropic level are doomed. The wheels I have set in motion cannot now be stopped, short of a cataclysm which will destroy the Prime Postulate itself."

"Ignore him, Roy," O'Leary advised his old comrade. "He's cracked."

Roy nodded. "Sure he is. But unfortunately, Slim, the data we recorded before everything shut down confirms what he's saying. Still, you might as well go on and try to see Daph one last time. S'long, kid." Roy thrust out his hard square hand. "We had a few kicks together, din't we? Good luck—and you better try the same spot, so's to catch the aura of temporarily enhanced permeability before it fades. Only lasts about ten minutes."

"I've been here nearly that long already," O'Leary said hastily. "And don't look so glum, Roy. Things have looked bad before, and we got out of it somehow."

"Do good, Slim," Roy urged solemnly. "Looks like you're the only chance we got. Make it count."

O'Leary nodded and stepped to the wall to stand facing it, the flat-walker in his hand.

"Little to the left, Slim," Roy advised from behind him. Lafayette nodded and stepped forward.

He felt the momentary resistance of the masonry, then thrust impatiently forward, ignoring the display of darting points of light which moved together and coalesced into a uniform dim grayness. Lafayette looked

quickly toward the central panel; Frumpkin was nowhere near it. He went over, looked at the safety-locked
knife-switch the Man in Black had been about to throw
the last time he was here. O'Leary looked around carefully for the first time, saw nothing but an immense
room like the deserted lobby of an out-of-date hotel, its
walls dim with distance through the grayish air. A blinking light on the panel caught his eye. It was one of a row
of amber, blue, and white indicators, directly beneath
which were tiny dials. They were cryptically marked:
MAYHAP, CINCH, GET READY, THIS IS IT, FOR-
GET IT. The one under the flashing amber lens read
LET'S FACE IT.

"Good idea," Lafayette said aloud. "I'm wasting
time. I need to get out of wherever I am, and back to
work." He started forward, met resistance, pushed
harder, and was abruptly clear, standing in another dim
light looking at the dangling skeleton. He turned at a
clanking sound to his right to see Duke Bother-Be-
Damned coming toward him.

"What—where's the scoundrel got to?" Bother demanded. "My eyes play tricks on me. It almost seemed
you were gone for an instant, lad. But as I started forward to search for a hidden panel, here you are. But
where is the wretch Frumpkin?"

"Take it easy, Bother," O'Leary suggested. "He's in
good hands, under guard. Excuse me; I have to find
Daphne—I mean Lady Henriette." He strode past the
man in armor and went to the open doorway through
which Her Ladyship had disappeared. His eyes strayed
en passant to the hardwood wall cabinet beside the dark
opening. On impulse, he paused to open the door.
There, amid dust curls and spider webs, was the tall,
old-fashioned black dial telephone which linked the lab
to Central. O'Leary hesitated, then lifted the receiver
and put it to his ear. A feeble dial tone sounded. He
frowned, wondering if he could remember the ten-digit
number after so long a time. . . . He dialed: nine five
three four nine zero zero two one one, and waited, not
even breathing. Then he heard the tinny rattle of the

ring signal. *Bawp—bawp . . . bawp-click, rattle.*

"Central," a tired-sounding voice said.

"Uh," O'Leary said, "Central—this is an emergency! I'm Sir Lafayette O'Leary, part-time agent, and I'm calling from a locus known as Aphasia. We've got big trouble here. A nut-case named Frumpkin from some far-out plane claims to be reshaping all Greater Reality, and he doesn't care what he runs over in the process. I need help to interrogate him and find out what we can do to save what's left, if anything. Artesia's gone, and so is Aphasia I by now; and Melange is in deep trouble—even Ajax doesn't have any ideas—so get somebody in here fast to straighten things out!"

"Please note," a tinny voice said, "that this line is for limited official use only. Please cite your priority and classification code."

"No time," O'Leary cut in briskly. "Listen: This is an emergency! The world—several of them—is, or are, coming to an end! We have to do something!"

"Yes, yes, Sir, ah, I'm sure things can't be as bad as all that. We at Central—" The voice stopped as a deafening *barr-room!* blasted in O'Leary's ear. He rattled the receiver hook frantically.

". . . Please note this line is for limited official use," the mindless voice parroted again. "Please cite—"

"Shut up, brainless!" Lafayette yelled. "Listen to me!"

There was no reply. O'Leary groaned. "It's a recording," he called over his shoulder to Bother, and tried again:

"Hello, Central!" he yelled into the instrument. "Are you still there? What happened—" Then an iron-clad hand closed on his arm, tugging him gently away.

"Easily, lad, be calm," Bother urged him. "Hast lost thy wits, Sir Knight? Why talketh thou to this ugly object here?" Gingerly, he moved the receiver from Lafayette's hand and let it fall to swing from its cord, uttering quacking sounds.

"It's a telephone, Bother!" O'Leary protested. "You're *supposed* to talk to it! Listen, somebody's on the line now. Let me hear what they're saying!"

". . . Your supervisor," a cold voice snapped. "I repeat: This is a limited access line. Identify yourself, please."

"I already told that dumb broad," O'Leary said, suppressing a desire to yell and choke the telephone. "Do I have to start all over? This is a crash emergency! Everything's coming apart, or it will if a screwball named Frumpkin has his way! Get me a squad of your best harness bulls in here double pronto. And no tricky undercover types like Mickey Jo and Lard-Ass! Plain old uniformed coppers with big billy clubs and packing plenty of iron—and ready to use it! Got me?"

"This is your final warning, sir," the unyielding supervisory voice said. "Do not attempt to make use of this classified circuit for personal calls. You will be traced and service discontinued."

"Discontinued?" Lafayette yelled. "What service have I gotten that you can discontinue? All I've had is a dumb recording and a dumber bureaucrat! This is disaster, I'm telling you. Do something!" He was cut off by a click and a prolonged buzz.

"No use, Your Grace," Lafayette told Bother dispiritedly. "It's up to us. I should have known better." He hung up the phone, then leaned close to examine the heavy black-insulated cable which ran from the base of the instrument through a hole in the cabinet.

"This is strange," he told the uncomprehending duke. "Back in Aphasia I, this line had been cut and the phone was gone. Now it's back again." O'Leary's eyes went to the gilded skeleton dangling in the gloom above. "And Mr. Bones hasn't been here for years. Something's funny here. Somebody's been tampering . . ." O'Leary sat in the decrepit chair beside the marble-topped counter, deep in thought.

"What troublest thee, Sir Lafayette?" Bother inquired.

Lafayette slapped the counter-top. "This isn't really the lab," he stated. "It's a fake someone rigged up for some reason. Probably Frumpkin's work. If I'm right that leaves the upstairs room back in town! You see, the lab is so firmly grounded that even though the loci come and go around it, it stays forever the same. That's why it's fifty feet above the ground level, and they had to build that scaffolding up to it. So let's go back, and this time I'll get inside!" As he concluded, Lafayette noticed a tiny vibration from the flat-walker still in his hand. He raised it to his ear:

"OK, Slim," Roy's voice came through, more clearly than before, "I'm going to try that area of permeability. If I don't make it in the next ten seconds, call out a strainer squad to look for me. Here goes!" The last words, spoken in full voice, came from behind O'Leary; he whirled to see the stumpy figure of Sprawnroyal standing by the wall, looking shaken.

"Wow," the Ajax rep said feelingly, "for a hour or two there, I thought I wasn't gonna make it. But then I thought to home in on the field from the flat-walker, and here I am."

"Glad to see you, Roy," O'Leary said. "But it's been only a second or two since you said you were on the way—but I know time gets all distorted in half-phase. Roy, it just dawned on me that this room is a fake—"

"It's Nicodaeus' old lab, isn't it?" Roy interrupted, looking around curiously. "I remember the alchemy department and the astrology section"—he indicated the star-charts on one wall, and paused, looking puzzled—"but seems like there was a high-tech electronic panel right next to it. When did he remodel?"

"I don't think he did," Lafayette persisted. "This is apparently a duplicate of an earlier stage of the lab. The question is, why?"

"Hard luck, Slim," Roy said mildly. "If it was the real thing, we coulda used the homing box we just installed a couple weeks ago."

"What's a homing box?" Lafayette demanded.

"A new item in our line," Roy explained. "One of Pratwick's best ideas—"

"Sure, but what does it *do*?" Lafayette cut in.

"Well, Slim, it's what ya might say versatile, is what it is," Roy explained in a leisurely way. "Instantaneous transport is the main function, but it's also useful for fast search-and-rescue jobs, you know? It's good as a substitute for a supply warehouse; you can tune to whatever you happen to need—got a zillion megabit storage capacity or something."

"But how could *we* use it?" Lafayette demanded, coming over to confront the Customer Service rep.

"What's it matter?" Roy countered. "After all, it ain't here. We onney installed it maybe a couple weeks back, and like you said, this is a copy off a early stage, prolly not long after Nick first set it up in Artesia."

"Never mind, Roy, just answer me. How could we use this gadget if we did have access to it?"

"Shift us right to the Ajax main office on Plane Two," Roy said. "Solid locus. From there we could gather in all the clues and find out what's going on."

"Why didn't you do it before?" O'Leary pressed. "If you had that kind of capability, why were you out beating the bushes in Aphasia I, instead of going right to the top?"

"Shoulda, I guess," Roy conceded. "But I had my orders. We didn't exactly realize how bad things were until it was too late, anyways. I tole you they cut our power source."

"Oh. Well, Roy, I think I'll try something: I'm going to make a real try to focus the old Psychical Energies—"

"What good's that gonna do, Slim?" Roy queried, frowning. "It's OK for you to duck out, maybe—though it ain't like ya—but how's about me and yer sheet-metal pal, here?"

"Oh, Roy, this is Duke Bother-Be-Damned," Lafayette made the intro hurriedly. "Your Grace, Sprawnroyal, Customer Service rep from the Ajax Novelty

Works, Melange branch. And what do you mean 'duck out'?" Lafayette went on hotly. "If my idea works, we're all home safe!"

"Well, it won't hurt to try, maybe," Roy conceded. "Go ahead."

"Just one thing first," Lafayette demurred. "I'm going to find Henriette and get a few answers."

"They'll all be 'no,' Sir Lafayette," Bother told him. "Many's the wight who's assailed my lady's virtue, but none, it's said, has scored."

"That's not what I had in mind," O'Leary advised the duke. "At least, not exactly. And I could have told you those local Romeos would bomb out. Daphne's true-blue—even if she's not really Daphne."

"I know, my boy," Bother said kindly. "None can expect reason and logic from a man bewitched by a maid. Seek out this witch, the while I search for the wily Frumpkin. He must have hid hereabouts; no man can, after all, walk through a wall!"

"Actually, Your Grace," Roy spoke up, "the scamp is well-trussed and locked in a garde-robe at this moment. We'll collect him in due course."

Chapter Eighteen

"That reminds me," Bother said testily. "Talking about walking through walls, how'd *you* get in here? I never seen you come through the door."

"That's just a little trick of mine, Bother," Roy waved the query away. "Maybe later I can show you how it's done."

"You, small sir, may address me as 'Your Grace,'" the nobleman said haughtily. "I overlook Sir Lafayette's informal mode of address," he added, "because, after all, his wits are addled, poor lad. In any case, tis 'neath my ducal dignity to perform tricks, like any wandering *jongleur*."

"No offense, pal," Roy muttered.

"Wish me luck," O'Leary said as he paused at the door by which the Lady Henriette in the Hill had departed. Nothing was visible but deep shadow. Lafayette took a cautious step, felt cracked paving stone underfoot. He felt his way carefully to where the top step should be, but the floor ended instead in loose rubble. Another step, and O'Leary's feet went out from under him. He yelled and grabbed, succeeding only in raking his palms across rusty metal; then he was falling.

"You OK, Slim?" Sprawnroyal's voice echoed from surprisingly far above, but before Lafayette had time to draw breath to reply in the negative, he struck. Hard.

Lafayette sat up, peered through dimness, and made out the shape of a large easy chair. He groaned. "Not again," he protested. "Not right now. I'm busy."

"Enough," Frumpkin's oily voice said above him. Then: "On your feet, fellow!" O'Leary got up shakily and opened one eye to see the Man in Black standing before him, a sneer on his pinched features. Before he could speak, Lafayette said:

"I don't know what good this hide-and-seek game is doing you. But you're going to do it once too often." He paused to feel for the flat-walker in his pocket.

"Don't bother," Frumpkin said curtly. "Your little engine of confusion has been confiscated."

"Fine," Lafayette came back promptly. "I'm eager for you to use it. Just align it—"

"I know all about that, O'Leary," Frumpkin cut him off. "All in good time." He turned away.

"This is as good a time as any," O'Leary decided, and threw his best punch at the angle of the jaw of the Man in Black; but something went wrong, he realized as he was swept up and away, then dropped with an impact which was surely sufficient to break bones—all of them.

For a moment, as he struggled to get his breath going again, Lafayette was quite sure that this time he had Really Done It. Then he found that he was hurting in too many places to be actually dead. He groped, felt underfoot the heaped rubbish which had padded his fall, and became aware of an almost tangible stink. Then he got his feet under him and stood up, peering unavailingly into circumambient darkness. He made his way forward a few steps and encountered rough masonry. Feeling over that, he soon discovered a doorway, barred by a splintery wooden-plank door. At his touch, it swung outward, and he stepped out into cool night air.

"OK, that'll hafta do," a half-familiar voice said nearby. "We got no time to be perfectionists like, so just get it tied in any old way."

"If it be ill-done, we'll blow ourselfs into the next continuum, Yer Lordship," a sullen voice replied.

"You think I don't know it?" the first voice came back hotly. "No more of your lip now, fellow; just do as yer told!"

"Sheriff Tode!" O'Leary blurted, recognizing the voice. "Where'd *you* come from? Look, I need help: I thought Lady Henriette came this way, but she couldn't have; she'd be lying here with a broken neck, because she doesn't have my knack of always landing on my feet, figuratively speaking."

"All right, Cease," Tode's voice spoke tensely. "You know whatta do. So do it!" There was a scrape of feet moving quickly on heaped rubble; Lafayette stepped aside, and someone slammed against the wall where he had been a moment before.

"Oh, Lordy," Cease's mellow baritone sounded shocked. "I . . . I think I've fractured my skull. . . ."

"That Cease," Tode said impatiently. O'Leary heard him approach and feel his way over the fallen man. "Always did have too soft a head for a deppity. Now, you, boy! Stand right where ye'r at!" O'Leary heard the double click of a heavy revolver action being thumbed back.

"You messed me up some, boy," Tode said aggrievedly. "Like to cost me my job. Now this time there's not going to be no slipups. You jest speak up to let me know jist where you're at, now."

"Where I am, you mean," O'Leary corrected.

"Sure: what I said. Now jest you don't move a muscle—" Tode's voice cut off as a dull *thonk!* sounded, followed by the crash of his body striking rubble.

"Don't get excited, Sir Lafayette," a voice Lafayette almost recognized said coolly. "Same orders, just a change in jurisdiction. I'm going to hand you a pair of handcuffs, and you're going to put them on," the voice went on, maddeningly familiar. Where, O'Leary demanded of himself, had he heard it before? Not here, in *this* Aphasia, he was sure. Then it came to him: Troglouse III, the Ajax deserter and sometime boss of Aphasia I.

"Where are ya at?" Trog demanded. O'Leary sensed him groping his way past; carefully judging the distance and angle in the dark, Lafayette directed his *ochi-dan* chop at the hairy tyrant's neck, connected solidly, and heard Trog collapse, the handcuffs rattling on the rubble underfoot. He followed the sound, found the cuffs, and fitted them around Trog's thick wrists and closed them with a solid *clack*. Trog snored. Behind him, Sheriff Tode was muttering to Cease:

"Hope he never hit the sucker too hard; din't like the sound o' that smack. Boss won't pay off for no dead body."

"I never signt on to get mixed up in no murder," Cease complained in reply. "Hey, Lousy," he called, "you OK?" When there was no reply he backed away, muttering, "What *is* this dern place anyways, Sheriff?"

"Don't matter a hang what this place is," Tode replied in the darkness. "We was tole to wait here, and I guess we got no choice now. Boss'll be along purty soon, Cease, straighten things out," he added more moderately. "Must be about done with the job. Be home soon."

"I whisht!" Cease said fervently.

"Hey, Slim," Roy's hoarse voice called from above. "Whyn't you take the stairs? You in a big hurry about sumpin?" There was a rasp of shoe-leather on rusty iron, then a thump, and Roy was at O'Leary's side, panting from the descent.

"I didn't know about the stairs," Lafayette informed Roy. "I had quite a fall, but I lit on a heap of old newspapers or something, and nothing broke."

"You got off lucky, Slim. Say, din't I hear voices down here? You talking to yerself? By the way, old Frumpie got outa that closet; don't see how he done it, with the cuffs on. Tricky rascal. Where are we at, Slim?"

"Apparently this trash pile Henriette lives on is hollow," O'Leary told his ally. "And it's full of suspicious characters."

"I heard that, son," Tode spoke up. "Who you talkin' to, anyways? Tole us you was the only one here."

"Where's 'here,' Sheriff?" O'Leary asked. "And

why are you after me? I thought we had a truce going.''

"Sure, onney we got word from Boss. Hadda get back onna job. Seems like you're in Big Trouble, son.''

"What did I do?'' O'Leary demanded. "Except try to stay alive and figure out what was going on?''

"Seems like you got old Boss plenty mad, son. Never heard him so worked up. Wants you dead or alive, and me and Cease here aim to oblige.''

"Why?'' O'Leary persisted. "I haven't broken any law.''

Tode chuckled comfortably. "Law, boy? Don't you know a big man like Boss can make up the laws to fit anything a feller like you up and does? We got you on everything from a twelve-oh-five—that's Expectorating Onto the Grass—to Cosmic Total. Put you away fer a few years, I guess, happen we bring you in alive.''

Too late, O'Leary realized that Tode had been steadily moving closer, zeroing in on his voice, no doubt. Even as he leaped aside, Tode's iron-hand grip clamped on his arm, and both men went down, Tode on top. Then the sheriff stood and heaved Lafayette to his feet.

"Now, son, no use adding Resisting Arrest to the charge sheet—'' Tode broke off with a yell. Then O'Leary felt a tug at his knee, and Roy's voice urging him to follow.

"Now, how'd that feller kick me onna shin?'' Tode was demanding of the circumambient darkness. He blundered away, calling to Cease.

Lafayette's feet groped over the strewn rubble, Roy tugging him along impatiently.

"Where are we going, Roy?'' O'Leary asked.

"Got to find the wall,'' the little man answered. "You still got the flat-walker, right? But you can't walk through no walls if you ain't got a wall to walk through.''

"Let's just go back up the stairs,'' O'Leary suggested. "Daph— I mean Henriette—is obviously not here.''

"Prolly took the stairs and got off at the next landing,'' Roy hazarded. "Good thing, too. Too much of a fall fer a lady.''

"Funny thing," Lafayette told Roy. "Somebody Tode calls 'Boss' knew I'd be here. He sent Tode and Cease ahead to put the arm on me."

"Figures," Roy replied. "I tole you Frumpy got aloose. He knew you'd go through that door and miss the top step. So *he* must be their Boss."

"Right. He told me he was planning on taking over the Cosmos, remember?"

"My boner, Slim, not securing the sucker better. But we'll find him—or he'll find us." Roy's pull at the knee of Lafayette's gold-striped breeches stopped. Abruptly, O'Leary slammed against a solid barrier of compacted rubbish. He called to Roy, but there was no reply. Carefully, he got out the flat-walker, oriented it approximately parallel to the irregular wall before him, and pressed.

Bright light, blinding him; a strident alarm bell. A voice shouting "—is it! Plane One, activate!" all cut off like a broken film. Then a deep-toned vibration that shook the floor beneath his feet—no, the bare earth, with tall weeds, dim lights, moving in curious patterns; the tolling of a bell, the perfume of night-blooming flowers, a clamor of childish voices, and the odor of chalk dust; a glimpse of an octagonal clock with the hands at high noon, the rush of water, a dash of cold spray; splintering sounds as of timber shattering before a high wind, the grating of massive stone grinding massive stone to rubble in utter darkness; the glare of a great blue-white sun, unshielded, close at hand; heat, turbulence, a deafening explosion. . . .

Lafayette shook his head and sat up, astonished to find himself alive and, as far as he could see, intact. The floor under him was smoothly carpeted.

"Good," he said aloud. "I'm out of that garbage bin, at least," he went on, and called Roy's name. No reply.

"You think it good, do you, fellow?" a cold male voice said above him. "Let us hope you're clever enough to ensure that you continue so to believe."

"Is that you, Frumpkin?" Lafayette demanded of the darkness above. He got to his feet, tucked the flat-walker away, and took a tentative step in the direction from which the voice had seemed to come. He tripped over something soft and fell heavily.

After half an hour of blundering about in what appeared to be a large room furnished with overstuffed furniture, pursuing the voice which spoke mockingly from time to time, O'Leary felt his way up onto a long chaise longue and collapsed, winded. He closed his eyes for a moment.

Chapter Nineteen

First Lafayette was aware of a mild clamor of voices, then of dim light. He sat up and saw that he was far from being alone in the big room. In divans, easy chairs, couches, davenports, and settees arranged in conversational groupings all across the rather faded pseudo-oriental carpets, were people of all ages, both sexes and many degrees of apparent cultivation. Most, but not all of them, were at least vaguely familiar to him. Only the Man in Black, now clad in a wine-colored brocaded dressing gown with a satin shawl collar, was near him. He stood rocking slightly on his heels, glass in hand, looking down at O'Leary with an expression of mild distaste.

"The time has come at last," he said blandly, "for me to confront you directly, my boy, and to discover precisely what has motivated your unexampled persecution of me. You've had a nice nap; would you care for a bite, or perhaps a spiritous beverage? Later we shall dine."

"That's a good one," O'Leary said bluntly. "I've been persecuting *you*, have I? Funny, I thought it was the other way around. Anyway, we've been all over that."

Frumpkin's eyebrows went up in a shallow mime of

surprise. "Why would I, in my position, trouble to persecute such a one as you, Sir Lafayette?"

"Maybe to get even for all the times I made you look like a jackass," Lafayette hazarded, a remark which netted a comfortable chuckle.

"You mistake me, boy," the dandified Frumpkin commented before taking a sip from his glass. "I employed a number of my analogs, of course, a few of whom you encountered in your mad course. It would be foolish of you to mistake any of them for my actual Prime-line self."

"What is this place, Frumpkin?" O'Leary demanded, looking around the big room—the gray room, he realized belatedly, which he was seeing for the first time in a good light. He noted the standing bridge lamps with their fringed, orange-parchment shades, the framed rotogravures on the flowered, brownish wallpaper, and on a nearby would-be Hepplewaite side-table, an Atwater Kent radio in a walnut-stained wooden cabinet. "It looks like a set for a Nils Asther movie," he commented. "Except for that." He nodded toward the control panel.

"I chose the decor for its ambience of complacent respectability, far pleasanter than bare, functional collapsed-matter," Frumpkin replied lazily. "As for the Big Board, it is of course a necessity. And you will call me 'Lord of All.'"

"I doubt it," Lafayette said. "As soon as your keepers find you, you'll be back in a padded cell."

"There's no need to be rude," the Lord of All complained. "I've told you I brought you here for a nice chat, after which we shall no doubt have agreed on a mutually satisfactory division of spheres of influence. I'm quite willing to go half-and-half with you, so long as my half is the larger." He finished his drink and put down the empty glass beside the radio, which he absent-mindedly switched on.

"Seem like to me, Brudder Andy," a resonant baritone voice said amid static, "you is jest temporaciously

regusted wid de taxicab business. But when de Kingfish
tell you about how we gonna redisorganize, you goin' be
singin' anudda choon.''

"I indulge you, boy, out of admiration for your
ingenuity, no more,'' the Frumpkin lookalike said
grandly.

"Where's Daphne?'' O'Leary demanded, rising
abruptly to confront his host, who stood his ground,
looking a trifle uneasy.

"*That* silly alibi again,'' Frumpkin commented and
flopped his arms as one despairing of reasonableness.
"Think, Sir Lafayette!'' he urged. "Once you've made
your peace with me, you'll have second choice of all the
wonders in all the worlds that are or might have been!''

O'Leary himself was surprised to see his left fist shoot
out in a straight jab to the middle of the fellow's smug
face. Frumpkin went down on his back, bleating. Heads
turned. O'Leary saw Chuck of Chuck-and-Chick take a
quick look and busy himself with lighting a cigar.
Sheriff Tode took a step his way and abruptly changed
his mind, pausing to engage in conversation with
Mickey Jo. Her cowgirl outfit was badly stained, but
her hairdo was in place. Neither looked directly at him.
Only Marv came forward, and with an apologetic look
at Lafayette, bent over the furious Frumpkin and
helped him to his feet.

"Don't waste your sympathy on that skunk, Marv,''
O'Leary said disparagingly. "He's the one who's responsible for all the problems we've been having.
Where've you been, anyway? I lost you in the crowd
back in Mudville.''

"Is that right, mister?'' Marv demanded of the no
longer dignified Frumpkin, who was dabbing at the
blood on his lip. "Is that what you told him?'' Marv insisted. Behind him, Trog was making his way forward in
haste, looking distressed.

"Hold on there, Marv,'' he called ahead. "I thought
I tole you and Omar to consider yerselfs under house ar-
rest!'' Marv turned to look coldly at his whiskery boss.
"Don't push it, milord,'' he said in a deadly tone. Trog

responded by turning aside to join a conversational group including Dr. Smith, still in her starched whites, talking to a man of oriental appearance, and Special Ed. But his eyes searched in vain for a glimpse of the Lady Henriette.

"Some guest list," he said shortly to Frumpkin when the Prime agent had resumed his position facing Lafayette but out of range of left jabs now. "It's pretty clear that you were herding me every step of the way," Lafayette went on. "And you had these people of yours planted to intercept me. Why? I think before this farce goes any further, we'd better clear up that point."

"As I've already told you, dear boy," Frumpkin began in an unctuous tone, "I acknowledge your expertise; you've unleashed forces which even I"—he paused to glance toward his guests, now busily chattering again as if no episode of violence had marred the tranquillity of the gathering—"skills which I admire, and indeed wish to learn from you. Do you have a drink, lad, and let's discuss way and means."

"Where is she?" was O'Leary's only response.

Frumpkin fluttered his hands. "Pray believe me, Lafayette, I haven't the faintest idea."

O'Leary shook his head. "Nope," he said. "I don't believe you."

"I have never so much as set eyes on this Daphne person," Frumpkin said loftily.

"You jostled her coming through the door of the lab not more than an hour ago," Lafayette stated flatly. Frumpkin threw up his hands.

"Dear boy, that was the Lady Henriette in the Hill, with her serving-wench, one Betty Brassbraid."

"Sure," Lafayette agreed. "I still want to talk to her. But you seem to forget that here in your gray room you call her 'Dame Edith.' "

"Wait here," Frumpkin said, his tone of command once more in working order. Without awaiting O'Leary's response, he turned and made his way briskly across the wide room. Once more, Lafayette examined the familiar faces among those present. Of all those he had encountered in his wanderings since the sudden shower in the palace garden, only Duke Bother-Be-Damned, it seemed, was nowhere to be seen.

—*and Roy,* O'Leary told himself. He took out the flat-walker and held it to his ear:

". . . Alpha Relay, via Forward Station Ten," a tiny voice whispered. "Kindly come in, whoever you are, *Raf trass spintern!*"

"*Raf trass spoit,*" Lafayette said softly. "Get Roy on the line, quick!"

A different voice responded: "This is your Plane Supervisor. May I help you?"

"Where's Roy?" Lafayette demanded.

"Kindly speak up," the supervisor said sharply. "I have in excess of ten-to-the-thirtieth Roys listed. To which do you refer?"

"OK, Slim," Roy's more audible voice cut in. "What happened? We started through, and—zap!—there I was in ultraspace, alone! But—maybe I got it! Slim, I'm glad you're OK enough to talk, but did you maybe not orient the flat-walker precisely like it says in the brochure? You gotta realize Ajax can't accept no responsibility if the unit is not used as directed. Says so right in the guarantee."

"I don't know, Roy," O'Leary came back impatiently. "But don't worry, I'm not planning to sue. Listen, every so often I get snagged by Frumpkin into a place I call the gray room. His HQ, it seems. Right now he's staging some sort of convention. Everybody's here but Bother. Can you get your strongarm squad in here to nab Frumpkin in a hurry?"

"Don't worry, Bother's OK. He's here, in fact, putting away a stack o' flapjacks higher'n me. I don't know about the squad; you're almost out o' range, Slim, right outside the whole of explored space-time! Fact is, I'm surprised we even got the voice link—" With those words, his voice dwindled amid rising static.

"See here," Frumpkin said sharply. O'Leary looked up; the Man in Black was back, confronting him in challenging fashion, two troglodytic men in waiter's togs at his side.

"I've lost patience with you," Frumpkin snapped. "You will now give me your complete cooperation, or I shall simply destroy you. Now, speak up!"

"You're a lousy liar," O'Leary told the irate autocrat. "You pretend I just stumbled around after I met you burgling the old lab—or whatever you were doing there—but it's pretty clear now I was herded every step of the way. Every time I almost broke the pattern, one of your boys or girls was on hand to nudge me back in line." O'Leary's eyes went past Frumpkin to the crowd. "Look at 'em," he added. "What is this, a convention of your hirelings?"

Frumpkin dismissed the question with a flip of his well-manicured hand. "After all, lad," he murmured unctuously, "when one can call on unlimited resources, why be stingy? It's true my cadres are extensive; but, far from docilely following my wishes, as you suggest they forced you to do, you repeatedly committed a curious act which cut across my complex pattern of causality, plunging my carefully constructed scenario into confusion! At last my experts were able to learn that it was at moments when you, ah—to employ your own curious term—'focused the Psychical Energies,' that my control of Destiny itself was broken. But"—Frumpkin paused to look triumphant—"they further established that it was also at precisely those moments that you were vulnerable to my own Prime Directive!"

"No bull?" Lafayette said contemptuously. "Professor Schimmerkopf didn't mention that part."

"I have also investigated this Professor Doktor Hans Josef Schimmerkopf, late of the University of Leipzig and the Homeopathic Institute of Vienna, in an obscure locus now forever dissolved both into the past and into the quasinothingness of the unrealized. He and all his works no longer exist and never did!"

"Too bad," Lafayette said carelessly. "I was going to write his estate a fan letter."

"You dare to jape at this, the crucial contretemps of all the cosmos?" Frumpkin demanded savagely. "Almost I incline to believe that you are indeed no more than an ignorant blunderer with an uncanny knack for precisely that paradoxical behavior which alone can seem to set my plans at naught. I say 'seems' because of course, in the end, I shall prevail!''

"You say Prof Schimmerkopf never existed?" O'Leary queried, unmoved by Frumpkin's outburst. "That has to mean that the locus he was a part of never existed, because without him it would be a different locus. And it follows that Colby Corners never existed, nor I— since he was on record in the local library, and he changed the course of my life. And if I never existed, then . . . who am *I*?" He glared at Frumpkin, who smiled sleekly.

"You begin to see the magnitude of the problem, lad. Your one chance is to attach your trifling destiny to the great engine of my own fate, and then to refute the unacceptable. But I'm wasting time.'' Frumpkin turned to wave a hand, and at once the cocktail-sipping crowd begain to drift away. O'Leary noticed Marv standing nearby. Noticing Lafayette's eye on him, Marv came over and looked curiously at Frumpkin.

"Now what, Al?" he inquired genially. "I guess this is the like showdown, eh? I heard what His Nibs here was saying, about how it was you or him. But where does that leave me?" He looked more keenly at the haughty Man in Black.

"What you got in mind for a honest fellow like myself?" he asked in an edged tone. Frumpkin waved him aside. "Later, my man," he said coolly.

While the two talked, O'Leary again put the flat-walker to his ear.

"—outside our jurisdiction, Slim," Roy's voice peeped faintly. "We got one chance: Focus the Psychical Energies one more time, and I can get a hard fix and rotate a strong-arm gang in there fast. Maybe—"

The message was interrupted as a hand grabbed Lafayette's wrist just as something swept his feet from under him. The flat-walker was wrenched away, and as Lafayette fought his way back to his feet, Frumpkin was saying:

"—my own inspection!" He was holding the Ajax device close to his face, studying it. Marv was at his side, looking anxious.

"Hmmm, yes," Frumpkin muttered. "One of the fiendish devices of Ajax, I see." He glanced up at O'Leary. "Oh, yes, Sir Lafayette," he commented. I'm well aware of the warped ingenuity of those little beasts. You'll recall that I retain in my employ one Troglouse III, a *renegado*, who has briefed me thoroughly on the Ajax bag of tricks. I can't tell you the trouble they've caused me. Seem to have links to high orders of reality. One day I shall deal with them as they deserve."

"In that case," a hearty voice spoke from low and behind Frumpkin, who jumped as if prodded with a pin, "you can gimme the medal *now*—quick, before you find out you been fired off the job." It was Sprawn-royal's bass tones. O'Leary thrust Frumpkin aside to grab the small man's calloused hand and greet him enthusiastically.

"Roy! You got through! This Frumpkin is even nuttier than I thought! Now he's talking about switching the basic planes around so that I—and Artesia, and you, and Daphne, and everything worthwhile—never existed!"

"Easy, Slim," Roy replied soberly. "It's not all bluff," he admitted. "What he's talking about is possible, theoretically. If he can reweave the lines so as to render Plane V-87 less likely than some alternate he's cooked up—then the rest follows naturally."

"Take him!" Frumpkin yelled, making a grab for Roy, who stepped aside and casually tripped the taller man as he lunged. Marv popped up from a deep chair nearby to seize Frumpkin's arm and haul him to his feet.

"I heard all that," Marv blurted. "And I, for one, got no intention o' being relegated to a unrealized status like Shorty here says. So how about it, sir?" Marv was making ineffectual efforts to assist Frumpkin to re-arrange his satin dressing gown.

"Leave me alone, you cretin!" Frumpkin snarled and

thrust the clumsy Marv from him. He assumed as
menacing an expression as his shattered dignity allowed.

"Whose side is the big bum on, Slim?" Roy asked
Lafayette in a stage whisper. "I thought he was a pal of
yours—"

"He is," O'Leary confirmed, watching Marv hovering at Frumpkin's elbow. "Or I thought he was.
Frankly, Marv has had me puzzled; he's stuck with me
through thick and thin, I'll give him that—but once I
overheard him throwing me to the dogs. Of course, he
had a logical explanation."

"Sure," Marv said eagerly, giving Roy a sour look.
"At the time, like I said, I hadda tell 'em *sumpin*. Why,
Al, they were planning on stringing me up!"

"What's this 'Al' business, Slim?" Roy asked.

"He pretends to think I'm some mythical character
named Allegorus," O'Leary explained. "Or maybe he's
not so mythical; I met him once. . . ." Lafayette broke
off, looking thoughtful. "It was right back at the beginning of this farce, just after I ran into Frumpkin here
for the first time, in the tower. He had some errand or
something he wanted me to do, but before we got
around to it, things started coming apart, literally."

"Enough of this idle chatter," Frumpkin barked.
"Allegorus, indeed! It's well enough known that he's a
figment—a demi-corporeal pseudobeing evoked as a
totem by petty minds in moments of stress—a mere
superstition, nothing more."

"I still talked to him," Lafayette said quietly. Glancing past Frumpkin across the low, now nearly dark and
almost deserted room, he realized that the guests had
been quietly departing, switching off bridge lamps as
they went. But from the shadowy corners others were
emerging: small, gnarly men in pink uniforms, carrying
in their hands complex apparatuses which O'Leary felt
sure were weapons. Noting Lafayette's expression,
Frumpkin turned to follow his gaze.

"Oh, good enough, Trog," he called brightly. "Just
deploy your troops loosely here and stand fast. I expect
to transfer this interview to the technical installation in a

moment. Here, you!'' he yelped at one stubby figure, forging in advance of the main body. "Keep back there! I told you I'm about to effect a transfer. Can't have any interference; it's a delicate technique.''

"Hard lines, Bub,'' the Ajax man replied jauntily. "Maybe you better lay down, face-first, hands out wide, flat on the rug.''

"You're not Troglouse!'' Frumpkin yelled, backing a step, only to recoil when Roy jabbed him sharply in the seat with a hard thumb.

"Better do like Casper says,'' the Ajax rep suggested mildly, "before he forgets his training about destroying evidence and gives you a jolt with the nothing-gun.'' Roy turned to wink up at O'Leary. "Now we'll get a few answers out o' the sucker,'' he said. "Old Casper's a real curious fellow, when I tell him to be.''

Chapter Twenty

As Lafayette opened his mouth to congratulate his diminutive ally, he noticed that the grayish fog had reappeared, which made even Roy's homely, good-natured face appear blurred, though he was only a yard distant. Lafayette took a step—or tried to: His feet seemed stuck to the floor by a gluey substance. He pulled harder, and realized that he was firmly trapped. He yelled, felt the glue flow into his mouth, immobilizing his tongue, and down his throat. He couldn't breathe.

Roy's mouth was moving, but no sound emerged. The light grew dimmer. Only Frumpkin's face seemed to glow through the opaque air, his eyes glittering like highlights on polished gem stones.

As Lafayette fought to draw breath, he saw dimly that no one was moving. Marv stood over Frumpkin, his arms folded as if he noticed nothing unusual. Casper was nowhere to be seen.

"As you see, Lafayette," Frumpkin's voice seemed to echo from an immense distance, "I still have a few resources on which to call. Don't panic; the difficulty with your breathing will clear up in a moment, just as soon as we've completed our transit across extra-time, a matrix with which perhaps you are unfamiliar. Only another, oh, perhaps ten seconds subjective, then we shall correct a number of inequities. Take a final look at your former companions, my boy, since you'll not be seeing them again. They will remain suspended in the Eternal Now forever, neither realized nor totally dissubstantiated, conscious and able to reflect at length on their treasonous folly in attempting to foil me.''

Still straining desperately to draw breath, O'Leary watched Marv, Casper, and a total stranger of Chinese appearance standing nearby, arrested in mid-motion, looking like waxworks. All but Sprawnroyal, Lafayette saw with a sudden access of hope. The little man was in the act of turning toward Marv. As Lafayette watched, he saw him languidly complete the movement, reach out deftly to pluck something from Marv's pocket, then turn to give O'Leary a slow wink. There was no one else in sight; the big room, looking like a deserted warehouse now, was deep in shadow. The silence was total. Roy took a slow step around Frumpkin, still supine, toward O'Leary who, striving mightily to draw breath, felt the resistance collapse and revivifying air rush into his lungs.

"Roy!" he gasped. "What happened?"

"The sucker was a little trickier than I gave him credit for," Roy said without apology. "But of course, his tricks only work in his own jurisdiction. I'm outside, because I'm not really here, Slim. You see, at Ajax we worked out what we call the counter-grid, a complete set of alternates to the natural grid, and to this bozo's own personal construct too. You might say nature and Frumpkin's setup lie at right angles, so to speak, in overspace. Well, we engineered the counter-grid vertical to that plane. So, we can operate anywhere we like—as long as we're within range, natch. After old Frumpkin here cut off our power-tap we were drawing from the natural entropic potential; gave us all the juice we needed and gave us a little edge in some of our more unlikely gadgets, too. We set up a jury-rig, drawing on Frumpkin's own pseudo-entropic energy, and that was just barely enough to let me punch through to this semi-half-phase layout here."

"Much good it will do you!" Frumpkin barked. "So

far, I've stayed my hand, out of sheer altruism; but now I'm at the end of my patience."

"Gosh," Roy said in mock awe. "What do you do when you run out of patience, you silly-looking maniac?"

At this insolence, Frumpkin literally began to foam at the mouth. Red-faced and with spit dribbling from his chin, he shook both fists and yelled.

"I dismiss you all back to the nothingness from which, after all, you were never really evoked!" He turned to a boxy apparatus beside him which until now Lafayette had not noticed. It was the same unit, he thought, that Frumpkin and Belarius V had had with them at O'Leary's first meeting with them.

"Don't let him use that gadget, Roy," O'Leary urged as he himself strove mightily, but without success, to make a move to intercept the furious fellow.

"No sweat, Slim," Roy said easily. "He's about to find out Ajax equipment won't work when it's directed against Ajax personnel—a little sort of safety device we install in all our stuff."

Then Marv was between Frumpkin and his infernal device. "Back off, brainless," Marv said roughly, pushing Frumpkin aside. "You heard what the little runt said."

"He's bluffing!" Frumpkin yelled, and lunged again.

"Maybe," Marv repled, "and maybe not." He turned his attention to Sprawnroyal.

"How about it, pal? Anything to it?" he inquired genially, thrusting Frumpkin aside to take a position beside the control console of the boxy apparatus. He glanced at the dials there.

"According to this readout," he said tonelessly, "this here whole set-up is going to go insubstantial in about ten seconds. So long, fellows. And Sir Lafayette, I knew all along you weren't Allegorus. Hang loose." With a wave, Marv turned and walked away into deep shadow.

Roy was frowning quizzically up at O'Leary. "Slim, how well you know this Marv?"

"Pretty well," O'Leary replied. "At first, he was just

my jailer, then we got to be fellow-sufferers, and we stuck together pretty well. You remember when we met in the woods in Aphasia I, he stood by loyally. He helped me out a couple of times, and somehow he seemed to be able to stick to me even when I had a wild ride in half-phase when I was totally lost. Once I caught him siccing the crowd on me, but he had an explanation: he was cornered, and it was the only way to save his own neck. Anyway, the mob didn't know me, so no harm was done."

"Unless maybe he was fingering you for someone," Roy suggested. "I don't like his sticking to you so close, Slim. How'd he do it? That would take all the Ajax equipment Frumpy here had, and then some."

"—like that last time," Lafayette continued thinking aloud. "He was washed away by the big wave, just like I was, and we fetched up on the same mud-flat."

"Slim, I checked out this Aphasia III," Roy said. "Funny, according to all readings the boys took on it, it's right outside space-time. Sort of scraps left over when reality itself, as we know it, was derealized."

"Why listen to this sawed-off intellectual?" Marv queried in an indifferent tone, as he came out of the shadows. "What we got to do now—we got to get outa here, before Frumpkin's boys arrive to finish the job."

"Any ideas how we should do that, Marv?" O'Leary asked, equally coolly.

"Sure, Al, just focus the old PEs," Marv recommended promptly.

"Wait a minute, Slim," Roy put in. "We better think about this. I don't know if you know it, but every time you pull that trick, you put out a signal that gives anybody that's interested a handle on you they can use any way they like—which is how old Frumpy here has been tailing you, I bet."

"Right," O'Leary confirmed. "He admitted it, even bragged about it—and he said the next time I do it, he'll be able to home in on the pattern and finish me off—and the whole pseudo-volume of probability I've ever occupied."

"Haw. Prolly could do it, too, Slim," Roy mused.

"All he'd hafta do is put a vitality tap on the anomaly flux and drain off all the entropic energy. That'd be the end of Artesia and all the nearby loci out to prolly a hundred parameters. Too risky, Slim. We need some kind of tangle-field to work behind. Lemme think."

"I just happened to think, Marv," O'Leary said. "Ever since I met you, you've been urging me to focus my Psychical Energies. I don't know how you so much as knew I knew how. Now it seems you might have had an angle of your own."

"Who, *me*?" Marv inquired in a raised-eyebrows tone. "Hey, Al, this is your old pal, Marv, remember? How about the old days, back when we were lodged in durance vile together and all, hah?"

"You waste your final breaths, poor fools," Frumpkin spoke up with renewed vigor. "All your petty problems will be solved very soon now, with no effort whatever on your part. Look about you."

"Holy Moishe," Roy muttered. O'Leary looked around and saw featureless gray walls which now were closing them in on all sides. It was as if they were at the center of an immense bubble of concrete. Frumpkin snickered. Marv growled.

"While you nattered of trivialities," Frumpkin said contentedly, "I busied myself by draining the vacuole of all energies; and thus, of course, I cut it off from all possible communication with the Greater Universe—except, naturally, for my own lifeline."

"You think you can get away with this?" Marv demanded, taking a threatening step toward Frumpkin, who waved him away casually.

"You know better than to contest me now, my dear fellow," he said. "At any move inimical to my best interests, the diameter of our little universe will shrink; and you will at all costs preserve the integrity of my lifeline, since it is your sole possible link with outside."

"Maybe so," Sprawnroyal grunted. "But we can make it mighty uncomfortable for you in the meantime. Slim, take his arms; Marv, you get on his head. I'll go for his legs." So saying, he launched himself, tackling the self-styled Lord of All, toppling him as O'Leary moved in and grabbed his arms. Marv flopped down across the fallen dictator's upper quarters. Beneath, Frumpkin kicked and flailed, uttering muffled cries.

"Just hang on to him a second, fellows," Roy suggested as he got to his stubby legs and dusted himself off. Marv rolled over Frumpkin's face.

"You won't get away with this," Frumpkin predicted, coldly furious now as he sat up, tugging in vain against O'Leary's grip while blood ran from his nose.

"Maybe not," Roy came back eagerly, "but it will be fun trying—for us, not you." He put his gnarled forearm in the angle of Frumpkin's elbow, and with his right arm forced the fallen man's wrist and forearm upward. Frumpkin rolled his eyes and yelled.

"Smarts some, don't it?" Roy remarked as he released the taller man's arm. "Want me to try the other arm?"

Frumpkin's reply was an inarticulate yell as he renewed his thrashing efforts to escape O'Leary's grip. Marv bent over and took a firm grip on a lock of Frumpkin's thin, well-oiled hair, and yanked gently.

"You can't really spare this, Frumpy," he said gently. "But it won't really matter much: you'll be bald soon anyway." With a sudden jerk, he pulled the tuft of hair out by its roots and held it before Frumpkin's wild eyes.

"Stop!" the tormented Frumpkin croaked as O'Leary manipulated his skinny arms behind his back. "All right, I confess I've no stomach for torture! I'll let you go—but only on your solemn promise to do nothing furthur to interfere with my great Plan!"

"You're in no spot to talk deal," Roy pointed out casually as he dug a knuckle into the muscle at the angle of Frumpkin's jaw, eliciting a roar of pain.

"Agreed!" Frumpkin yelled. "I'll release you unconditionally—and you'd best hurry; time is running out!"

O'Leary looked up: The domed 'ceiling' of the spherical chamber was noticeably closer. Even as he watched, it shrank in furthur as Frumpkin uttered a long drawn-out howl. O'Leary glanced toward him. Marv was now sitting at ease on the formerly arrogant Frumpkin's face. He caught O'Leary's look and rose. "It ain't comfortable anyways," he explained. "That sharp nose'd be hell on a feller if he's to sit there any length o' time."

Roy bustled forward and bent over the supine Frumpkin. "You ready to be reasonable?" he inquired solicitously. Frumpkin grumbled, which Roy took as assent. He hunkered down beside the fallen dictator. "Go ahead, spill it," he ordered.

Frumpkin sat up, wiped blood from his nose across his lower face, and gulped.

"Very well, you inhuman beasts," he started. Marv promptly knocked him flat.

"Just the facts, big shot; skip the insults," he prescribed. Frumpkin nodded and cautiously sat up again.

"Started with a little accident," he blurted. "I was on duty in the probability lab, and I noticed some anomalous readings on the main monitor panel, and I, well, I did a little investigating, and made a curious discovery." Frumpkin paused as if to savor the moment.

"Something was playing hell with the energy equipoise in a minor locus out on Plane V-87. Looked like every few years there'd been a drain that shuffled the loci like playing cards. No repercussions had showed up outside the manifold, but that didn't mean it would never happen. I should have reported it to YAC-19 at once, I know—but all of a sudden I saw it! If I could deduce just what was happening, I could use it myself, to shape this sorry scheme of things entire closer to my heart's desire, as the poet hath said. Ahem!" Frumpkin cleared his throat and fussed with the lapels of his rumpled dressing gown.

"As even you are doubtless aware, all of existence rests on the principle of entropic equipoise. For each ordering force, there is a balancing force of disorder; and all this vast matrix of interpenetrating forces is modulated by the universal-probability field. To tamper at any one point with the probability flux is to cause the

matrix itself to readjust so as to bring all forces back
into balance. When you, Sir Lafayette, fecklessly employed the gigantic forces at your command, the nature
of which still escapes me, to make certain minor local
realignments in defiance of the pressures of local probability, you occasioned readjustments which resonated
at vast distances. These caused realignments of reality
on a scope unthinkable. But I soon saw that, at bottom,
your method was simple enough; and used systemati-
cally, one could realign the natural forces so as to produce results specified by oneself—or *my*self, that is.''
Frumpkin paused again. ''At first, I envisioned only
local readjustments which would place me in a position
of total authority, and provide such trifling comforts as
the disposal of all the wealth in existence, my choice of
all the world's delicacies of food and drink and luxury
goods, plus the unselfish devotion of the Lady Xan-
thippe, the only person beside myself whom I considered deserving of the fruits of reality. Speaking of
which—'' Frumpkin snapped his fingers. There was a
stir in the shadowy distance, and a lone figure came
slowly forward into the light: then two more people appeared, one tall and broad, the other slim and graceful.

''. . . somehow unsatisfying,'' Frumpkin was droning
on. ''So, I asked myself why. The answer was simple
enough: While there remained planes of probability outside my sway, what joy could I take in my petty rule of a
portion of All That Is?''

''I've heard enough,'' Marv said roughly. He stepped
close to Frumpkin and spoke quietly to him.

''It's far too late for that, Marv, old boy,'' Frumpkin
cut him off curtly. ''You erred in not acting at once,
while my path was still unclear.''

Marv replied to this by taking a firm grip on Frumpkin's neck, causing his victim to squirm ineffectively,
while his face became purplish. Then Frumpkin's cold
eyes met O'Leary's.

''Sir Lafayette!'' he cried, ''I call on you to intercede
in the interest of justice. Don't you see? I lied just now,
I admit, but only in a desperate effort to save what I

have built—and that includes Artesia and all that outlying area—from utter dissolution. I did all I claimed, but
not as a free agent. I made the error of telling of my
discovery to the janitor who mopped up in the Prime
Vault—a cretin, but I was bursting with the knowledge!
So I told him. And rather than merely gaping at me in
incomprehension, the low fellow began to behave most
strangely. He went to certain controls and manipulated
them with surprising deftness, then stood aside and
dared me to look at the results. Unless, he said, I agreed
to do as he dictated, he'd bring about a cataclysm which
would set all of reality at Entropic Maximum—a state
of which you have a sample here, in this vacuole—an
eternity of absolute stasis. So I had to do as he said. He
himself, he told me, was now far above such petty tasks.
I was but a slave, but he—he was Lord Marvelous!"
Frumpkin's trembling finger pointed at Marv, who
backed a step, almost colliding with the foremost of the
three advancing from the dimness: Duke Bother-Be-
Damned. Even as the armored hands of the big man
clamped on Marv's arms, Lafayette's eyes went past
him to those behind him.

"Daphne!" he yelled and started toward her, then
checked as he recognized Betty Brassbraid at her
mistress's side. "But you're Henriette in the Hill," he
groaned. "And you don't know me from Adam's pet
mongoose."

"Fie, Lafayette!" the pretty brunette replied after a
moment's hesitation. "Do you not know me, your own
true love? Of course I'm Daphne, silly," she added
more gently. "And Lafayette—if it really *is* you, my
love, and not another beguiling dream—oh, how I've
longed for this moment, and somehow knew that, in
spite of all, at last it would come—someday." She
broke off and began to cry silently. Lafayette stumbled
to her and took her in his arms. Now Betty was sniffling
behind her mistress, while Bother hurrumphed and fiddled with his sword-hilt. Marv stood to one side, looking sullen.

Chapter Twenty-One

"What it boils down to," Bother was saying after hours of intense discussion, "is a contest of strength between the miscreant Frumpkin or his master, Marv, and you, Sir Lafayette—they with their vast technical expertise and all the potency of the apparatus to which Frumpkin is linked, and you with your native naïveté, your simple faith in some abstraction you think of as 'right,' your single-minded devotion to this fair lady, for the which I blame you not, begad!"

"What contest?" O'Leary demanded. "He's been sitting on the floor bragging about all the terrible things he's going to do, and I've been standing here wondering what I could do about it." His agonized gaze went to Daphne who, comforted by Betty, had been weeping.

"What happened, Daph?" Lafayette implored her. "How did I lose you? You were right in front of me."

"Two men," Daphne replied, calming herself. "These two villeins." She looked contemptuously at Frumpkin and at Marv, who was still protesting his innocence. "They fell upon me as I gained the terrace, threw a dirty cloth over my head, and dragged me away, then left me in a thicket. I heard you call, my Lafayette, but my own cries seemed remote, even to me. Then, later, I saw George, and together we bowled over someone called

Omar, and fled to the woods. There was a flood, and we rode it here—or *there*—wherever it was, and then *he* came back one day.'' She indicated Frumpkin. ''He demanded that I submit to him. I struck him, and he swore I'd never escape him. But I knew somehow you'd come, my Lafayette!''

''I'm sorry it's taken so long,'' Lafayette said, going to her to embrace her slim form again. His eye fell on the faded pale velvet rag around her shoulders.

''That was my brand-new cloak,'' he said. ''It must have taken years to fade that much! How long *has* it been, Daph?''

''I know not, my Lafayette,'' she replied, sniffling. ''After the first year I lost count—everything was so strange.''

Lafayette patted her comfortingly. ''Poor kid,'' he murmured. ''For me, it's only been a few days—I think. But it's all over now.''

''Sir knight,'' Bother spoke up beside him, ''pray forgive my intervention at this tender moment, but we must make certain decisions in haste. As you've heard, I am Chief Inspector Mobius, carrying Catagory Nine credentials, empowered to act for the Council. Now, it seems that if I'm to credit this fellow's boasts''—he paused to look without approval at Frumpkin—''matters are in an even more parlous state than we had assumed. I defer, of course, to your unique status; what's to be done?''

''What *is* my 'unique status'?'' Lafayette demanded of the stern-faced inspector. ''I'm just a dumb guy who got in over his head!''

''Be none so modest, sirrah!'' Bother boomed. ''The time for pretense is past. Now you must act!''

O'Leary turned to Roy and squatted down to put his face on a level with the Ajax rep's. ''What do you think, Roy?'' he appealed. ''What does he expect me to do? Who does he think I am?''

''Beats me, Slim,'' Roy said sympathetically, ''unless he knows about the Category Ultimate Anomalies and all. But how could he?''

"He's an inspector, from Prime. Prime outranks Central, I understand. But wht's a Category Ultimate Anomaly?"

"Come on, Slim, you don't need to fake it with *me*. A CUA is what you make every time you focus, you know. By the way, I was right about Daph. The louse told her if she didn't cooperate he'd do you in, painful. That's why he kept pulling you back here, so she'd see you in trouble. But how do you focus the old PEs?"

"I don't know, Roy. But if I did know, what should I do now—before the bubble closes in the rest of the way and squashes all of us?"

"Except maybe me, Slim," Roy pointed out. "I'm not really here, remember? But to heck with that kinda talk. You use the flat-walker"—he handed it over—"and I'll see if I can punch a signal through to Ajax's field office for this quadrant. Doubt it, but I can try." Noting Lafayette's surprise at seeing the flat-walker, Roy added, "Marv lifted it off Frumpy when he was doing the Alphonse and Gaston routine, dusting him off. I taken it outa Marv's pocket. Right now, I got Marv on 'hold,' till I can check out Frumpy's story."

"What should I do with it?" Lafayette asked helplessly, holding the flat-walked gingerly.

"Oh, just try the wall here." The concrete-like surface of the contracting sphere was only a few feet away now, crowding all its remaining occupants together like fraternity men in a phone booth.

Lafayette took a last, lingering look at Daphne's anxious face, kissed it lightly, said, "Here goes nothing," and faced the wall.

"If you get into trouble, Slim," Roy said behind him, "reorient the walker at right angles, OK?"

Lafayette nodded and pressed forward, the flat-walker held parallel to his body. The wall yielded easily, like dense fog, and the display of darting lights was dazzling. He took a cautious step, then another. Then the floor was gone and he was falling—or so his first impression was. Then he seemed to be hanging motionless in still air. The tiny sparks of light whirled about him more quickly than ever, vast numbers of them, which became a dazzling, whirling glow that consumed him.

The floor was hard and cold. Lafayette grabbed at it and willed it to stay under him. The darkness was as dense as the brilliant glare had been a moment—or an eternity—before. He blinked, saw a faint glimmer, held it, got to his feet, and groped toward a dim-glowing rectangle at a remote distance. He bumped against it and, feeling over it, found a door latch. He lifted it and the door swung outward, letting in cool night air. The light sprang up behind him.

"No, no, over here, my boy," an urbane voice spoke behind the glare. Lafayette blinked and groped his way toward it, averting his eyes from the bank of fluorescents above the marble-topped counter.

"I know you've had a shock, Lafayette," the voice said kindly. Lafayette turned toward it and saw a tall man in a black hooded cloak, sitting at ease in a large leather easy chair beside the crackle-finish instrument panel.

"Allegorus!" Lafayette blurted. "And I'm back in the lab! How—what?" His voice trailed off as he covered his face with his hands. "Or am I just off on another bad trip?" He looked directly at Allegorus.

"Ye gods!" O'Leary said feelingly. "Nicodaeus! Why the spook getup? If I'd recognized you the first time I ran into you, back when Frumpkin and Belarius V were conning me, we could have saved this whole thing! All the torment poor Daph has been through, for example."

Allegorus/Nicodaeus shook his head. "No, Lafayette, life is not after all so simple. What will be, will be. One way or another, the equations had to balance, and just as Bother told you and Roy—in the end it had to come to a face-to-face confrontation between you and your opposite number, so to speak—Lord Marvelous, as he's calling himself. Yes," Allegorus held up an admonishing hand. "I am indeed Nicodaeus, or at least I am the Prime-line original of the ego-gestalt of which he is a manifestation—rather a close manifestation, too, only a few zillion parameters away. But in spite of that, when elemental forces are in flux, only a rascal (Frumpkin) or a fool (yourself—no offense intended) can influence them. You see, Lafayette, when an individual of ordinary potential places himself in the path of what we may loosely call destiny, he is simply ejected from whatever locus he is occupying; thus the unexplained disappearances and other weird experiences sometimes reported—and as often ignored by the more pedestrian personalities who indeed provide the stability of such mundane loci, as for example Colby Corners."

"Sure," O'Leary dismissed the subject. "But just what was going on back there in Aphasia I? I saw the palace in ruins. And Trog, who turned out to be nothing but one of Frumpkin's hirelings, was in charge—or he seemed to be. I guess I was gullible to accept him at face value. And that Marv! Lord Marvelous, that's short for —he seems to be Mr. Big. Some disguise, coming on like a hired thug taking orders from his own servants."

"Lord Marvelous is less elementary than he may seem, my boy," Nicodaeus pointed out. "Don't be misled by the persona of Marv which he was forced to adapt hurriedly when you appeared on the scene. He assumed you'd be dealt with by Frumpkin. But he reckoned without me," he added almost with a smile.

"What did *you* do?" Lafayette demanded. "Except let me walk out there and get clobbered again."

"I remained here, with my equipment at hand," Nicodaeus answered coolly, "until the moment when I could safely snatch you across the plenum to relative safety. I tried a number of times, actually: each time you ventured into half-phase. But I was blocked by your Lord Marvelous—though it did give me an opportunity each time to keep Ajax informed."

"What connection do *you* have with Ajax?" O'Leary demanded.

Nicodaeus raised a hand. "Quietly, Lafayette. No need to adopt that hectoring tone. I don't wish to pull rank on you, but after all I *am* First Secretary to the Prime Postulate at Nuclear City. Why, actually, it was I who established Ajax in a small way of business back in Artesia's early days, long before you were born, of course, Lafayette. The little chaps proved surprisingly ingenious as well as industrious, and soon expanded the scope of their operations far beyond anything I had envisioned. Still, I never interfered. I did, however, keep them posted as to your constantly fluctuating position in the plenum, and even supplied the Words of Power of which you made such good, though random, use."

"You mean, 'raf—' " Lafayette was cut off in mid-word by Nicodaeus' hand clapped over his mouth.

"Never speak the Words of Power lightly, Lafayette," he said severely, then removed his hand and used it to pat Lafayette's shoulder. "Your pardon, my boy. I know you've been through a lot."

"So has Daph!" Lafayette cut in. "And Roy and Bother, too, for that matter! I've got to get back to Daphne—you have to help me! Roy told me he and his boys had planted something called a transfer box or something back here in the lab—the *real* lab, I mean." He looked up: The gilded skeleton was not in its accustomed place. "No skeleton," Lafayette told himself. "That's OK, because it was taken down right after the first time I was here."

"Umm," Nicodaeus agreed. "Trifle too much, eh, lad? But let us remain calm. Transfer box: just where did Roy install it? Useful gadget, if it is indeed present."

"We'd better hurry, Al," O'Leary said tensely. "That bubble's getting smaller by the second, and Daph's probably being squashed between Marv and Frumpkin!"

"To be sure," Allegorus replied mildly. "A happier fate than those two deserve." The hooded man paused thoughtfully, then spoke soberly:

"Understandably enough, Lafayette, you've expressed bafflement as to the motivation behind your persistent persecution. . . ."

"In other words," Lafayette shot back hotly, "why does this big shot—Marv or Frumpkin or whoever—have it in for me? I'd like to know!"

"Consider, Lafayette," Nicodaeus said soothingly. "Here we have a petty fellow who comes to a great realization. Performing menial labor in the Prime Probability Laboratory, he became aware in time that the forces being monitored there, the great basic flows which energize the fluctuation of any given alternative among the three states, could, if properly—or improperly in this case—manipulated, bring into actualization those elements of potentiality most conducive to the aggrandizement of his own ego-gestalt."

"What are these 'three states'?" O'Leary asked humbly.

"Why, you can deduce them for yourself, Lafayette. Consider: Reality *is*. Being reality, it is not subject to change." Allegorus paused significantly. "Consider," he went on. "While reality is immutable, our perception thereof is constantly undergoing modification. Any real event, artifact, or phenomenon, while existing eternally, can be perceived serially in anticipation, experience, and retrospect. This shifting viewpoint is the basis of the construct we call time. Now, time comprises, in its entirety, the past and the future. The plane of intersection of these two great realms, the zero-duration interface we call the present, persisting for no length of time, clearly has no 'real' existence. It is analogous to a line bisecting a plane, or indeed a plane which intersects a three-dimensional volume. It is merely a location, not an artifact." Allegorus pulled out the endless paper strip from a computer printout station on the counter-top. "Now, my boy," he said as he took a pair of shears from a drawer, "if I snip this strip in twain"—so saying he clipped the paper across —"every molecule, analogous to elemental units of reality, remains a part of one piece of paper or the other. The past"— he indicated the paper left on the roll—"or the future." He tapped the other loosely flapping end. "There is no paper between them. The cut—the present moment—is only a position on the seamless fabric of past/future."

"Fine," Lafayette agreed impatiently. "But let's *do* something."

"I'm getting to it, lad," Allegorus said soothingly. "It is, after all, a rather heavy realization with which you are about to be confronted, and it can't be simply dumped on you all unprepared."

"I'm prepared to do whatever I have to do to get Daphne out of that hole," Lafayette rapped out. "If there really is anything I can do . . ." he finished doubtfully.

"There is, Lafayette," Nicodaeus reassured him. "Very well. Considering the fallacious nature of the conviction we all hold that only now is real, and the only reality, it should be clear to you that while in nature the flow of entropic energy must follow some specific course, there is no predetermined pattern which must of necessity be followed. Water will surely run downhill, but by precisely what path is a matter of random indeterminability. Thus, a pebble placed to block a potential outlet—a new channel cut across the route—and the trickle will be diverted. So it is with the realization of one chosen actuality among the myriad potentialities. Reality is, after all, not a sheet of paper. It is a book of infinitely numerous leaves, an endless library. The page we turn to is a matter of choice. With a small movement of the fingers, we can turn a page, or select another volume. So it was when our Lord Marvelous found himself free to reset the equipment in his care so as not only to monitor the entropic flow, but to redirect it. His plans were grandiose, complex—and even as he saw their fulfillment at hand, something went wrong, aborting his grand pattern, forcing the mainstream of actualization into channels not of his choosing. He took desperate measures, even altering the role of spontaneous conversion of energy to protons in the general area to which he had tentatively traced the mysterious counterforce. Inevitably, the new matter thus generated coagulated into galaxies, in turn influencing adjacent galaxies, all of course on the locus where he imagined his rival existed. Local observers who noted the resultant phenomenon of the diffuse X-ray background, attributed it to something they called *bromsstrehlung,* and ignored it, even as the newly created matter, created, as it must, a new galaxy.''

"You mean," O'Leary cut in, "that *I* didn't put a new star in the constellation Ursa Major?"

"You mean Unicornis Maximus, I suppose, Lafayette," Allegorus corrected gently. "My boy, the Great Unicorn has been well-known from antiquity. It is in only a few anomalous loci that Marv's galaxy-building eliminated C-51, thereby producing the pattern usually called the Great Wain, or wagon. See for yourself." Allegorus/Nicodaeus indicated the sky visible through the open French doors to the balcony. There, upside down against blackness, he saw the familiar Great Bear.

"It's not there!" he blurted. "There's no horn for the unicorn!"

"In any case, Lafayette, it was Lord Marvelous, and not you, who tampered with the stars in the sky. You saw the results in the aborted loci to which your recent travels took you: the presence of a new major galaxy relatively near at hand—only twenty million lights distant, and thus an intruder in the Local Group—had massive repercussions in our familiar Milky Way, which perforce was distorted in response to the gravitational pull of the newly created universe. This distortion placed Sol in unexampled juxtaposition to a minor sun we may call Nova Centauri, at a distance of only a fractional light; thus the Solar System was perturbed and forced to strike a new equilibrium. Luna was thrust from its orbit by the approach of Ceres to within half a million miles of Sol, and began to fall, passed within Roche's Limit, and disintegrated. Thus the spectacular phenomena you saw during your sojourn in that clump of loci—and of course, in some loci the effects were even more drastic. You drifted for a while in matterless space, Lafayette, on a locus where Earth herself had fallen into the sun. Luckily, your passage in half-phase did not expose you to the local influences, to which you owe your survival. Ajax will be embarrassed to learn that it was due only to a malfunction of one of their devices that reality as we know it was preserved—or will be—as soon as we face up to the moment of truth. Are you ready, my boy?''

"Ready?'' Lafayette echoed incredulously. "I don't know what you're talking about! What's all this stuff got to do with getting Daph out of that trap?''

"There is a force, lad,'' Nicodaeus/Allegorus said solemnly, "greater than the vast, blind workings of entropy: the force of human aspiration: the dreams of perfect harmony. Harmony, justice, peace, order, love, loyalty, truth, and beauty—these all are human inventions, Lafayette, along with honesty, decency, courage, integrity—all the qualities we think of as virtues. None exist in the impersonal extra-human universe. You, Lafayette, dreamed a dream that shattered the master plan of Lord Marvelous. Not that you knew; you merely opposed what you considered wrong, and thus aborted the false destiny of the madman.''

"Gosh,'' Lafayette said dully, "and I was getting myself all psyched up to step up and do something dramatic.''

"Drama aside, Lafayette, your moment is at hand.'' Nicodaeus/Allegorus rose and went to the wall cabinet housing the telephone. He lifted the receiver and spoke briefly, then hung up and turned back to Lafayette.

"You'll recall,'' he said grimly, "that when you first encountered Frumpkin here in this room—so to speak— he was accompanied by one Belarius V, whom he deserted to his fate. Belarius is an official not without power, and due to his marooning in half-phase by his treacherous subordinate Frumpkin, he escaped the general dissolution of the existing power structure known as GHQ. He alone of the Presidium of the so-called Masters of Destiny, the not notably modest council controlling the Probability Laboratory at Prime—I myself am a member—survived. I found Belarius and showed him the route by which he could return here. He should be along at any moment.''

"So *he's* going to put everything back the way it ought to be," O'Leary said contentedly. "And I can relax."

"Not quite, Lafayette," Nicodaeus said sternly. "Belarius V can assist you, but ultimately it is you versus Lord Marvelous."

"Some match," a harsh voice spoke from the balcony. Frumpkin, once again immaculate and arrogant in his black costume, swaggered into the room. "It took me a few moments to marshal my resources so as to nullify the vacuole into which you tricked me, Allegorus. Now I shall dispose of you at leisure."

═══Chapter Twenty-Two═

Another black-clad man came through the
door behind Frumpkin. He took a grip on the latter's
shoulder and spun him around.

"You didn't listen to this defector's lies, I hope,
Belarius!" Frumpkin blurted, attempting to pull free of
the slightly larger man's grasp. "Why, I was planning to
turn back for you just as soon as I'd dealt with this
saboteur." He jerked a thumb at O'Leary, who came up
behind him.

"Where's Daphne?" Lafayette demanded. "You got
out and left her there to be crushed, I suppose."

"Never mind, Lafayette," Belarius said smoothly.
"All his fell deeds are about to be relegated to the realm
of might-have-been. Help me now: Focus your Psychical Energies as you've never focused them before!"

O'Leary paused only to cast an imploring look at
Nicodaeus; then he closed his eyes and concentrated:

"Daphne's all right," he told himself firmly. "And
Roy, too. In fact, Roy got her out and they're in the
Yggdrasil Room at Ajax, having a nice lunch. Come to
think of it, that's where I am." He visualized the cheery
dining room at the novelty works, the rose-cheeked
diminutive waitresses, the view from the wide window,
the heavenly aroma of bacon-and-eggs. It was all there
pictured in his mind, clear in every detail. The clock on
the wall said one-thirty. Daphne was smiling at him. He

monitored the passing moment, remembering Nicodaeus' dictum that now is nonexistent. "But this is real," he told himself, believing it. There was a gentle tremor, as from a distant explosion. He opened his eyes and blinked against the glare. Nicodaeus was just coming through a door across the room, surrounded by waist-high Ajax personnel, all vying to be foremost to welcome him. He came across to Lafayette.

"So far, so good, my lad," he said briskly. "Can you keep it up under stress?"

"What stress?" Lafayette demanded genially. "I guess everything's just about perfect. Sit down, have a cold beer—"

"Lafayette," Nicodaeus said gently. "Look behind you."

Puzzled, O'Leary turned, saw the Man in Black, Marv at his side, guns in hand, both weapons aimed at his head.

"Here, now," Allegorus/Nicodaeus expostulated, rising. "There's no need for any show of primitive violence."

"Not so primitive," Frumpkin grated. "This nothing-gun will annihilate the wretch's ego-gestalt over an entire manifold. Tell me one good reason I shouldn't use it—and put an end to this nuisance."

"That's an easy one," Lafayette said with a show of nonchalance. "You can't." He concentrated on the appearance of the part of the weapon which was out of sight in Frumpkin's fist. The firing stud was almost concealed under a mound of crudely applied brass welding rod, he assured himself.

"Never mind, Frumpy," Marv spoke up. "There's other ways." He looked past O'Leary to the table.

"All right, sister, Lady H, or whatever," he snarled. "On yer feet. Get over here and put the cuffs on yer ex-boyfriend, and put some snap in it!"

"Aroint thee, sirrah!" Duke Bother-Be-Damned's voice cut in. Coming around from behind Marv, he struck the gun from his hand, then knocked Frumpkin down with a backhanded swipe. "I took no oath to treat

ungently with a lady." Bother executed a courtly bow
and extended a hand to Daphne, who stepped forward
to Lafayette's side.

"Oh, Lafayette," she cried. "Can't we go home
now? I'm so tired of struggling." As Lafayette took her
tenderly in his arms, Roy's hoarse voice spoke in the
silence:

"OK, Slim, better late than never, eh, kid? I guess I
and the boys can try the old transfer box now. We got it
remoted, you know, so we don't have to fetch it back
from the lab to use it. Good thing, too: with our power
cut, the lab's direct line to the Primary Event is the only
reliable power source around. Ready to go?"

While O'Leary was rather dazedly framing his reply,
an intangible force gripped him, ripped Daphne from
his embrace, sent him tumbling head over heels. He
yelled and grabbed, feeling fine fibers like spiderwebs
that broke as he clutched them.

"Easy, Slim," Roy's voice spoke in his ear. "Get out
the flat-walker, and orient it ninety degrees out of phase
—quick." Lafayette complied hurriedly. At once, with
a shriek like a silk tent ripping open, the blackness
which had folded around Lafayette split to reveal bright
sunlight on pink rubble. Rose bushes, trampled flat, still
bore fat pink blooms which raised their fragrant heads
above the mowed grass stems.

"Roy!" O'Leary gasped. "What's wrong? It looks
like Aphasia I!"

"Just a little problem of calibration, my lad," Nicodaeus supplied. "Curious; I personally guided and
amplified the effect of the transfer box, drawing on my
own emergency power-tap. It appears Lord Marvelous
has managed to hold a bit of ground, after all. Now,
let's look around." Allegorus/Nicodaeus came forward
from behind Lafayette and nodded to Daphne who resumed her place hugging Lafayette. Roy trotted at the
side of the First Secretary of the Prime Postulate, talking with both hands.

"—way I see it," he was exhorting Nicodaeus,
"Slim's gotta get him on the carpet, eyeball to eyeball,

and shrink him down to size. Otherwise, he'll have that one last-ditch hope to hang onto: that Slim can't really beat him in a showdown.''

"Very well," Nicodaeus said and halted. He was muttering under his breath, his eyes closed, his face strained. Roy came over to O'Leary and Daphne.

"He's gotta try to link up with HQ," he told them seriously. "A guy like old Al, he's got connections—but only if he can punch through. What you got us to here," he added, glancing around at the ruins, "is a fair approximation of Artesia-that-would-have-been; it's all Frumpkin could hold onto when you put everything you had into shifting the energy flow from the pseudo-realized version back to the recollected aspect. You almost made it, Slim. Like looking in the rearview and putting yourself back on the road before the accident that kilt you—speaking figurative, o'course. You're still alive, but we were pretty well marooned on the other side of the Primal Front in this almost-Artesia. Uh-oh, here's Frumpy now, and Marv, too." Roy fell back and Lafayette was alone, facing the conspiratorial pair across a yard of rubble-littered turf. Daphne had slipped away.

"Ah," Lord Marvelous said comfortably. "Shot your bolt and fell short, eh, Lafayette? Pity, and all that. Here you are, separated from all you hold dear by a barrier so thin and so insubstantial as to be indetectable by the subtlest instruments of mankind. Yet you can never cross it. Look yonder. . . ." Marv paused to wave a hand toward the pink-spired palace gleaming rosy in the early sun. Chauncy, the assistant chamberlain, appeared briefly on the terrace, setting out the morning's wash for the laundry truck. Other familiar faces were in sight, including on the upper terrace Adoranne, slim and blond and beautiful as ever, Count Alain at her side. O'Leary made a tentative step toward them, felt himself stopped cold as by a resilient but infinitely tough film. Daphne was coming toward him along the walk, but appeared not to see him.

"It's not really there, lad," Nicodaeus' voice said at

Lafayette's ear. "This is a shadow of what might have been and almost was. Something—I don't know what—is preventing our reality from shifting that microscopic distance to merge into full identity and give it all the flush of life."

"We're closer than before," O'Leary said. "The palace was in ruins at first; now it's back in place, as perfect as ever. Nicodaeus, I *have* to get across the barrier. What can I do?"

Daphne came closer, seemed to brush past Lafayette almost within reach; but as he turned to speak to her, he felt the impalpable membrane close in on him, stifling his breathing. He fought clear, stood breathing hard, looking after his wife's retreating image.

"She's real enough, Slim," Roy told him. "Just out of reach. Something's not meshing quite right. Wait a minute." He went to Nicodaeus, who had herded Marv and Frumpkin aside.

"Maybe we can squeeze it outa this pair," Roy said. Nicodaeus turned, shook his head. "It's nothing they're doing, Roy. It's some sort of residual resistance preventing our matchup."

"Scratch your heads in vain, petty wretches," Frumpkin said in his haughtiest tone. "As you see, in the eleventh hour my dream of glory is the master of your protégé's soulful yearnings. Let him face me if he dares!"

"I heard that," Lafayette said, regretfully taking his eyes from the ghostly Daphne retreating along the path while the real Daphne dabbed her eyes, beside him.

"Oh, Lafayette," she wailed, "I saw how you looked at her, and even though I knew it was really me you were admiring, I'm still jealous. Never mind her," she went on briskly after blowing her dainty nose on a bit of lace; she rose, and suddenly her expression was one of astonishment and alarm. "Lafayette!" she screamed. Her face went slack as she collapsed on the grass. Lafayette reached her first and knelt down at her side. Nicodaeus bent over the girl, then gave O'Leary a look of commiseration.

══════Chapter Twenty-Three══

"Pity, Lafayette. The stress of the juxtaposition was too much. Her vital energy has merged with her other self, beyond the barrier. Wave good-bye, lad. You're fated never to touch her again."

"Hard lines, Slim," Roy comforted O'Leary. "Nice dame, but now we still got a problem. Think hard: Focus the Psychical Energies one more time."

It's easy, Lafayette told himself. *All I have to do is realize that this is Lord Marvelous' doing, and it's not binding—not if I can just think. What should I do?* He looked up to meet Nicodaeus' sympathetic gaze.

"Look carefully, Lafayette," the older man said. "Can you find something, some tiny flaw that will invalidate this almost-world, and allow your own vision to emerge into full reality?"

Beyond Nicodaeus, Lafayette saw Marv and Frumpkin with their heads together.

After all, he informed himself doggedly, *it's only their world view against mine. They believe in lies and treachery, and I don't. It's up to me to be right. I have to be right!*

"What is it, Lafayette?" Nicodaeus broke in on his thought. "Have you noticed something that would tend to discredit the actuality of this construct?"

"The facade of the real palace is perfect," O'Leary replied, his eyes fixed on a small but unsightly scar on the polished pink marble slab inside the ballroom entrance. He walked across to it.

"Laugh, honey," a feminine voice came from behind Lafayette. He turned. Mickey Jo, slim and radiant in a trim white uniform with gold shoulder boards, was hurrying toward him across the lawn.

"I don't suppose it's important," she went on, "but my conscience got to bothering me. Remember when I put your pocket stuff in your new suit, back in the motel? Well, I kept something as sort of a souvenir, you know, to remember you by and all. Just a pebble. I figured it wasn't worth anything and if I asked you about it you'd throw it away. So I kept it. Now, it came to me I ought to give it back." She extended her hand, on which rested a lump of pink marble, polished on one side. Lafayette remembered picking it up and casually dropping it in his pocket long ago, before Trog's throne.

"Is it your lucky stone?" Mickey Jo asked wistfully. Lafayette took the bit of rock, turned and fitted it into the raw wound on the wall before him. It seated perfectly, leaving not even a visible seam. At that instant, a subtle *change* came over the scene. Behind Mickey Jo, Lafayette saw Daphne hurrying toward him.

"I guess it was," he said as Daphne's fog-soft hair brushed his face and his lips met hers.